I0734422

A Change In Crime
By D.R. Perry

Change comes with the strike of a match.

Leo Riley loses his whole family when mobsters burn his home to the ground. His only ally now is Oguina, a vengeful woman-turned-monster. If Leo walks her path, at least they're not alone.

As Leo plots his demise, Giacomo Bianco gazes into an abyss that stares back. His fall to madness is a one-way trip Leo aims to stop at all costs before Bianco orders another hit.

Monster and Mafioso fight for dominance over Fall River's streets. But powers change everything. Can Leo roll with the punches or will it all go up in flames?

Read this 2017 Dragon Award shortlisted book today!

D.R. Perry

It was just a piece of paper, dated November 27, 1929, but it felt heavier than an anvil. The red ink stamped across the carbon copy of his application to the United States Armed Forces looked greenish-black in the street light. Leo Riley thought it was a nice sickly color to match how useless he felt.

At least skipping dinner hadn't done him in. The doctor who'd examined him declared him fifteen pounds underweight. There was no way he'd have packed that much on with a plate of Ma's potatoes and cabbage. Military service was the only way to get them out of this town. He couldn't afford medical training anywhere, not even with his grades. The Army was picky when there wasn't a war on.

His feet traveled the street by rote, avoiding loose bricks and cracks in the pavement. That sidewalk would have tripped up anyone else trying to navigate the route at night while staring at a piece of paper. The November air was cool and dry, and there was a hint of smoke to it that was stronger than fireplaces or burning leaves. That ink-inspired greenish-black feeling dropped from his head to his gut. Leo slowed his steps and looked up.

The end of the street was full of smoke, too much

smoke. Leo ran past the next two houses, stopping at the building next to his own. By then, he could see it was his house on fire. There was a car parked outside, with two men beside it. The brawniest one wore his suit like a soldier wore a uniform. Even with his back turned, Leo saw the revolver. The man held the gun like Ma held a wooden spoon. He'd never get past that guy.

"I had to set it on fire, Jimmy." The big man wiped his gun with a handkerchief. "We can't let the Boss think we did a half-assed job."

"Jeez, Niccolo." Jimmy fidgeted with the cap on a hip flask. "You couldn't even do it, what else were we supposed to do? You think I don't know how serious this is?"

"Yeah, that's what I think. You're making less on milk runs with that Jones Act malarkey. The Boss still thinks your mother is a mark against you. That kid missing is gonna be another one. You don't want three strikes."

Niccolo turned to peer at his reflection in the car window, then put the gun in a holster under his arm. Leo had a better view of Jimmy now; he had bronze skin and stood more like a man in an Arrow shirt advert than a Mafioso. He thought about trying to get by them to the house, but Jimmy would see him.

"Bianco's going to have us all out hunting that kid down, even that irregular, Fallon." Jimmy jerked his chin in the direction of the park. "Someone'll take him for a ride."

"Yeah." Niccolo wiped the latch on the front gate with the hankie. "But look. I gotta scram. I wasn't here. They're iced except for what we already talked about.

The fire's cover for that. That kid Leo's only part Irish. He stands out, red all over instead of just in the face if you know what I mean. Spitting image of his grandpa. Anyone sees him, the Boss'll find out he wasn't here. Best if you tell him yourself."

Leo's hand curled around his rejection slip, crumpling paper with a crackling sound. Niccolo turned in his direction, but only to step around the front of the car and walk across the street. Jimmy was looking right at him. Leo froze for just a second, then ducked behind a shrub in front of the neighbor's house. He peered out at Jimmy.

The hoodlum bent his head as if he hadn't seen anything. Jimmy walked around the back of the car toward the door on the driver's side, his gaze the keys he'd just pulled out of his pocket, instead of Leo's hiding place. All the same, Leo collapsed under the shrub and puked his guts out.

By the time Leo stopped, his head was pounding. He heard a fading sound of crunching gravel. Peering out from behind the shrub revealed an empty street. Niccolo was gone too. He wiped his mouth with his handkerchief.

Leo reached up and ran his hand through his hair and down over his face. It came away wet. He hitched his satchel of sneak-out gear so it hung cross-body. All he had left in the world were the clothes on his back, a tie and the Daylos he'd inherited after his uncle's death in the trenches of the Great War.

Leo knew he'd better start walking. He could hide out for a couple of nights at the High School. They'd turned the heat down for the Thanksgiving weekend, but he'd be warm enough in the boiler room. He got to the end of the block, passing a heavyset guy in a bulky scarf and trench coat coming the other way.

"Hey, buddy." The big guy was holding something. "You want to keep this?" Leo ignored the man and kept walking a route that would take him to the school. That guy might have had something he wanted, but he could also be one of Bianco's. Hadn't those hoods said everyone would be out looking for him? He had to hide until he could figure out what to do.

Leo turned down the street on the side of the school. He saw a bald black man and a blonde woman sitting on a bench just inside the park. He thought about asking them for help, but no. A pair like that alone in a park at night? They'd take off before he could get over there. He put his head down, kept walking. There would be a window he could use on the other side of the building. The army wouldn't take him and the police were in the Mafia's pocket. Grandpa had been Wampanoag, so he couldn't try and join an Irish gang.

Leo wriggled through the casement window into the cellar, then made his way to the boiler room. The little hideout was small and dingy, but warm. All the more mischievous guys he'd graduated with had used it to skip class. He didn't bother with the little stash of comics. Stories of concrete good versus overt evil meant little to him now.

Leo sat on the floor, tilting his head up to gaze at the familiar faint outline of pipes that carried hot water to radiators throughout the school. He looked down to rub tears off his face and saw the line of tin cans kids hiding down here used as ashtrays. He picked one up and peered inside it, finding it hadn't been used yet.

The can made him remember the first, and only time he'd tried a cigarette. He'd cadged the smoke by offering to tell Grandpa's story about the lady monster with the crazy looking sharp teeth. Every kid in Fall River heard about that monster showing up around town and scaring people, but Grandpa had told a different story. Grandpa's story had always felt like it was true.

The monster had been Wampanoag just like Grandpa, a young woman out for revenge against the Pilgrims. She wasn't a fighter, but she had brains so she went into the woods and came back a monster. The story used to fascinate Leo, but he hadn't really believed someone could want revenge that badly. He'd been wrong. If that lady monster were here right now, he'd have more than a few questions for her.

Leo yawned. He'd have to stay put until at least tomorrow night. He curled up with his head on his satchel, soon dreaming of running through woods with a raging fire crackling behind him like his crumpled rejection slip.

Pearl sat on the bench and stole glances at her friend while he stared into space. His huge shoulders slumped slacker than his jaw. She wished she could see what horror he remembered now. She ran her tongue along the inside of her sixty-two teeth, a habit she'd grown to replace nipping her lower lip after the time she'd nearly bitten it off.

"I never thought there was anything wrong with him until the night he went bad and killed those sailors. You're lucky you didn't have to see that." Sampson's jaw tightened, but his shoulders drooped even more. "I should have noticed something was wrong sooner. I still don't know if I could have stopped him. It's probably my fault."

Pearl slipped her hand into one of his, glad that the skinny young man across the street had kept on walking. Her ears told her there were no other wakeful creatures around. One never knew who would protest about a white woman and a black man touching, but that's what Sampson needed right now. It was the closest semblance of human comfort he could get. It wasn't what it looked like, but then again neither were Pearl and Sampson. They'd been Changed forever. Tonight, she hoped to help Sam stay strong. He didn't want to become something worse. "Hey now. What did I tell you about that kind of thinking?"

"You said I need to think positive. Remember the good more than the bad. Find balance." He sighed, squeezing her hand. She squeezed back. "He used to say things like that. In some sick way, I think that's the reason he picked you. Back then, he could still remember being like you. Maybe he was trying to do something to save himself." Pearl knew better, but she only nodded. "Are you ever going to tell me why you dropped a wall on that man for me? You, who won't even learn to fight?"

"I was only waiting for you to ask again. I knew him."

She tucked a stray lock of hair behind her ear, taking a deep breath before speaking again. "That man's name is Jack. He's the reason I went with Daniel in the first place. He and my brother have been trying to find me for years, so the only reason he was following you is because of me."

"So you've been helping me out of guilt?" He dropped her hand.

"Sam." She turned to face him. "Would you have let me help you before that?"

"No, I wouldn't have." He twitched one corner of his mouth. "Would have gone on thinking you were weak, just like Daniel. Funny how a little guy like him can't see there're all kinds of strong."

"And that's something to keep in your mind. You've been strong before, in exactly the way you need to be." She turned her head and grinned, keeping her lips together. "Remember your mother's smile. Remember the first time you saw it snow. Remember being the man who helped all those people make the journey north to freedom. When you live a memory, live one of those."

"Remember being that man?" Sampson uncurled his hand, turning it palm up on the bench between them. "I remember all those things. But I wasn't a man anymore by the time I worked the Railroad, Pearl."

"Even better." She placed her hand over his, let him fold his fingers together with hers. "You acted like one despite what you became, and that makes all the difference. Keep that, and it will keep you."

"He's getting impatient with me." Sampson kept facing the street. "Sooner or later he'll figure out you've got a resistance going. If he does, it won't end well."

Pearl laughed. "Let him figure it out." She squeezed his hand.

"Aren't you afraid?" Sampson relaxed his grip.

"Yes. I'm used to that." She untangled her fingers from his.

"He's likely to kill you." His hands curled into fists.

"That doesn't matter." She pulled a black cloth with one white edge from her pocket.

"How?" He clenched his jaw to match his fists.

"Because I'd die on my own terms. I'll have stayed Pearl, not turned into some evil thing wearing Pearl's face and using her name. I'd die, but it would prove something to everyone in that warehouse." Pearl smoothed the fabric, tracing the attached combs with one fingertip.

"Why prove something they already know? They've all seen Daniel kill."

"It would show them that his way isn't the only way." She turned the fabric so the white edge faced away from her, then lifted it to a spot just behind her hairline.

"The hospital again." His face relaxed back into its usual absence of expression. Pearl nodded, securing combs and adjusting fabric to cover her hair.

"While I'm in there doing what I have to, think about something?" Pearl stood up, smoothing her plain gray dress.

"Name it." He raised an eyebrow.

"Daniel's over a hundred years old, but he's not the first. There have to be others even older. We'd have seen signs, heard of them if they all acted like he does. There's another way for sure. So far, what seems to work is getting into the right habit." She turned in place, then gave a flourish with her hands pointing out the wimple now covering her head.

The sound of warm startled laughter echoed out of Sampson's throat and through the park. Neither of them noticed the large fluffy cat watching from the tree beside them. It hadn't been breathing, after all.

Oguina thought he was trying to pick her up in the alley outside the speakeasy. This sometimes happened when she came to listen to the music. Her feminine yet dangerous appearance was like a stream to spawning salmon. This shivering buck was babbling away, trying not to chatter his teeth. Vapor from his mouth punctuated each word. Why wasn't he inside the building, dancing and drinking with the rest of his kind? Curiosity froze her, focused her ears on his words instead of the singer's inside.

"You know what it's like? Being alone, I mean. Completely alone?" He looked her in the eyes, something no one had done in years.

The skinny young male smelled like smoke, dust, and ashes. She heard his words, also his blood as it moved through his veins. His question distracted her just as she'd been getting ready to pounce. He was bold but bashful, both peculiar and familiar. Contradiction distracted her like a stray hair on the cheek. Something was different this time.

"Knowing everyone you care about was taken from you is pain without value." Thin lips hitched out a wry grin. "Pain that gets inflicted on you uses you." He inhaled, then exhaled slowly, twitching his eyes sideways. He was nervous, but hiding it well. Had she let her expression change?

His blood hadn't sped up. She'd kept her lips closed around her inhuman teeth, then. His words itched around in her mind. What could this skinny youngling know about the pain of loss?

He looked up at her eyes and spoke again. "The most valuable pain is chosen. Pain you choose is pain you can use." He was either brave or stupid.

The alley, the bony buck, and the music filtering through the brick wall all faded from Oguina's mind. One of her fugues engulfed her like ice storms cover trees. She remembered.

One unknown night after she'd been Changed, Oguina lurked hidden near where she had grown up. The men on watch spoke of who was ill and who had died. When she heard the name of her youngest brother, she nearly killed them. Confused and ashamed, she sneaked in to see the boy. At first, she couldn't find him. The only male here was well past his prime. She leaned over for a closer look, peering into eyes like muddy water. He looked dead, but she knew better. His blood hissed and rushed like rapids.

His dry voice whispered softer than the skin crinkling around those eyes, but she could still hear it. "Oguina. How do you look the same, after all these years?"

Years? It couldn't have been long enough for her brother to grow up, let alone age this much. Still, it was him. This dried-up, dying old man was her brother.

Oguina couldn't answer. She knew her hideous fangs

would frighten him. Instead, she shook her head regretfully, remembering the dimple-faced boy her brother had been. He smiled. She willed tears to stay behind her eyes.

"Quiet as always." He chuckled, but age changed it into a cough. "No… you are a spirit, Oguina, here to witness your old brother's death."

She shook her head again, trying not to be distracted by memories of their childhood. She didn't notice he'd moved until his hand was on her wrist.

She clenched every part of her to halt her movement. Oguina wasn't hungry, but the beat of his blood on her skin crushed her will. She stopped bare inches short of biting into his face. She leaned over him, mouth wide open. He saw rows of pointed teeth, the only visible change she'd experienced in all this time. Her brother's mouth opened, his eyes wide, blood racing like lemmings toward a cliff. She inhaled his breath, stealing his strength to break his death-grip. His throat rattled and shuddered as he reached out again.

Oguina ran faster than any mortal creature. She still couldn't go fast enough to escape that erratic pulse and gasping breath. Alarmed voices from the men on watch called after her, but she ignored them. That night she traveled as far away as she could. She stayed in the wilderness for a time she didn't bother measuring. She returned to paths of stone and stacked tenements. No one remembered her face, but the pale children told tales of a copper-skinned woman with monster teeth.

She blinked back the distracting haze of old memories. That talkative buck was still here, his blood moving slightly faster now. He asked a question she couldn't focus on. She was certain now: he was not like her brother but like someone else from long ago. Who could it be?

"Didn't you hear me?" His voice tightened with desperation. "I said, I know the stories. The ones about you, Oguina." He knew her name.

She didn't know him. She recognized herself in him. That had been her expression the night of her own Change. This was not her hunt. It was his.

Oguina arched an eyebrow at the fragile creature. His expression remained unchanged; he'd even stopped shivering. He was not prey. He had stalked her like a cougar cub stalks its mother's tail. More than that, his clumsy pounce had startled her.

The audacious youth held a knife, and an empty tin can out between them and said, "I want the strength to avenge my family, to kill Giacomo Bianco. You can give it to me. Or you could kill me. I'd rather you do it than him."

The defiant cub would choose death in her teeth over death at Bianco's hands? She'd heard stories of Giacomo Bianco from the men in blue who were supposed to enforce the law. They called him the leader of a "crime ring." By seeking her, the cub had already beaten this Bianco. The criminal couldn't kill him if she did. And if she Changed him, he had a chance to fight.

Without touching him, Oguina took the knife and held one wrist over the can. She grinned, showing as much of her teeth as possible, but the young one had no fear left in his heart. The knife bent nearly in half, only just scratching her hide with her strength behind it. She bit her wrist instead and a trickle of blue-black syrupy liquid dripped into the cup. It smelled rich and deep, like autumn leaves under thawing snow. Seconds later her arm healed.

Oguina spoke for the first time in more than three hundred years. "Never forget cub. For this kind of power, there is always a price."

"What price?" She couldn't believe the soaring audacity of this cub. She would need to shoot that down. A cub's place was to learn.

"You will be told everything you need to know if you drink." Oguina's smile was wide as a bride's and toothy as a crocodile's. She may not have spoken for centuries, but she had smiled. "If you do not drink, what you know will not matter."

"F-f-fair enough." His voice cracked. "Down the hatch." His hands trembled as he reached for the can, taking one last glance at the bent knife in Oguina's hand. He turned his eyes away from the can as if that might help him drink the syrupy black blood. She had looked.

But this cub was different from her, to begin with. He was of a new time and a different people. What if he changed into a different kind of monster? She wasn't ready for this. She ought to stop and kill him now. But it was too late. While she hesitated, he rushed ahead. His mouth was ringed with black. He licked his lips and blinked eyes the color of honey with moss-green flecks.

The tin can rattled and bounced as it hit the pavement. Oguina stood like stone while the cub clutched his face and curled on the ground in pain. To his credit, he made no noise, just the same as she had. Oguina's hands twisted like hair in a flame. What would she do if he ended up her opposite? She remembered her own Change with perfect clarity but hadn't seen it happen to anyone else. Were monsters supposed to differ from their creators?

He rolled and slumped against a barrel of trash. A few minutes later, he turned his head and opened his mouth. He watched his teeth rattle to the pavement, then turned his eyes on her. She knew from her own memories that he saw her through a reddish haze. His fallen and too-blunt human teeth decayed into dust. Had she truly wanted to do this?

His breath came short and shallow. He was dying. His heart sped up, then gradually slowed as blood grew cold and thick in his veins. The song of life in his body piped out its final note. And finally, there was something familiar again, a face full of recognition and fear. His senses had sharpened just in time to hear and feel the moment of his own death.

His eyes widened, and his lips drew into a thin, flat line. Smiling down at him, Oguina heard a hiccupping sound coming from somewhere. She poised for an attack, then recognized the unfamiliar sound. She was laughing. His eyes stayed wide, but one corner of his mouth turned up. He blinked, glanced at her heaving shoulders, grinned. There was something feline in that expression.

His lips parted, showing sharp white points along his gums. His new Changed teeth would reveal what he was every time he opened his mouth. He touched one of the little points, then pulled his hand away from his mouth. The teeth were sharp enough to cut metal with some effort. He watched his finger heal in seconds.

"Hungry." He gasped. "I'm hungry." He paused, then pounced behind a trash can, coming up with a cat. He took the blood from it in seconds and stripped its entrails and flesh in under a minute. His hunting instinct was strong, as hers had been. She needed to curb it now.

He stood, trying to get past her out of the alley. Oguina was short and weighed even less than he, but she had centuries of experience. She blocked him, locked her arms around his neck and pulled down. His head clunked into hers, stunning him.

"This is not the forest or the countryside. You will not go out in the street like a bear just out of hibernation. You want sustenance? Follow me." Oguina bared her teeth and stared steadily into his eyes until he looked away. Now he would follow and listen.

She made sure he was watching, then crouched low to leap and catch the top of a fire escape with one hand. She looked down at him as she dangled, then pulled the rest of her body up on the metal platform. It only took a moment for him to follow. She led him north, jumping from roof to roof until they were out of Fall River.

They stopped when they came to Joshua's Mountain, a hilly formation of rocks and caves surrounded by woods and the deer that lived in them. They killed some animals on the way to sustain themselves, leaving only bones and skin behind. Oguina made a campfire. The Changed needed no light or heat, but there had been a fire on her first night. There would be a fire on her cub's first night.

"What is your name, cub?" Wide eyes stared from his pale, bloody face. He looked down at his hands, then wiped them on his trousers to remove some of the gore. He extended a hand in a gesture she'd seen before.

"Sorry. Guess I never mentioned it. Name's Leo. Leo Riley." She reached toward him, unsure what the custom meant. She hadn't tried it before. He took her hand, then moved their hands up and down four times before letting go. What a strange thing to do. "Do you have a surname?"

Surname? She wasn't sure why he'd think she had one, considering he knew what she was. Did he know nothing of her people and their history? She had too many questions, and this wasn't the time. The one who Changed her hadn't asked anything. That was the only example she had of how to conduct herself.

"I do not." She dropped a branch into the fire and watched Leo out of the corner of her eye. He made more attempts to brush dried blood from his hands. He would learn to do things more neatly. There would be time for that later.

"Now you will hear of the power you have gained and its price" Leo nodded absently, rubbing a twig under his fingernails. She rushed up behind him faster than the wind and smacked him across the face with the palm of her hand. The cub toppled on his side. Bits of earth clung to the sticky blood on his hands and face.

"You are not listening." Oguina frowned down at him, hoping she looked stern and severe. "If the new facts of your life are less important than having a wash, there is a stream just west of here."

"I'm sorry, Oguina." Leo folded his hands together to keep them still. "I'm listening now." She glared until he cut his eyes away from hers again.

"Your hunger is controllable, as long as you hunt something larger than a wolf each evening. Animals will sate you, but human prey gives us more strength. You know we can hunt for blood and flesh, but we can also steal breath to survive. That takes more control than you have right now, but you will learn that in time." He opened his mouth for a moment, then closed it and nodded.

"You will want to chase and kill anything that runs from you, anything with a pulse you can feel, and anything that attacks you. You will learn to control this." She paused because the next truth still held mystery for her.

"All Changed sleep when the sun rises. We lash out at anything disturbing this sleep." Leo narrowed his eyes and opened his mouth again. "What is it?"

"Where am I supposed to sleep during the day?" asked Leo, "in a bed? A basement? A...coffin?" She heard that hiccupping sound and knew she was laughing again. She hadn't laughed this much since years before her change. "Did I say something funny, Oguina?"

"Tell me, Cub Leo, where you think creatures like us slept before humans buried their dead in boxes?" His mouth opened and closed like a newborn's, and she grinned. "Sleep comes to us at dawn, wherever we are. It is wise to hide where nothing will find you before sunrise." She remembered waking once with the limbs and entrails of three men scattered around her. "There is space to sleep in a cave nearby." She saw the tension go out of his shoulders.

"Your body will not age or change more than it already has." Oguina bared her teeth to make her point. "This may be difficult later when your peers are old. It is best to avoid people you knew before." His face grew slack and inexpressive. He'd said his family was all dead. At least they had that in common.

"You can no longer see your own likeness." Leo's brow furrowed. "What is it this time?" She tapped her foot.

"So, I won't show up in a photograph, or on film? I can't use a mirror?" He raised a skeptical eyebrow.

"You cannot see yourself, though others will be able to. We are unable to see ourselves now that we are Changed." She hadn't considered the vanity of modern humans. Oguina wasn't sure about films or photographs, but knew about mirrors.

"So, even if someone made a sketch of you, you can't look at that drawing? What if I drew this tree with you standing in front of it?" He tapped a finger twice against one bony knee.

"I could see the back and the edges of the paper, the tree, or anything else in the picture, but I would not see the image you drew of me. Our eyes reject the sight of ourselves."

"All right. Sorry about getting distracted. I'm ready to hear the rest." He tapped his knee again. This one was curious, likely to test everything.

"Finally, your hide is tougher than any other

creature's. Few things can pierce it. This makes you extremely tough to kill. Fire and your own teeth will damage you severely."

"What about your teeth?" Leo stilled his tapping. "Could those, um, damage me severely?"

"Yes, and the teeth of other Changed as well. That is highly unlikely to happen, though."

"How do you know?"

"I have only met one other, and that was more than four hundred years ago." Had it truly been that long?

"So that's all? All there is to this?" He grimaced, pointing at his sharp and slender teeth.

"All there is to be told in so many words, yes. The rest you learn over time by experience."

"Time." Leo sighed. "So, when can I get some practice?"

"We start tomorrow, after the sun goes down. Dawn is coming." She poured dirt on the fire to smother it out.

The next night, they came out of the cave under Profile Rock and Oguina brought him to the nearest stream for a wash. Leo splashed water over his face and hands, surprised it didn't feel like it took his skin off. So, Changed didn't have to freeze their marbles off? If he left now, he could beat Richard Byrd to the South Pole.

The whole experience of his Change was so painful, he'd immediately tried to forget about it. He couldn't. Leo remembered everything, from the taste of the loamy blue-black liquid to the sound of his old teeth on the ground. Even worse, it came back in exact detail. He'd come so close to being killed without even knowing it. He shook, but not from the cold. He washed his shirt and jacket, draped them across a naked shrub.

Leo couldn't think about it anymore, so he dragged his sketchbook and charcoal from his satchel. He drew lines, made dots, smudged. Mom and Siobhan in the kitchen, laughing at Colin's first steps. A drop of water plopped on the paper. It wasn't raining. Leo turned the page, started again. A more recent scene took shape under his charcoal, silhouettes in front of a burning house.

"You have talent, Cub."

Leo started. If he'd still had a heartbeat, it would have skipped a beat. He and his sketchbook were thirty feet up the nearest tree in a blink; looking down, clinging to the trunk, wondering how he got up there. Oguina laughed. Again.

She laughed an awful lot for a monster who'd spent centuries alone. Maybe she'd gone loopy. Maybe she'd always had a good sense of humor and no one to show it to. There was so much he'd expected from the stories, but a laughing straight-shooter wasn't one of them. Leo shimmied down the tree.

"I brought you these." Oguina held a bundle of fabric. Clothes. The shirts had a rectangular dent in each shoulder like they'd been on a clothesline. She side-eyed his damp shirt and jacket.

"Are we doing something messy again?" Leo held the stolen shirt up to his chest. It'd be big.

"Perhaps." Oguina shrugged. "Perhaps not. That depends on you. There is this also." She tossed a smaller bundle at him, and he caught it easily. It was a pillowcase wrapped around pencils and more charcoal.

"How'd you know about my drawing?"

"How do you think?" Oguina tapped her nose and smirked. Of course. She'd smelled the paper and charcoal in his satchel. He slid one arm into the new-to-him shirt.

"No." Oguina shook her head. "After we hunt. Go as you are, or suffer the task of more laundry." Her eyes and tone were serious, but the corners of her mouth turned up.

She ran between trees and Leo followed, ducking branches and skirting underbrush at a speed he couldn't have matched a few nights ago. She stopped at the edge of the woods near a fenced pasture. He saw a barn in the distance. He heard heartbeats and breathing, slower but stronger than humans. He smelled the ruminated grass.

"Cows? You're bringing me for hamburgers?"

"There's more to this exercise than a meal. What's out there besides cows?"

He listened harder, heard something like an over-wound wrist-watch.

"Is that a dog?"

She nodded. "We hunt cows tonight and leave them alive, taking only a little blood. You will fight the urge to kill. If you wake them, the dog will alert its masters. Hunt neatly and quietly, and it won't. Then get out." He nodded, watching her leap the fence without touching it. Leo went after her, smiling. Easy jumping was the most fun part of this monster business.

Oguina crept up to a cow lying down. She leaned in

where its pulse was closest to the surface and bit. Leo couldn't see blood and the cow made no noise. He moved toward a standing cow, but she waved him away from it. That made sense. A standing animal would fall over as it lost blood. What was he supposed to do, act like some kind of overgrown mosquito? He stood by one of the ones on the ground, scratching his head. Why couldn't Changed eat actual hamburgers? Leo had no idea, so he shut his eyes and thought about ground beef. He might as well have remembered folding laundry. His appetite stayed flat. So much for that idea.

All that blood just under the cow's skin made his teeth itch. He bit. Hot blood stung, splashing his chin and then his chest. He'd been messy, but not like last night. The blood tasted like metal, its temperature like a cup of tea that would only just scald the tongue. Now he felt a chill, but his hunger damped down.

Leo opened his mouth wider to get his teeth out of the cow's hide. Blood splashed him in the face. He didn't know how to make it stop, but then Oguina was there. She did something, and the cow stopped bleeding like it hadn't been bitten at all. The animal blinked at them, then put its head back down. Leo glanced at Oguina's peacefully sleeping cow.

"How did...." she placed one hand over his mouth and pointed at the dog with the other. The canine moved its legs in its sleep and snuffled. It might be dreaming now, but it had smelled the blood for sure. It would wake soon. Oguina led them quickly and quietly back the way they came. She waved a hand at his mouth. Good, he could talk now.

"How did you get it to stop bleeding like that?"

"I put my blood on its wound."

"Our blood cures wounds?" Oguina nodded. If Changed blood could heal cows, what could it do for people? But that was crazy. Should he expect the blood of a monster to work miracles? Could it cure polio? He could hear the snake-oil pitch now, "a monster cure for monstrous ailments." It was such a powerful idea that he didn't dare speak it. He filed the thought away for later.

"We have more to practice this night, Cub Leo." Oguina led him back through the woods, in a different direction. They came to a place with older and taller trees. Leo heard dozens of tiny heartbeats high up in the air. He peered up, trying to guess what in the world could possibly be so active at night. He shrugged, stumped.

"Now we catch bats. Watch." Bats? What could she want to catch flying mice for? Oguina stood still with her eyes closed, then she was gone. Seconds later she was back again, eyes open and holding one of the struggling creatures in her left hand. Oguina was a southpaw, like Babe Ruth. She handled a different kind of bat, though. Leo laughed out loud. She laughed, too. At him or with him, he couldn't tell. He was okay with that now.

"Now you, Cub."

"Now me? I don't even know how you did that." He jerked his chin at the bat.

"I hear them." She shrugged, blinking owlishly at him.

Leo listened, heard one of the tiny rapid heartbeats off to his right. He jumped up in that direction. There were no bats anywhere near him in the split second he was at peak altitude. He landed, holding empty hands out to Oguina. She laughed again.

"You listened for their blood. Listen this time to the sound the bats make before they change course. Try again."

He knew the noise she mentioned. This time, he closed his eyes. This time, he followed the sound like she said. Two squeaks, the second an echo. This time, the bat flew directly in his face. He made a panicked grab before falling back to earth. An instant later he stood on the ground, bat in hand. The animal shrieked pain in a high pitched little voice, wings crumpled like an old newspaper. How could he not remember tiny creatures were so delicate. Leo's frantic horror paralyzed him. Oguina crossed the distance between them. Cleanly and quickly, she snapped the bat's neck.

"Why did you kill it?"

"It was in pain."

"But you could have healed it, like the cow."

"It is only a bat. If you care so much, be more careful. Mistakes have consequences." Her voice was stern, like a Sunday School nun's. "You will try again."

They stayed until near dawn, but Leo didn't catch another bat that night.

"Boss, why do I gotta go to Confession today?" Jimmy the Hooch walked easily up the steps of St. Mary's. That bastard.

"Because Jimmy, I'm going to Confession, and you're driving the car." Giacomo Bianco took each step slowly, making it look like a deliberate swagger. A Boss couldn't show weakness.

"But Boss, Niccolo coulda drove you." They stood by the door. Jimmy opened it and kept right on complaining. "I coulda just gone before Mass this Sunday, like usual."

"Jimmy, don't you think your immortal soul is important? Accidents happen, kid." Bianco put a hand on Jimmy's shoulder. "Say, what if you took a tumble down those stairs and died? You'd go to Hell for sure." Jimmy's face went from bronze to olive, but the kid was smart. He didn't glance at the stairs. Still, he'd screwed up, and he knew it. He shouldn't complain.

They genuflected at the font inside the door. The kid walked to the reconciliation room, opened the door and stepped inside. Jimmy was good at exactly three things; chasing skirts, preening, and importing the hooch which was the source of his nickname. Bianco only put up with him because Jimmy had an uncanny instinct for exports. He'd been pinched a couple of times but never lost a shipment or payment.

Jimmy Delaqua's biggest flaw wasn't something he could fix. His mother was from Puerto Rico. Bianco was a traditional man. He didn't think half-breeds like Jimmy belonged in leadership, but he couldn't afford to kick the kid to the curb. Jimmy made big money and followed orders, most recently even did wet work. Of course, that was why they both were here. He always preferred Niccolo's company, but Jimmy was the one who'd iced the Riley family. The Fall River Famiglia faced more than police on a regular basis, so staying right with God was important to Giacomo Bianco. What was important to Bianco was important to his men. Unless they wanted to be taken for a ride, that was.

Jimmy shuffled out of the reconciliation room, hanging his head. Good. Bianco walked deliberately into the booth, closing the door behind him to create comforting darkness. The hard bench gave firm support for his unstable limbs. This was a rare place where no one would see his tics and tremors, so he let his body relax.

"In the name of the Father, and of the Son, and of the Holy Spirit, Amen." That was Father Francis on the other side of the booth.

"Bless me, Father, for I have sinned. It's been five days since my last confession." His hand shook as he genuflected, his left heel lifted off the ground. Damn Parkinson and his cockamamie disease.

"Father, I've had wrathful thoughts, committed

wrathful acts. I have anger at this world, the circumstances of my life, and the people around me." His words were true, but he'd never thought of anger as a bad thing. He always faked that apologetic tone, but technically Bianco wasn't lying to the Father.

"My son," said Father Frances, "you've carried so much anger the last five years." The old Priest sighed. "You keep coming to me with contrition and do penance, but every time you return, you bring the burdens of wrath with you. When you were a boy, and I was just starting here, you got into mischief, not fights. When you were a younger man, your sins were greed or lust, sometimes gluttony. Now, your sins harm others. And you do them over and over again. Giacomo, look into your heart. Find where that rage comes from and control it."

"Yes, Father." Giacomo almost laughed at that irony. Control his anger? He could barely control his body. His right pinkie finger hopped like a flapper in a juke joint. "I'll try to find the source of this anger." Of course, it was the damned disease messing with him. He was so close to a solution for that. He'd be cured once he had enough of what he needed.

"Then, my son, what are your sins?"

"I am responsible for seven deaths," Giacomo said a silent thankful prayer that courts of law couldn't subpoena priests. It was silent on the other side of the wall.

"How are you responsible?" asked Father Francis finally.

He had to give some kind of detail. "Those people

saw me in a compromising position, and you know how loyal my men are." His left heel hopped, tapping his toes against the inside of his shoe.

"You should tell the earthly authorities what you've told me. But if you won't, at least reflect on your anger and pride. Humility's a virtue. Come to confession, attend Mass, remember whosoever shall smite thee on thy right cheek, turn to him the other also. God gave us his only Son as our Savior, and with true repentance in your heart, you can be saved. If you can't stop your feelings of anger, then stop acting on them. Stop and think about the human and spiritual cost of giving orders to kill. Take a day or an hour or even a minute and come up with a solution to your problems that isn't murder. Will you say the Act of Contrition?"

"Yes, Father." Giacomo cleared his throat. "Oh my God, I am sorry for my sin with all of my heart. In choosing to do wrong and failing to do good, I have sinned against You, Whom I should love above all things. I firmly intend, with Your help, to do penance, to sin no more, and to avoid whatever leads me to sin. Our Savior Jesus Christ suffered and died for us. In His Name, my God, have mercy."

"God the Father of Mercies," said Father Francis, "through the death and resurrection of His Son, has brought forgiveness of sin to the world. Through the ministry of the Church, I grant you pardon and absolution for your sin in the Name of the Father, and of the Son, and of the Holy Ghost. Amen. You may go."

"Thank you, Father." Instead of genuflecting, he took a swig of rum from his hip flask and rose carefully.

Giacomo dropped the weight of pain and rigidity back into his muscles. He checked himself for any hint of a tremor before leaving the booth. Jimmy the Hooch still sat in the pew, waiting for him.

"You ready to go, Boss?" asked Jimmy. Bianco stifled a weary sigh. Riding in Jimmy's cologne-reeking automobile seemed a heavier penance than anything Father Francis had laid on him.

"Yeah, Jimmy." Bianco paced like a pallbearer up the center aisle. "Let's shake a leg."

Leo surprised her last night. He had more efficient digestion if one cow was enough for him. On the other hand, the incident with the injured bat told her he had an overgrown sense of compassion. That could put them both in danger. She'd never been so afraid.

Oguina wasn't afraid of Leo, she was afraid for him. Even the idea of his destruction frightened Oguina. How could the one who changed her leave her alone after only seven days? Nothing could have prepared her for this. It had been four hundred years since she'd cared this much about anything.

How could she teach him on her own? She'd needed decades of trial and error to control her new instincts, then twice as long figuring out how to use them. After that Oguina had observed the new human ecology, considering what her place in it might be.

Oguina remembered being human, so she understood their fear of her. There was no way she could reveal her true self and be accepted. Silence, self-control, and secrecy were her only recourse. Three threads of will woven into a delicate veil let her pretend to blend into the crowds coming and going from mills or factories. The wolf was least lonely in sheep's clothing, motive enough for wearing it.

Years earlier, Oguina walked with the third-shift workers at the same mill for several months. When one of the does politely nodded at her, she nodded back. It was the first gesture of kindness since her youngest brother grasped at her hand on his deathbed.

She tracked the doe back to her crowded tenement, shared with a buck and two small younglings. Oguina knew by scent these were the doe's children. On the other side of the window, one of those little, bundled forms rolled to face her in its sleep. The boy opened his eyes, then smiled and waved. His eyes grew round and frightened, mouth opened in a scream before Oguina realized she'd smiled back. She'd leaped from the building immediately. Oguina had to stay away after that. What could she offer this small herd if they'd been willing to tolerate her company? Would she leave dead rabbits on their doorstep in winter? Kill their wealthy relatives so they could inherit money? Accidentally slaughter them some night because they got too close to her? Solitude buried her like an avalanche after that.

Before Leo, she hadn't bothered with laughing. She'd come to terms with being alone and unchanging and found a strange peace in isolation of her own making. "Pain you choose," as Leo had said. And he had been correct in a way. Burying herself weighed less than being buried, though she couldn't say why. She thought solitude would crush her if Leo's choices left her alone again.

She cared too much. Was some unknown fact of Changed life at play here? Oguina had never been outgoing or talkative, preferring physical tasks to social pursuits. Her friends had been her family. And Ahanu, though that was a different kind of caring. Was Leo like family now? Had she changed herself by changing him?

"What's on the agenda tonight, Oguina?" Leo's hair was still wet from the stream. He'd made a habit of a nightly wash, as she had for her first fifty-odd years.

"Tonight, we walk past a group of humans without attacking them," she said. He laughed. She couldn't.

"That's it? We just have to walk past them?" He smirked. "No jumping over them or convincing them we're a couple of dogs guarding cows?"

"Yes, Leo, that is all. We walk past them without frightening them or attacking them. We walk past them leaving them ignorant of what we are and what we are capable of." She watched his face for signs of gravity and found none. "This is something you need to learn before you face Bianco."

"Well then, let's get to it. Let's go walk past some people." He wore an overconfident smirk. This would be hard for him.

"First we hunt." They went to a place where the deer were plentiful, then past the edges of town. Oguina brought him near a trolley stop on North Main Street. People were coming and going, but not many. They pretended to wait for the next trolley until a mostly empty inbound train came. An elderly doe got off the train, hobbling toward them with a cane. She was dressed all in black, carrying a small sack of groceries.

Leo tensed and stared like a wildcat preparing to pounce. Oguina nudged him and they walked in the opposite direction of the aged doe. Oguina walked between her cub and the tempting living target.

This doe smelled familiar. Could this be the woman from her nights mingling with the factory workers? But she was so old. Had it been so long since then? She had to stop the remembering and the pondering and get Leo over this hurdle. His hand reached toward the elderly doe but Oguina clasped it against her side.

Leo looked at her, came back to his senses. His jaw clenched as he set his gaze straight ahead. Just as they passed, the old doe stopped and spoke to Oguina.

"I remember you," rasped the old woman. Oguina stopped walking as well, but did not turn around. She kept a firm grip on Leo. Oguina knew instantly that the old woman had worked all these years at American Printing Company. Her breath smelled like wet fabric. "You were at the mill years and years ago. You look just the same." Shock stilled Oguina's legs, or she would have dragged Leo away. Instead, Oguina stood where she was and spoke.

"You must be mistaken. Perhaps you knew my aunt, who worked at the mill. Good night," Oguina tugged Leo's arm, but he didn't move. She closed her mouth firmly and turned around to give him some encouragement. His eyes carried a feral gleam and his jaw twitched. If they did not leave soon, this woman would meet a messy end in the street.

She gripped Leo's arm tighter, but he was staring off at nothing. She knew he was hearing the song of blood in the woman's veins. She tugged his arm, nudged his foot with one of hers but his trance remained. The doe spoke again.

"My son said he saw a monster outside the window. He said she was a dark and pretty young woman until she smiled. She had monster's teeth. He drew pictures." The doe came closer. Leo's legs bent like a cat's before it pounced. Oguina looked around. The street was empty. Oguina slipped her other arm around his waist to clasp her hands behind him.

Oguina turned her head away from the woman and spoke. "Yes, it was me at the mill. Yes, I frightened your son years ago. But you must go home. This boy is like me, but new." Now she turned so the old woman could see her face. "If you value your life, leave now!"

The woman's eyes grew round and frightened, exactly like her son's all those years ago. She turned and hobbled away as quickly as she could. Leo struggled against Oguina's grip but couldn't break it. A few minutes later, it was safe to let go.

"Can we go back to the woods now?" His eyes were as round as the woman's had been.

"No. This, like the bats, takes practice."

"But if I fail here, innocent people die. I can't do this all in one night." She didn't understand his sudden reluctance. He was the one who wanted vengeance by murder.

"These are not your people anymore, Cub Leo. You are a monster that feeds on life." She couldn't keep her weariness out of her voice. "You came from them, but are no longer of them. Think of them as bucks and does or bulls and cows. That makes it easier when you inevitably kill one."

"So you just lived separate all this time? Alone?" He looked like she'd slapped him. "I said some stupid things the night we met. I was an arrogant bastard, and that's no way to treat a friend."

A friend? She wasn't sure how to respond.

"Oguina? What's wrong?" he asked.

"You will practice more with the bats. We can try this once a night and then hone another skill with the rest of our time." She would have considered this coddling last week, but she wanted better things for him than for herself. Oguina wasn't sure why.

They left town stealthily, heading back to the clearing with the bats. She watched him leap up to catch the small creatures, wondering what she had gotten them both into. Neither of them noticed they were being watched.

A Change In Crime

"Forgive me Father for I have sinned." Pearl fiddled with the combs on the wimple in her lap. She forgot to say something the Father on the other side of the screen expected of her.

"And how long has it been, child?" She recognized the voice of the older Priest. That was good. He was kind.

"Oh. Sixteen years, Father, forgive me." Pearl would have blushed if she could.

"Forgetfulness is not a sin, child. But one of those must have brought you here?"

"Yes. Father, I disobeyed and dishonored my parents. I caused a man to have lustful thoughts and take action on them." Those were definitely not all of her sins. She had to start somewhere.

"And were these sins recent?"

"No, Father. That all happened years ago."

"My child, where there's life there's hope. These things must have weighed heavily on your soul all this time if you come here with them now. But I have to ask, how did you cause that man to have such thoughts and act on them?"

"We were childhood friends, Father, he and my

brother and I. He went to my parents with an offer of marriage. But I've said all my life I'd rather be a spinster. I never felt carnal passion, Father. Those desires never interested me. Jack knew, but he just wouldn't believe I only wanted friendship. I must have done something without realizing to make him think...."

"A friend you trusted failed to trust you? That's his sin, not yours. Tell me more about disobeying your parents."

"They, um, accepted his offer. I was supposed to marry him, but I didn't want to." Pearl took a deep breath, trying to calm herself, to keep the memory from coming back. "Mama went on and on about how handsome she thought Jack was. And Papa was all for Jack becoming part of the family. I tried to talk him out of it later that night. He wouldn't hear it. He said I just needed incentive. So he kissed me, put his hands on me, tore my blouse." She took another deep breath. "I told him trying a new tea was more of a thrill than his advances, but then he threatened to do worse. I only got away because he heard someone." She might have continued telling her story to the Father, but the next memory from that night brought her down like a cougar does a deer.

Pearl shut herself in the bathroom. She used the hand pump to fill the basin, then tried to scour away any trace of Jack's touch. Once she'd washed, she wrapped herself in her robe. The torn blouse went in the trash bin. She wished she could throw Jack in a bin, it would serve him right.

Pearl went up the back stairs to her room, avoiding

her brother and parents. She locked the door, then slid the "hopeless" chest in front. Desperate for fresh air, she opened the window. Pearl put on her nightgown behind the screen. Even though no one could get in the room with her, she found the barrier comforting. Her window was flush against a flat, brick wall. No man could climb it.

She reached for the brush on her dressing table but hovered between it and the shears in her sewing basket. As Pearl hesitated, a rustling sound came from behind her. It was too loud to be the wind in the curtains. She snatched the shears, her heart pounding like it would leap out of her throat along with the remains of her supper. She swallowed and turned around slowly, intending to defend herself if Jack was behind her.

A boy she'd never seen before sat in her window, leaning against the frame. Though most of his face was in shadow, the boy leaned so casually she didn't think he meant any harm. All the same, Pearl stayed absolutely still with the shears pointed toward him just in case.

"Go on, cut it." He nodded at her hair. "It won't deter him, but you'll feel better. I know. I did something very like what you're about to do."

"I beg your pardon?" Pearl was too shocked to scream. It didn't seem right to call out for help against a boy who couldn't be more than thirteen. Besides, she had to know what he'd seen.

"Don't you want to talk about it? Finally discussing it is what helped me escape the man who kept me." His accent and manner of speech reminded her of old Captain Rodgers, her great-uncle who'd defected from the British Navy before the Civil War. The breeze shook the curtains slightly, revealing more of the boy's face. His features were lean but beautiful with haunted gray eyes.

"Talk about what?" She knew better than to reveal information before getting any. He only answered after the breeze rustled the curtain and his face was back in shadow.

"Your fiance." He sounded angry. "Things could have gone worse for you if he hadn't heard that noise I made. He's cunning, but a vile sort. His plan was to get you in a family way tonight, whether you wanted it or not. You'd have been forced to marry him. If you don't talk about it, at least do something. Don't you deserve a better life?"

Tears ran down Pearl's face. She wanted to answer but risked hysterics if she spoke. How could he know what Jack had whispered as he'd pressed against her? The boy's gray eyes glittered, as though he held back some strong emotion. Was it sympathy? More anger at Jack? Did it matter? She raised the shears to the side of her face, just below her jawbone. The boy nodded encouragingly.

Pearl opened the scissors with her right hand then held a clump of her pale yellow hair away from her head with the left. As she closed the blades together, weight lifted from her head, her heart, her soul. The first cut felt so freeing, she pulled another clump away from her head and did it again, and then again.

"Good girl." The boy nodded. Pearl smiled, and he gave her a closed-lipped grin back. After a few more minutes, there were no more long locks for Pearl to feed the devouring shears. At her feet were remnants of the girl she'd been. The hair was like broken shackles. Without its heavy weight, she thought she could do anything. The boy stood up on the bit of roof just outside the window.

"I feel so much better, Mister..." Pearl still had no idea who this boy was.

"Denton." He chuckled. "But please call me Daniel. After all this, it seems silly not to be on familiar terms."

"Then you can call me Pearl," she said.

"What will you do now, Pearl?"

"I'm not sure, but I can't stay here."

"My friends and I are leaving town tomorrow." He leaned against the outside of the house. "Some come from circumstances much like yours. You could go with me tonight and meet them, decide whether you want to travel with us." Pearl looked around the room, then down at her nightgown.

"There's time enough to dress as you wish, Pearl." He turned his back to her and assumed a posture of waiting.

Pearl grabbed some clothes from her bureau, got behind the screen, and put them on more speedily than a child on Christmas morning. When she came to the window, Daniel offered his hand, and she held it despite the fact that it was cool as the evening air. By the time she saw his wickedly pointed teeth, it was too late for her to change her mind. Instead, she Changed forever.

"Child?" The elderly Father's voice brought Pearl back. "You told me you escaped your former intended. That must have taken courage."

"Oh, Father, I'm sorry. I've wasted your time." What

was she doing here? She should leave. Changed didn't belong in churches.

"No, child. You're not the first to pause at a brink like this, and you won't be the last. Take whatever time you need to finish your reconciliation." The priest's voice was soft, undemanding, serene. Pearl stayed.

"I changed that night, Father. I ran away with some people. I never went back to my parents, or even wrote them to try and explain. I was angry at them, but also ashamed of what I'd become to survive. I'm still ashamed."

"Why?"

"I had to steal. The people I was with expected it of me, it's what they taught me to do. But I found another way. If they find out I'm doing it, they might kill me."

"And is it fear of this that brings you back to God after so many years?"

"No, Father. Shame brings me. It was wrong of me to go with these people, and wrong not to explain things to my family. But I still believe it was right to leave them and try and make my own way. I'm here because I want to escape these people. I want to be better, make amends, live honestly. I'm just not sure that's possible for someone like me."

"All things are possible in God's love, child, if only you're willing to get right with Him. I'm glad you've come."

"Thank you, Father. I'm glad, too."

"Work on getting to safety first. You must try not to steal again. If you're hungry or cold, there is help for people in your situation. If you can find honest work, take it. Some of the mills here in town even have dormitories for single workers. I'll gladly help you with contrition any time you need it. For now, let us pray."

The words of the sacrament came back to her more clearly than the memory of Daniel. As Pearl prayed along with the Father, hope kindled in her heart. She couldn't do exactly as he said, but she had ideas about how to survive away from Daniel. She could bring Sam and anyone else willing to leave with her. All she had to do was figure out how to get away. Daniel would never willingly let anyone go.

Leo wrung his hands as they headed into town again. He didn't want to be near any people this soon. Last night, he'd almost killed a little old lady like some kind of big bad wolf. What would his next embarrassment be, a little girl with a basket? He would bet all of his inherited Daylo flashlights that Oguina'd been better at this when she was "new." He couldn't imagine her being any other way. She was so much stronger than she looked, too. She could have just slung him over her shoulder and skedaddled.

He'd been humbled at just how long she'd lived alone. When he went looking for her, he'd thought she'd been around since maybe the Civil War. He hadn't imagined an undersized woman from the Plymouth Colony days would have had the courage to go find a monster, and ask to be one herself. He'd barely been able to do it himself. She must have had a damned good reason.

That old woman had somehow recognized Oguina, but they couldn't be the source of the stories he'd heard. The woman's initial greeting had been friendly. It was a testament to Oguina's ability to hide herself in a crowd without making people uneasy. He wondered how many people over the centuries remembered her as an innocuous face in a crowd. And he'd made her blow her cover. Shame washed over his face.

And just how many recognized her later in life? He'd bet a whole box of Daylos that there were even more stories about a woman who never spoke and never aged. Weren't those traits often attributed to ghosts? There were even more stories about the ghosts of Fall River than monsters. Would those would turn out to be true? What about the story of the silent Sister at the hospital? Was that Oguina, too?

"Where are you going?" asked Oguina. At the edge of town, Leo thought about running back to the woods. Oops, he'd actually almost done it.

"Just bracing myself." He grinned and looked back the way they'd come. Was that something up in the branches, a dark crouching shape? If it was more than a shadow then it was probably some kind of wildcat. He faced the city again and rolled his shoulders. "I'm ready to go now."

They went toward Highland Avenue. The men and women here were more well-off than those on North Main Street. Some of them were heading out to the cinema, restaurants, or speakeasies. He hung back for a few moments, then tried walking down the block alongside Oguina. There was a couple coming out of a house across the street. He heard their individual heartbeats and, worse, he smelled them. It was different from animals, like the difference between smelling oatmeal and smelling a steak. He stopped walking.

"Keep walking. It serves as a distraction." Oguina

pulled him along. She had a point, sort of. Moving his feet at a casual pace was difficult enough to need focus. The smell lessened as he moved away, though heartbeats were so easy to hear. It was impossible to drown them out.

"Can I ask you something kind of personal?" Leo hoped talking would be even more distracting. How in the world had Oguina done this all alone? "Why didn't he stick around? The one that changed you, I mean."

"I do not know." Oguina's pace stayed steady.

"Well, didn't you ask him for help learning about all of this?"

"No, I did not." Her arm stiffened.

"Why?"

"I thought things would be easy with all this power. I went away almost immediately, and made mistakes."

"So you went back for help? Because of the mistakes?"

"No."

"Then why?"

A low growl came from her chest. "Do not press me for an answer, cub."

He stopped his questions, remembering Oguina was one of the only things that could kill him. He shouldn't keep pestering her. They turned the corner, revealing more people. What she'd already said would have to do for now.

As they neared the four men on the other side of the block, Leo tried to imagine why Oguina would go looking for that other monster again. Was it the anger? She'd said over and over how important control was, but he hadn't seen her come close to losing it until just now.

Everything she'd done so far seemed as emotionless as it was effortless, a necessity. Violence and anger were not the same thing.

And he also wondered what these mistakes of hers were. He had no idea why she'd chosen to become what she was. Maybe he should have asked her in the first place, instead of condescending questions about being lonely. That's exactly the kind of polite thing to ask someone new. What do you do for a living? How did you decide to be a seamstress instead of a nurse? But Oguina was a monster not a seamstress. Thinking of things to ask was like trying to think of a joke. What does one monster say to the other monster? What do you do when you're not eating the living? Were those appropriate questions in polite monster society? Was there even such a thing?

But then, Oguina was a solitary monster who had not been amongst monsters. Maybe there was no such thing as a monster society, and even a pair of monsters was unusual. Then again, everyone told stories about monsters even if they didn't generally believe in them. There might be too few monsters to make a society, but then they'd have to be too rare for stories also. Oguina couldn't answer these questions for him, but that just made him more curious. He had a sudden urge to go searching for more monsters. It was the only way to find more answers.

What was he thinking? Did he want revenge or roots? It would have been simpler to hop a boat to Ireland and track down some cousins. He had to still want vengeance, right? He'd Changed, sure, but had he also changed his mind? Oguina turned them around to walk back down along Highland Avenue, and he smelled something that almost made him bare his teeth.

More men had joined the ones across the street. They were standing around next to an expensive car, smoking cigarettes. He glared in their direction, but their faces were lost in too many shadows. That smell though, it was some sort of cologne. He'd last smelled that outside his house while it was burning.

One of the men took a step siceways, revealing dark hair and fine features covered with bronze skin. Jimmy. A haze came over Leo's senses and all he could hear or see or think of was blood until he felt rough stone on his back and something like shackles on his wrists.

"Have you returned to me, cub?" Oguina stared up at him, searching for something. Was she worried?

"What happened?" He blinked, clearing the last of that haze.

"That is exactly what I planned to ask you." They were in the Beattie Granite Quarry. Oguina had him pinned against an upright slab of rock. Had she gotten him that far from Highland Avenue by herself? He looked around. They were alone.

"I saw one of Bianco's men. He was standing by that car." Leo shuddered. "I don't know what I would have done."

"One thing is certain, you need more practice. You were running away from them, but toward the hospital. I chased you here instead." She released his hands. "Let us return to our camp."

Too ashamed to say anything else, Leo followed her.

Something was wrong when Oguina woke the next evening. The extra clothes were missing. Even worse, she had left the clothes right beside her as she slept. What could have done that without disturbing her rest?

She saw Leo just beginning to stir. Had someone followed them? If so, why had they only taken the clothing? Oguina looked around, saw no blood and no signs of disturbance. Could an animal have dragged the clothes away? A more thorough search found nothing. She could not think of any animal that would leave so little trace, not even a scent. As she peered up into the trees, she heard Leo approach.

"What are you looking for?" He stretched, then scratched his head.

"Who or whatever stole our spare clothes." Oguina chose another tree to scrutinize. "Will you assist in the search?" He nodded, then searched the ground around the clearing.

After several minutes, he shrugged. "I guess we have to raid another clothesline."

"That is not the problem. Whoever took them got past us and covered his tracks. He could still be here. We might be in danger."

Oguina lifted her head, trying to catch any scent at all. Still, nothing was out of the ordinary. She smelled an owl's nest, four nights worth of campfires, the stream and some deer taking a drink from it. She focused her efforts on listening instead, but there was a distraction. She turned to look at Leo, who had his eyes closed.

"Do you smell those deer?' He inhaled deeply through his nose.

"Yes. Go and get one." He dashed off in the direction of the stream and the unsuspecting animal beside it. Moments later she smelled its blood. Oguina applied herself to listening again. This time, she heard something. "Reveal yourself or die," she hissed.

"Die? Don't make me laugh!" That voice was familiar, but she couldn't pinpoint its direction. Before she could reply, Oguina was on her back, pinned down by a pair of bulky arms. She looked up into the attacker's pale blue eyes. His familiar face was half obscured by an unkempt red beard, which parted in a savage razor-toothed smile. "So, Bersadottir, you've finally extended our family." Here on the other side of centuries was the one who'd Changed her. She supposed she was his daughter, after a fashion.

Something hit him over the head from behind. He laughed. Leo's hands groped for the attacker's eyes, an instinctively sensible move but ultimately futile against this creature. She also laughed.

"Where have you been all this time? And let me up before you answer."

Bersi kept hold of her arms as he stood, lifting Oguina off the ground. "That is a long and boring tale." She found herself swept over his shoulder, carried a few paces, then put down on a log next. She took in the fact that he was wearing Leo's missing clothes. He gestured at Leo, then pulled out a knife to trim his beard.

"No." Leo crossed his arms as he shook his head. "I won't sit until you tell me who you are and what you're doing here." His refusal was almost funny; Bersi weighed at least twice what Leo did. But then, Leo bared his teeth.

"I am Bersi Olafsson." The bearded man's tone turned serious. He gazed at Leo. "I am here to meet you."

A Change In Crime

Pearl noticed the dark-haired man perched in the rafters right away. He watched Daniel Denton intently, sizing up the Changed who had once served in the British Navy aboard the HMS Centaur. She tried not to look up again because she didn't want Daniel to notice him. He'd killed or pressed all of the Changed they encountered. To keep herself from giving away the man in the rafters, Pearl looked over at Sampson.

Sampson still managed to hold onto himself. He stood at Daniel's right, glaring down his nose at everyone including Pearl, but it was an act. After her Change, it was Sampson who helped her adjust. Without his help, she'd be just like the haunted masses doing Daniel's bidding. Instead, she'd kept her conscience.

Daniel had plans Pearl could only guess at. He made his Changed duel each other as "training." He'd bring in humans also, usually derelicts, and order them gruesomely slaughtered. Pearl learned to hide so she could avoid being singled out, but Daniel caught her sometimes. Her rebellion inspired others. Sampson feigned uncontrollable bloodlust, killing the victims before Daniel could find everyone. Daniel laughed at this, slapping Sampson's back and telling him how far he'd come since the Underground Railroad.

Less than a year ago, Sampson's act started turning real. He'd lose himself in memories frequently, and come back from them with a hard ironic smile instead of tears. Sampson said he'd gotten the jitters, acting out of instinct before he could even think about controlling himself. Every night she could, Pearl would wander off alone so they could talk. Together they would reminisce about the better parts of their pasts. It was the only thing that helped.

There were others at that jittery stage, and Pearl couldn't be so secretive about getting them together for remembrance of better days. Daniel noticed, of course, and banned "story hour" with Pearl. But he couldn't keep track of things like that when they were out, so Pearl took her groups outside on a walking tour. They'd appear to be hunting as long as Daniel didn't come close enough to hear what they were saying. He'd started to notice the effects of this and kept Sampson with him more frequently now. Pearl hadn't figured out what to do about that yet.

Sampson noticed Pearl looking at him. He gave her a smile disguised as a menacing grimace, then twitched the left corner of his mouth twice, as his gaze flickered to Daniel then up to the rafters. He was letting her know Daniel had spotted the man up there. The man looked down. Did he know he'd been seen? Daniel stared up directly at him. Whoever this fellow was and whatever his reason for being here, he'd lost his chance at surprise.

Just as Daniel opened his mouth to speak, the man dropped from the rafter and landed lightly on the balls of his feet. He had no heartbeat and didn't breathe. He was Changed, just like them. The man from the rafters wasn't much taller than Daniel but was more solidly built. He carried himself with confidence. He also looked more human than the rest of them, like he was newly Changed, maybe like the others said she seemed to be. He looked about as human as she felt herself. That hope she'd started feeling in the reconciliation booth grew.

"Daniel Denton." The man had a commanding voice. A brief flicker of surprise crossed the monster boy's face. "You and your Changed have been carrying on in dishonor long enough. I challenge you to single combat, to prove that your way is wrong and to take responsibility for those pressed into your service unwillingly."

"Oh look, we've gotten a visit from a Vaudeville performer!" Daniel winked and then smiled, showing as many of his teeth as possible.

"I am no stage performer, but Sir Hrafin of Mercia. Will you continue to mock me, or will you take my challenge?" The newcomer smiled a little less widely than Daniel but somehow showed more teeth. Hadn't she heard somewhere that Changed grew more teeth the older they got? Pearl believed this man was who he said he was.

Smirking haughtily, Daniel tried to stare Hrafin down. That didn't have its usual effect. Some Changed in the room were either too afraid or apathetic to care, but most watched intently. Daniel sized up the knight from under his veneer of feral bravado. There would be a fight, and this Hrafin had a chance to win. Even though

Pearl wasn't sure God would care about the prayers of a Changed, she still sent one His way.

"Challenge?" Daniel laughed. "No such thing could come from you for me, but sure. Duel me if you want. It's your end you're chasing; who am I to keep you from it?"

The knight's nostrils flared, and Pearl sniffed as well, wondering what he was smelling. She didn't detect anything different from what was normally in the warehouse, except Hrafin of course. Then she realized that Hrafin's scent, musky and earthy like the start of heavy rain, was familiar somehow even though it shouldn't be. All the Changed she knew smelled of driftwood, dry with a hint of old brine.

"No," said Hrafin, "you must either accept or say you decline. Do you not know how to properly answer a challenge? The one who Changed you ought to have taught you better, Cousin."

Pearl watched rage occupy Daniel's face for a few seconds before he covered it with his usual veneer of sarcasm. Her eyes flicked back to Hrafin, and she could tell he'd seen that slip of facade. He nodded slightly as if he'd been expecting it. Pearl knew now that Hrafin must have smelled something important, but didn't have time to wonder what that meant.

"Then I accept." Daniel sauntered toward the middle of the room. "As the one being challenged I choose the weapon, right?" Hrafin arched an eyebrow, then sighed and nodded. Pearl saw the knight's mistake. Daniel would name some other Changed to duel in his place.

Daniel's saunter carried him right up to her. "Pearl

Fallon. You're my weapon. Take care of this." He waved one hand absently in Hrafin's direction and blinked like a lizard in the sun. If her heart could still beat it would have been loud enough for a regular human to hear. Hrafin blinked. His face was as still and close as the moment before a rainstorm.

As Pearl approached Hrafin, she remembered something from all those stories she'd read as a girl about King Arthur. She caught the Knight's eye and winked, then watched the small, enigmatic twinkle light his eyes. Pearl turned her back to Hrafin. She faced Daniel, steeling herself.

"I request a champion to fight in my stead." She prayed again to God that this was valid under Hrafin's rules and not just some device Lord Tennyson put into his verses. "Daniel, you are the most capable combatant I have ever known. I choose you as my Champion."

"That's not good form." Daniel's lilting tone chilled Pearl more than a snarl would have. She pressed her knees together to keep them from shaking, thankful she favored long and modest dresses.

"Oh, but it is." Hrafin's voice carried authoritatively to every corner of the warehouse. "A Lady facing mortal combat may always choose a champion, and Changed Ladies are no exception." The knight smiled at Daniel, and Pearl went back to stand with the others.

"Fine," Daniel spat, "When I win I'm discarding my weapon in a most satisfying way."

"As the challenger, I choose the time and place of the duel. I choose here and now." And then Hrafin said, "Cousin."

Enraged, Daniel flung himself at Hrafin. Hrafin's hands moved so swiftly Pearl couldn't follow, but somehow Daniel ended up on his back on the floor. That had never happened in the last fifteen years. Pearl's mouth dropped open in shock. Sampson's jaw clenched.

Daniel snarled, kicking up from the floor, clearly too angry to plan his next attack. Whatever this "cousin" business was that Hrafin kept bringing up, it was working. Pearl saw Daniel resort to a hackneyed move he'd used nearly automatically before; a feint to the left with his arm while attempting a leg sweep on the right.

Hrafin wasn't fooled. He shifted away, dropping to one knee and grabbing Daniel's right calf. He pulled and Daniel toppled pronely. Hrafin was on him in a fraction of a second, pushing his face against the floor. There was no way for Daniel to get leverage and no chance for him to get at the knight with his teeth. Wood splintered as he gnashed them against the hardwood.

"Do you yield?" Hrafin's voice was even and calm. Daniel growled out a word that Pearl couldn't make out, but she assumed it was never. She was wrong.

Pearl shouted a too-late warning. A streak of red arced toward Hrafin as a Changed made a flying leap. It was Bloody Bess, Daniel's first follower. She kicked Hrafin in the head, knocking him off Daniel's back. He went flying to land in front of a pile of crates.

"Treachery!" Hrafin shifted to get up off the floor. Bess kicked Hrafin while he was down, and the knight skidded off into the shadows, knocking crates over on the way. Bess threw back her head and coughed out a laugh that sounded like a cougar's scream.

"I'll be back, Cousin." Hrafin's voice came from a pool of shadow behind the crates. "This isn't over." A strange crackling and shifting sound came from his direction. No matter how hard Pearl listened, she couldn't figure out what he was doing over there.

Pearl should have used that time to run. Bess grabbed her, pinning her arms to her side. She wasn't strong enough to break away.

"I've got just the punishment for you," Daniel smirked, then bit his wrist and forced the wound into her mouth. For the second time in her life, Pearl's mouth was filled with a taste like the smell of the compost out back at her home in Worcester. This time, she felt no pains of Change. She felt nothing at all. Her skin numbed, sound dwindled, scent faded, and sight dimmed.

Pearl tried to make one more prayer, aloud this time. Her lips moved too slowly. She knew someone else would have to stop Daniel.

Crouched outside the cave next to the ancient monster, Leo had to stop thinking about how old Bersi might be. He shouldn't want to know. Hell, getting a definitive answer might just drive him insane. It was bad enough contemplating one hundred years alone after Bianco was dead. What if it turned out to be a thousand or more?

Then again, haunting the shores of humanity's oceans might be tolerable with some company. Bersi was jovial where Oguina was sober, brash where she was subtle. Leo felt more normal with Bersi here than with Oguina alone. He'd gotten a dose of slow-acting impatience in her company. He could find those men from Highland Avenue, follow them to whatever destination they had for the evening, let go of all his control. He just wasn't sure he could live with himself if anyone besides the murderers got hurt.

Bersi nudged him, pointed upward. Oguina was crouched above the four-foot high mouth of the cave. She dropped the deer carcass to the ground, then stilled. Something that rustled and snuffled moved inside the cave, then he heard a noise of something large taking a breath and a slow, steady heart pumping a large volume of blood.

A bear emerged. It was the largest animal Leo had ever seen; six feet long and solidly built. Scars on its muzzle and other areas of its pelt indicated a life of successful fighting. Puffs of dust were displaced from the ground as it paced to the dead deer. It paused before inspecting the carcass, looking around as if it smelled something. Bersi threw a small stone opposite from where they hid to draw its attention away. The old bruin wasn't fooled by the ruse. It spotted Oguina, reared up, and batted at her with a paw bigger than her head.

Oguina sprung off the small ledge just in time. The bear's paw hit the rock where she'd been a moment before, and chips of granite went flying in all directions. Oguina landed behind the bear, on her feet but in a crouching position. The bear growled, and threw itself backward to scrape her off on the rock behind it. Somehow, she pushed back, throwing the bear off balance until it landed directly on top of her.

"Go help her!" Leo looked at Bersi, too surprised to answer. Why send the little guy to fight this behemoth? "Does your nursemaid catch dinner for you every night, or just when you have company?"

Leo growled instead of delivering some scathing remarks about age before beauty. The bear was on its back rolling from side to side. Oguina was getting crushed under there! Leo jumped up to tackle the bear. It was like running into a parked car. Better than a brick wall, at least.

The bear growled, rolling to swat Leo with its paw. Leo almost got out of the way in time, but the animal caught his arm, shredding his sleeve and the flesh under it. He heard a crack, felt an intense and sharp pain, then couldn't feel anything from the elbow down. The bear reared up on its hind legs, about to fall on him. He couldn't move in time so that half-ton of rancid smelling bear crushed him.

Leo panicked before realizing he had no need to breathe. He tried to use the ground for leverage to push the bear off him, but his limbs were in the wrong places. His ear was against the bear's belly. He could hear and feel all that blood moving around making him nearly mad with hunger. He opened his mouth and bit down. The bear got up with a bellow and began charging at something, dragging Leo along the ground. Blood was running hot into his mouth so he held on, drinking.

There was a jolt as the bear hit whatever it had been charging. It bellowed again, quieter this time. It staggered a few steps to one side, its blood flowed more slowly. Leo heard its heartbeat slow down as it keeled over. He let go when its heart finally stopped, then sat up to look around. He turned his head to spit out a matted clump of bear hair.

Oguina climbed off the bear's back. Her face was covered with blood that also matted her hair in red-black tangles around her face. Clumps of the fur looked glued to her clothes with blood. Leo heard a hearty laugh and a clapping sound from behind him.

"Now that was a hunt! A real fight." It was Bersi clapping. Of course. "None of that sneaking and walking away without a mark." The big red-haired man winked at Leo. "Give me your arm." Leo wondered why but wasn't in the mood to ask questions.

Bersi took the injured arm in his big callused hands and looked it over. Leo looked with him. He'd regained sensation but hadn't been able to move it as usual. Now he knew why. Leo's arm had broken and then bent backward halfway down his forearm. Worse, it had healed that way. It sat at a right angle below his elbow, with most of his forearm pointed toward his back. A shadow fell over them, Oguina stood over him with unusual concern. She must have been a model of femininity in her days as a regular human. Leo looked at her bloody face and tangled hair, wondering again why she'd chosen to be Changed. He knew all the stories, but now that he knew her those stories didn't fit.

"It must be broken again if it is to heal properly." Oguina stared at Bersi until he nodded.

"You are right, Bersadottir." The ancient man cracked his knuckles. "Hold him."

Leo got up to run as fast and far away as possible. Oguina was too quick for him. She had grabbed him around the neck, tangling his legs up with hers. All Leo could do was flail his twisted, deformed arm around wildly. Bersi just stood watching for a few moments, then grabbed it like a person would pick an apple off a tree. He felt sick-green pain before hearing a sharp snap as his arm was re-broken. His throat burned with the intensity of the howl he made. Leo looked down at his arm. It looked exactly the same as it had before the fight with the bear, except for the ripped sleeve. He really had to start taking better care of his clothes, or else Change them so they'd heal themselves.

"Next time, let's go after a smaller and less messy bear." Leo waved a hand in front of his nose. "Maybe one that's had a bath in the last seven years?"

Oguina laughed, untangling herself from him. She looked down at herself, at Leo, and then at Bersi. "You owe us fresh clothing. These are too torn to use again."

"What do you need clothing for?" asked Bersi. "Your bellies are full, and deer are still plentiful for the next few weeks at least."

Oguina nodded at Leo.

"I have a particular hunt I need practice for," Leo answered. "I need to pass some humans by so I can get some specific ones."

"Oh ho!" Bersi rubbed his hands together. His clean hands, the stinker. "Tell me about this hunt you need so much preparation for. What is your quarry?"

Leo thought his answer through before giving it. If he could phrase it right, Bersi might help. "I hunt a...herd...or whatever you would call it of human monsters that kill other people. They don't kill for food, and they never give a fair fight. They kill just because they can because they think they're the strongest. I went looking for Oguina to prove them wrong."

Bersi threw back his head and laughed. "Then I will steal us some clothes, and later this season we will all hunt fools!"

Oguina went alone as far upstream as she could get before bathing. She needed time alone to think. After hundreds of years alone she needed a break from constant company, especially with Bersi there. She'd wanted him to come back, but his presence could complicate this situation. She could stop worrying and just ask him some questions, but had to be sure to ask the right ones.

She could use some of the paper she'd stolen for Leo to make a list. She'd done it before to foster contemplation. Her thoughts felt immature while they remained trapped in her head. But other people were more complicated than paper. She needed to nurture ideas about Leo's vendetta against Bianco. But first, she'd need to make peace with Bersi.

Oguina finished washing away the blood, her hair still tangled worse than it had ever been. She'd practiced and honed her abilities specifically to kill cleanly and keep tidy since her earliest and most out-of-control nights. Bersi seemed to revel in blood and gore as though that was the glory of battle. Hunting a bear over four times her own weight held no glory for her. It was inefficient and wasteful. Combined with its flesh, even a small bear was more than the three of them would need in one night.

"More like gory than glory." Oguina was halfway up a tree at the sound of the voice before recognizing her own. Her voice was like another person's after so long, and the words themselves sounded like something Leo would say.

What would happen when Leo finished his vengeance and Bersi ambled off again? Could she hibernate like the bear had been preparing to do? There was one thing to ask Bersi, at least. She found a pointy rock to try and untangle her hair, since her comb was back at the cave. Her hair was impossible without a comb, but she didn't want to cut it. Hair took twice as long to grow back for Changed, she'd learned that much on her own at least. Hearing footfalls behind her, Oguina turned her head. Bersi was standing there, holding something.

"Bersadottir." Why did he always call her that? Did he forget her name? "Here are some clothes and also this." He held a woolen dress in one hand and a comb in the other. She had expected the dress from him instead of trousers as she'd prefer, but not the comb. That was uncharacteristically thoughtful.

"Thank you." Oguina stood and took both items. She pulled the dress on over her head, and then started putting the comb to good use. She glared at the water, wishing she could see what she was doing. "I went back to try to find you only a week after you changed me, and you were gone. Why?"

"Because you Changed strong." Bersi crossed his arms over his chest. Oguina glared until he looked away. "I knew you'd be a good warrior. I didn't expect you to come back once I'd told you everything I knew. I hoped you would win your battle."

"Have you seen the people in the cities? Is it not obvious that I lost?" The comb was stuck in a snarl. She had to work to get it free.

"Fail?" His teeth glittered in a smile that dodged his eyes. "Look at you. You never want for prey, you fool the people into thinking you're one of them, and you Changed Leo. He'll be at least as strong as you are."

"Bersi, I mean that I failed in my battle." The comb was stuck again. "I told you I wanted my enemies dead. But look around; my enemies overran my people. You don't see many like me anymore because all of my family died. I could barely control my hunger those first nights. I woke after a day in the open sometimes, surrounded by people in such small pieces I couldn't tell which were my foes."

"No one would know that now, watching you." Bersi sighed. "The past is carved in our minds like stone. You've learned since then. You lost then, but this is now. What troubles you here in the present?"

"I didn't learn enough. In the end, a sickness killed my people. No inhuman strength could have saved them. I lost due to circumstances beyond my control. And I'm supposed to teach Leo how to win?" She wiggled the comb out of her hair. If anything, she'd made the tangle worse. This one was much worse than the last. She gave up and reached for a knife.

"Oguina, you were alone." Bersi's hand covered hers and most of the knife. "Saving your people would have been like trying to keep a wave on the beach. You shouldn't have been by yourself. I failed, not you. I thought anyone I Changed would need nothing but facts from me. I was wrong. I wasn't there to help you then. But I am here now. And I'm sorry, Oguina."

His apology was late, and couldn't change the past. But he did have a point. He was here now. Perhaps Leo wouldn't fail. Perhaps there was more to learn about being Changed even as she taught. Perhaps, if she was like the moon, that was the third phase she had to look forward to. Bersi reached for the comb but hesitated, waiting for her reaction.

"Yes." She nodded and handed over the comb. "We are both here now. Let us all use the time wisely."

Bersi's face relaxed. He began untangling her hair in silence.

D.R. Perry

Howard Fallon loitered, studying everyone who walked down Bradford Avenue. It was something he usually did in Fall River on the nights he wasn't under orders. Working for someone was still a strange experience. He'd worked with his best friend for seventeen years until Jack's accident. They'd figured things out together ever since his sister had gone missing from her bedroom on her eighteenth birthday. Ten of those years they'd chased rumors and strange stories until finally, he ran into her back in Worcester.

He'd been in an alley less than a block from Saint Vincent's Hospital when something knocked him down. He hadn't been able to scream, hadn't wanted to once he saw it was her. All that time looking and she'd been the one to find him. He was so relieved to see her face that at first, it hadn't registered what she'd been doing to him.

She'd pulled herself off of him. If she hadn't, he would have been in his grave nine years ago. He remembered her staring at him with blood all over her mouth until she wiped it off with inhuman speed. He hadn't figured out why she'd dragged him across the street to the hospital until he smelled the blood. If she hadn't had that unnatural speed, he would have died. The doctor she left him with was an old hand at stitches, the hospital did transfusions and had a donor of his blood type. His sister had hoofed it before anyone could ask her questions.

Jack Houlihan found him on the second hospital check. That was something they'd agreed to do if one of them didn't come home some night. Jack had been relieved to find Howard in recovery instead of in the morgue. He and Jack hunted monsters with the same kind of camaraderie they'd had playing stickball as kids.

Until that night, Howard thought he trusted Jack implicitly. Jack had asked him if he'd been hurt on the steps of the hospital. When Howard answered in the negative, Jack got angry and accused him of lying. They couldn't talk about monsters while Howard was at the hospital. A private or even a semi-private recovery room was too rich for Howard's blood, and Recovery was busy that night.

Once he was discharged, Jack inundated him with questions, but Howard just told him he couldn't remember anything about how he got attacked, only that it had happened in an alley. He always followed his gut. That night it told him to keep his sister's identity a secret. When he had time to think about it, he figured it was for Jack's own safety. Jack could end up dead if he went up against her alone, and Howard still wasn't up to a battle.

When they'd gone back two weeks later to the same alley, he saw Daniel for the second time. Howard knew the monsters didn't age but never saw the same one more than once until that night. He kept thinking the boy should have looked more like a man by now, gained some bulk and height. Daniel hadn't changed one bit, of course.

"Your sister's worse than useless." Daniel smiled. Howard had seen these things do that before, but he still had to fight the impulse to run. "I should have taken you instead. Kill them." Daniel pointed into the back of the alley. A tall, lanky monster with a weary expression and physique like a stick bug stepped forward. This monster chased Howard and Jack around Worcester for the better part of an hour. Howard figured out it was a klutz and tripped it with a trash can. Jack killed it with a kerosene lamp.

Each monster had individual strengths and weaknesses. Some were more agile, some weaker, some tougher, and some burned faster. The one thing they all had in common was always those teeth. They all had tells, and Howard had some kind of knack for reading them. It was like playing poker. Howard had a knack for that too, which kept them fed. He could watch the monsters, then plan how to kill them. The only time they'd made a mistake was two years back. They were about to kill one of Daniel's lieutenants when scaffolding fell on Jack's legs. The doctors had to amputate, leaving Jack stuck in the hospital for good and all. Howard still visited him twice a month.

Daniel was the only one who seemed not to have a weakness. His two lieutenants were stronger than the others. The one from Jack's accident was Sampson, a black monster who had tunnel-vision. Bloody Bess was easily distracted, but only when she was killing someone. Laying a trap for her would mean setting someone up to die. Bess killed even more people than Daniel and seemed less calculating than him. Howard thought monsters got more insane the more they killed but had no way of testing it.

A woman with red hair walked by, so Howard focused his attention on the present. He checked her gait, hip to waist ratio, and height. Nope, that wasn't Bess. She called out a friendly greeting to another woman. Howard ignored it, letting his thoughts go back to a few months after he got to Fall River.

Howard had been watching people just like he was doing tonight. He caught one of Bianco's muscle men, Niccolo, following his sister. They almost fought each other, but they got attacked by another one of Daniel's worn-out looking followers.

That night when Niccolo had asked if he would go and meet with Bianco, Howard knew there was no real choice. He had already heard around Fall River about what happened when you crossed Giacomo Bianco. That was one reason he agreed to the meeting. The other reason was Bianco ran all the area poker games.

He'd been surprised when he met Bianco. It was easy to imagine a crime boss as some brute of a man with an intimidating and threatening demeanor. The thin, calm man spoke slowly, his voice calm and even. He seemed harmless. His stone-faced expression was nearly legendary, and he used it to catch people off-guard. Howard's knack gave him no clues, so he had to go with rumors and stories. All of those said Giacomo Bianco was dangerous.

From July to late October he'd thought that working

for Bianco might not turn be all that bad. Howard didn't like working for Bianco but damn if it didn't pay well. It paid for the automobile and kept him and his mother in comfortable quarters with plenty of food. He could play cards for fun now. He could even buy slippers and pajamas for Jack.

Howard saw a bald, dark head in a crowd of other heads covered with hats. Could it be Sampson? Monsters didn't feel the cold and sometimes forgot to dress for the season. The bald man turned right on Bradford instead of left like the rest of the crowd, coming toward Howard. No fog of breath was coming from the face, and the height and gait matched. That was Sampson, all right.

Howard counted down backward from seven, then started walking to follow Sampson on the opposite side of the street. He was wearing gloves with handkerchiefs tied around his wrists, a vest he'd sewn thick woolen padding into to cover his heartbeat and a padded scarf around his neck. Nothing could completely block the sound of his heartbeat from the monsters, but the padding muffled it so he sounded farther away. It also had a risk of heat exhaustion in hot weather. Wintry weather was best for hunting.

Sampson wasn't just strolling along looking for someone to kill. The bald monster walked deliberately and with purpose, as though he was on the way somewhere important. This could be the break Howard needed. If he could follow Sampson all the way back to Daniel's lair, he could burn the place to the ground during the day while the monsters slept. Jack had done that to a different group in Springfield.

Howard counted the pros and cons of his idea. A fire was one of the few things that could kill Daniel, if he got stuck in it long enough. The monsters shrugged off most things that killed people, but fires weren't one of them. Fire would kill monsters. One point in favor. Daniel was the most powerful monster Howard had ever seen. Howard probably couldn't even injure Daniel in a fight, but he could burn Daniel while he slept as long as he didn't get too close. Another point in the burning method's favor.

But Daniel might not sleep in the same place as its followers during the day. Howard could destroy an entire building and risk the others without getting Daniel. Firemen could get hurt fighting the fire. And if the monsters had humans in there, they would die too. Two points against.

Bianco would be angry if Howard killed Daniel right now. Bianco was using Daniel for something; Howard didn't know what. He figured the crime boss would want him dead someday. But until he gave an order, an attempt to kill Daniel could cost Howard his life. If Howard were going to go against orders, he'd better make it count. He'd have to be absolutely sure Daniel would die. He'd also have to make sure his sister wasn't in there. Two more points against.

So far, the cons were winning by a landslide. Before Howard could follow Sampson or his train of thought any further, Howard heard a truck behind him. It slowed as it approached, and then paced him. Howard looked to the left and saw Jimmy the Hooch peering at him out of the passenger side window. His shoulder was moving up and down as he rolled it down.

"Hey, Fallon." Jimmy talked to Howard like he'd known him for ages. "The Boss wants to see you." Howard stopped walking. The car stopped too.

"I'm tailing someone right now. This important enough to interrupt that?"

" Affirmative." Jimmy nodded.

Howard opened the door and got in. He unwound the scarf from his neck and put it in a satchel he wore across his chest under his coat. That was a wise idea; the air in the car reeked of the cologne Jimmy used to cover up the smell of gin. If Howard didn't put his scarf away, it would stink like Jimmy's cologne by the time they'd reached their destination. Monsters might not hear him coming, but they'd smell him. Howard had some respect for Jimmy. They were both creatures of instinct, making observations and snap judgments in the field. Was it such a big deal if their jobs were different?

"The Boss has a proposition for you." Jimmy took a swig from his hip flask. "I think you'll like it."

"What kind of proposition, Jimmy?" Howard took off his gloves, tucking them away with the scarf.

"It's about a dame. The Boss got an offer from little Daniel the bastard, and he wants your professional opinion on it."

"An offer?" What could Daniel offer Bianco?

"He's giving a dame to the Boss." Jimmy chuckled. "Can you believe that?"

"A monster dame?"

"That's right." The car bumped as they crossed the trolley tracks on North Main. "Not that it matters, but

Daniel says she's easy on the eyes."

"Does she have a name?" An odd feeling started in the pit of Howard's stomach.

"Yeah." Jimmy took another swig from his flask. Howard was glad it was Niccolo driving. "*El pequeño bastardo* says her name is Pearl."

"Well, then. What are we waiting for?" Howard stunted the growth of his sudden smile just in case Jimmy was watching him instead of the road.

Pearl was his sister.

Bersi was impressed with Leo. His instincts were sharp, and he had a sense of humor. He was a good choice of companion, but Bersi couldn't figure out why Oguina had gone this long alone. He would have Changed someone much sooner if he'd been alone, someone he could relate to. She'd grown crafty and deadly on her own, though nothing like he had.

He watched her with Leo, catching moths attracted to lamps made from deer fat. He supposed it was one way to teach bravery, but the fire was puny. Getting near it proved nothing. He'd learned by leaping over bonfires and would have taught it like that. But maybe his Bersadottir used the right method. Leo flinched each time he tried to snatch a moth too close to a flame. But he also kept cheating, waiting for the insect to fly away from the fire before he moved his hand.

"Why do I even have to bother with this moth-catching thing? It's just like bats."

"If it's like bats, it should be easy." Oguina put her

hands on her hips. "What will you do if you go at Bianco when he's smoking a cigar? What if he's sitting by a fireplace?"

"Okay, I get your point." Leo's hand flew at the flame again but came back empty. "Bersi, what do you think?"

Bersi didn't speak an answer. He fixed his gaze on one of the moths, got up, and plucked it out of the air without flinching. He flicked the insect at Leo's face. The youngster caught it.

"Ugh, fuzzy." Leo grimaced and let go of the moth, shaking his hand.

"You see? That's easy after hundreds and hundreds of years. You only have weeks to get half that skill." Oguina met Bersi's gaze, and after a moment she nodded. Bersi turned around to face the campfire. Then he jumped over it.

"Hot Damn! Can I learn that?" Leo clapped his hands.

"I don't know. Can you?" Bersi chuckled, grinning widely at the youngster. He saw hesitation in Leo's stance, but when he stretched his limbs to relax, and it vanished. Leo went to the edge of the clearing and then took a running leap. He landed next to Bersi, laughing. Bersi immediately pushed Leo to the ground, rolling him vigorously while the bewildered Leo tried to fight him off. The smell of singed fabric and ashes mingled with dust from the bare earth. Leo stopped struggling.

"Ugh, what a goof. But it was leaps and bounds over catching moths." Leo stood up, patting his jacket. "No offense, Oguina."

"Will you try it again?" Bersi smirked. Leo hesitated.

"Before you do, I shall get some water." Oguina

picked up a bucket, staring into it grimly. "If it gets windy, this exercise ought to be abandoned." She walked away from them, toward the stream. She was prudent, intelligent, cautious, and correct - but boring. How had she lasted like this for hundreds of years? Safe from everything but ennui, which was more dangerous than she knew. Bersi thought he'd arrived just in time.

"Bersi?" Leo brushed moth dust from his hands. "You said that you were here to meet me. How did you even know I was Changed?" His eyes narrowed. "Were you watching Oguina all this time without bothering to say hello?"

"No." Bersi sighed, then sat as near to the fire as he dared. "Until recently, I've been too far away to watch her. We can tell when someone nearby or in our line has been Changed. It's something we can do, but I don't know how it works."

"So Oguina hasn't Changed anyone but me. You really haven't Changed anyone since her?" Bersi felt too guilty to give an answer so he just nodded. "Well, why not? You seem like the kind of guy who likes company. I can't imagine you alone all that time like Oguina."

"I was not alone." Bersi wasn't ready to explain about Hrafin or the girl in Plymouth yet. He changed the subject. "You might think we always stay separate from people, but that is not true." Leo raised an incredulous eyebrow. Bersi rose to its challenge. "So Oguina never discovered it. You don't know. We don't need to stay in this shape." He stood and moved away from the fire, preparing himself.

Bersi felt his bones begin to lengthen and thicken. He

felt his skin stretch, his shoulders draw together. His skin sprouted thick red fur with an undercoat of gold. His teeth changed shape as his jaws jutted forward, and his nose got wetter and rounder. He had to look up at Leo, who sat still as a corpse. Bersi's transformation had even stopped Leo's habit of breathing and blinking for a few moments.

"Holy cow." Leo blinked round wide eyes. Bersi lolled his tongue out one side of his mouth, panting a surrogate laugh. "You're a dog."

Oguina was back from the stream. She almost dropped the bucket of water when she saw Leo staring at a big red dog. Why hadn't she smelled a dog, or heard its heart? She sniffed and listened again. Still nothing dog-like. She checked the clearing for anything else out of place and didn't find Bersi. There was something familiar about the dog's fur. She set the bucket down then went to Leo's side. Leo looked at her and took a deep, long breath.

"Oguina, Bersi..." Leo pointed at the dog, otherwise speechless. Was the dog Bersi's? But no, it wasn't alive, and animals couldn't be Changed. So what did this dog have to do with Bersi? As she thought, the dog started losing fur, shifting its form and posture. Soon, the dog changed into Bersi. He'd kept all his clothes and belongings during the transformation.

"It has drawbacks, but it means that you can find some company in disguise. Information too." Bersi scratched behind one ear. "You still have the urge to kill anything that lives, but you're learning to control that."

"So I could hang around people shaped like a dog if I want to?" Leo smiled. "That sounds like the bee's knees."

"You still want to spend the day somewhere alone," said Bersi. "But your shape might not be a dog. Each Changed only gets one animal. You won't know which yours is until you try."

Leo walked away from the fire. He stood there just waiting for something to happen and, of course, nothing did. Bersi watched Leo with a smirk. He glanced at Oguina and dropped her a wink. What was the cub missing? What kind of animal would he be? On his first night, she'd equated him to a cougar. His first kill had also been a cat. Something feline then, she guessed.

"Close your eyes." Bersi continued after Leo followed that suggestion. "Imagine yourself, then decide what you would look like as an animal. Would you have fur, scales, or feathers? Would you be brawny or lithe? Then imagine what it would feel like have those traits. Your animal will reveal itself."

Images of animals came to Oguina. She closed her eyes, imagining herself a wolf, but no. She was not a pack animal and that also eliminated dogs. She thought of a bear. Again, no. Too blunt and overt. She almost laughed when she thought of a deer. But there was a predator that glided silently unseen by its prey and took only what it needed with speed and efficiency. Her skin prickled and her shoulders hunched. Her neck thickened and shrank to meet her shoulders.

"Watch, Leo, see how it's done!" Bersi said.

Oguina opened her eyes again, her perspective closer

to the ground. She had four toes tipped with talons that anchored her to the log by the fire. She turned her head to look at Bersi and Leo. She turned it some more until it made a full circle. She blinked, then stretched and felt wings extend out from her body. She felt air move through her feathers as it went to feed the fire.

"An owl?" Leo leaned down to peer at her. She flapped her wings and let go of the log with her feet, lifting herself into the air. She hit a branch in a nearby tree instead of managing to perch on it. Determined, she screeched and hopped at the tree's trunk, claws gaining purchase in the time-scored bark. She climbed until she reached a different branch, this one a comfortable distance from the ground. Leo straightened to look up at her. She bobbed her head, blinking and hooting out owl laughter.

Leo shut his eyes until crinkles formed along his forehead, at the corners of his eyes and mouth. He tried for the rest of that night, but his animal didn't show no matter what he did.

D.R. Perry

It had snowed all day. Snow was a problem for Leo because it made them easy to track. The Changed left footprints like anything else; footprints that looked human. They could have come and gone as animals, but he still hadn't figured that out yet. Leo took one of the lamps into a corner to try some drawing since he was stuck in the cave anyway.

He drew Oguina right after she'd caught a bat, then added Bersi into the sketch. Leo had always been above average at drawing, like most things from his human life. Back then it was easy to ignore the things he wasn't automatically good at. Changed life was different. He'd need all the skills Oguina and Bersi could teach eventually, but he needed a pursuit of his own like he needed to hunt. The things he'd learned before were important to him, too. Like this drawing experiment. He knew they'd only given him paper to humor him, that they saw no point to it. But one monster's ceiling is another monster's floor.

His sketch was rough but done. In it, Oguina held a bat in one hand, crouched with the force of her landing. Bersi leaned against a tree, arms crossed over his chest with his usual smirk. Now he could test Oguina's rule.

"Hey, Bersi?" Leo beckoned with his hand. "Come have a look at this and tell me what you think." The large Changed man approached, peering over Leo's shoulder. Feathers rustled as Oguina flew into the cave. She landed before changing back to her usual self.

"This drawing looks just like my little Bersadottir." Bersi laughed. "That's an unhappy bat, though."

"What about the rest of it?" Leo stretched the drawing between his hands in front of him, under his chin. He felt like a little boy showing school work to his parents.

"You draw some happy trees." Bersi stroked his beard.

"You don't see the other person there?" Leo pointed at the sketch of Bersi.

Bersi squinted at the picture. When he reached out for the paper, Leo handed it over. He turned the drawing around in his large callused hands, looking at it sideways and upside-down. He took it near the lamp, then farther away. He pulled it close to his face, then to arm's length. He shook his head. "Maybe for a moment I saw something under that tree, but..." He shrugged, handing the drawing back to Leo.

"Oguina," said Leo, "would you look at something for a minute?"

"She won't be able to see it." Bersi stroked his beard again.

"What won't I be able to see?" Oguina raised an eyebrow at Leo. He handed her the paper, and she laughed. "Bersi, if only you could see this drawing of you! It's perfect!"

"That's not a drawing of me, it's a drawing of you.

And a most unfortunate bat." Bersi pointed to the Oguina on the paper. "You're right there."

"He must have drawn us both." Oguina turned toward Leo. "I told him we couldn't see our own likenesses. This is a test?"

Leo nodded. Bersi picked up the drawing, looking at it every which way again. With his artwork occupied, Leo decided to draw another one. This time, he tried a self-portrait. Leo put the charcoal to the paper. In a few minutes, he ended up with a drawing of his father instead. He and his father looked quite a bit alike, so he tried making the face thinner and the hairline further forward. That was a total failure. The man on the paper ended up with a completely colored in face.

"Bersi, do you know how to draw?" Leo flipped the useless drawing over, holding it and the charcoal out in front of him.

"You want me to draw you?" Bersi handed the paper to Oguina. "You want to test this for yourself." Bersi took the paper and charcoal and spent the next several minutes scratching paper with charcoal. He smirked the entire time. Leo hoped to see something that would settle this question.

Sure enough, he could only see two things in Bersi's child-like drawing. There were two stick-figures. One had long hair and a triangle on the lower half like a dress. The other was large and bulky, with a filled-in face like the one he'd tried to do of himself. There was room between the two crudely-drawn people for a third.

"Let me guess. Leo tapped the empty space. "That space is where you put the drawing of me."

"Exactly so." Bersi laughed and slapped Leo on the back. "We are snowed in. We've drawn pictures. Why not tell stories next? You must have at least one."

"What kind of story are we talking about here?"

"I want to know what tales they tell about my Bersadottir." Leo heard paper crinkle behind him.

Leo relaxed. He thought Bersi wanted to hear about an epic battle, a night of drinking, or some romantic conquest. Leo hadn't done any of that, but he'd been telling his grandfather's story about Oguina since he could talk.

"One thing children do in the city when they're bored is tell stories. Sometimes, they see who can tell the scariest story. Mine was always about a lady with long black hair and big brown eyes. But the lady was also a monster who lived in the woods. At night, she comes down into town because she wasn't always a monster. She used to be an ordinary woman, like any other. You know how your mother or your older sister tries to protect you? Well, the lady turned into a monster so she could do exactly that.

"My great-grandpa was friends with a man and that man's grandfather was the woman's little brother. His big sister, Oguina, went out one night and disappeared for years and years." Leo saw Oguina at the cave entrance, looking out. He hesitated. Could his simple tale have caused Oguina's tense shoulders, set jaw, and flared nostrils? Could words harm someone as stoic as her?

"Go on, Leo." Bersi slapped his shoulder again, smirking. "You tell a good story." Leo grinned back, his pride glittering and hard as it swelled in his chest.

"Everyone had thought that she was dead. There was something horrible in the woods, a thing from an even older story than the one I tell you now. More people went missing, but these were found. Pieces of them, anyway, but mostly pieces of dead settlers. Nothing living was safe from this thing. It killed anything that happened to get in its way.

"The brother was on his deathbed. There was a disturbance one night, so everyone asked him what happened. He started by saying that he knew what the horrible thing was in the woods. He said his missing sister had visited him, looking exactly the same as she had on the night she disappeared, except she had enormously long teeth.

"And everyone who tells this story knows the monster lady is still out there. She still looks for her brother because she's forgotten that he's dead, just like how Peter Pan forgot Wendy's all grown up. If you're in bed and hear someone at the window, you should pretend to be asleep. Peter Pan's not real, but Oguina is. If she sees you awake, she'll try to scare you, and if you run, she'll kill you."

Bersi jumped up, clapping his hands. "Such a legacy you have! Tell me, Bersadottir, what parts are true?" Bersi and Leo looked around the cave, finding themselves alone.

Oguina was gone. Leo gulped, trying to swallow his mortification. He loved telling stories to entertain, but he'd always stop when a tale upset his audience. He peered at the snow outside the cave, finding no marks on it. Leo couldn't even try to find her and apologize.

"Women." Bersi shrugged. "Who knows what they'll do, eh?"

Pretty much the same thing a man would do, from where Leo was sitting. But maybe men and women were different in Bersi's time and place. Oguina apparently hadn't wanted to hear her history turned into a hokey ghost story.

"Ah, now that she is gone, I have a story to tell you." Bersi rubbed his hands together.

"You were trying to get rid of her? That was a cruel way to do it." Leo crossed his arms. "Why didn't you just ask her to go get more paper or something?"

"She has a weakness." Bersi sighed. "She should be able to hear things like that without overreacting. I'd do the same to you if I thought you were the same. Does that mean you won't hear my story?"

"No, I'll hear it." Leo sat down. "But I have to ask: is it something I shouldn't talk about?"

"For now." Bersi put a log on the fire, then took the pad and charcoal. "My story starts in Greenland, in the town around Hvalsey Church. As I grew up, the town shrank. Winters got colder, and summers got shorter. There was only fish to eat, and many fell ill. One winter, a third of us died. We would have left, but all the shipwrights were among the dead.

"One night, a ship came to the docks. It was from the east, unusual for that time of year. It was so well-made it might have belonged to a king. But something was strange. The ship had only half the men it needed. It was going to Vinland, so the Captain wanted more men for the crew. My father, my brothers and I joined up in exchange for my sister and mother's passage. We gathered what little was still worth taking and left the next evening."

Bersi sketched as he spoke. Leo saw he'd drawn a boat. His words hadn't done it justice. The craft was large, with a square sail, oar holes on each side, and a massive dragon as its figurehead. The dragon had teeth like needles like his own teeth were now.

"You were holding out on me before, with the stick figures." Leo shook his head. "Why?"

"Never judge a creature who is testing you by your first impression of him." Bersi winked, then continued his story.

"Setting sail at night was unlucky, but we didn't complain. We wanted to leave Hvalsey that badly, you see. The captain had a cat. It was large, thick-furred, and so fierce no rat dared set foot on board. The cat had its own covered basket in the Captain's quarters, but one day it slept on the deck. One of the men dared stroke its fur, and it flayed the skin of his foot to the bone.

"We'd stop every few nights, to get fresh water and forage for fresh food. The cat went out at these stops but came back before we set off. During one stop, the man with the mangled foot was found dead in the brush. There was talk of the ship being cursed.

"The settlement at Vinland was better than Hvalsey. It was warmer, and more crops grew. But we had problems after we arrived. Something killed livestock every few nights. Soon, the Skraelings came to us, accusing our hunters of murdering theirs. They attacked any time they saw us and dismantled the traps we set to catch game, saying they'd only stop when the killings did.

"One night, my oldest brother decided he would fix our problem with the Skraelings by catching the killer, be it a Skraeling, settler, or beast. He went into the woods with his ax and shield but never came back. We searched, finding his shield in pieces and the ax bent nearly in half. Father decided a monster had killed my brother and the Skraelings. He painted charms with protective runes on our house to bar monsters from entering. He even convinced Mother to sew monster-repelling charms into our clothes. Everyone thought he'd gone mad. They all thought my eldest brother was killed by a bear.

"My other brother armed himself to hunt bears, to make the settlement safer. He went out one day at noon and came back at sunset, dragging a dead grizzly. Soon every house in the settlement had a bear skin rug just in time for winter. One day he was late going out, leaving about an hour before dusk instead of at noon. He never came back. Almost everyone thought his prey must have killed him. We found his corpse, missing a few parts, and gave him a proper funeral.

"My father raged. A monster had killed two of his sons, and he swore an oath to do something about it. He found prayers to ward off monsters, painted them on his skin, gathered every spear he could find. He went out in the afternoon, and I snuck out to follow. He came to where we'd found my oldest brother's shield and ax, then made camp. I climbed a tree with a good view of

Father and waited.

"At first I wondered why a man so driven would sit in a camp, but my father knew something I did not. What if his monster fixation was a cover for something else? After sunset, I heard someone approach. It wasn't a bear because it came on two legs and walked with a limp. It was the ship's Captain, and his cat was with him.

"Father accused the Captain of bringing a monster to Vinland that broke our peace with the Skraelings and killed two of his sons. The Captain denied this. He said there was no way a monster could have come by boat across an ocean. My father said it must have been disguised as the figurehead. While they argued, the cat looked on as though it understood speech.

"Father shouted, drawing my attention away from the cat. In moments, another man was in the clearing with them. He was short, wiry, and pale with dark hair and light eyes. I looked for the cat, but it was gone. The small man glanced up the tree directly at me and nodded. Then he stood between my father and the captain, who had almost come to blows. The small man spoke, turning his head away from them and me. Whatever he said made my father hopeful, then relieved, and finally angry. He lunged at the small man with his spear.

"He leaped out of the way and grabbed Father's spear, twisting it. Father fell to the ground.

"Those are my terms," the small man said. "Accept them and live or refuse them and condemn everyone."

My father got up, brushed himself off. He took a deep breath and sighed. Then he said, "it's Bersi's choice."

"The small man was in the tree with me a moment

later, without having to climb. He asked me to come answer a few questions. He'd changed form, had inhuman speed and strength, and was here to bargain. I thought he must be Loki. He said there was a monster in the woods, that he needed help tracking it. There would be a risk; I could die.

"Of course I said yes. Here was a chance to help everyone and avenge my brothers. I took a knife and food from my father and left that night.

"The small man told me to call him Hrafin. He said he'd been a knight of the Britons when my people still raided their northern shores. Hrafin had been Changed in the prime of his life into a kind of creature that never aged or forgot anything. The killer used to be a creature like him but gone evil. He called it a Feral.

"He showed me tracks that looked like any ordinary person's. That didn't make me doubt his story. Hrafin's tracks looked that way, too. I wondered what use I would be against something stronger than him.

"When the sun came up, I understood. He fell as though dead the moment the sun touched him. I remembered the cat on the boat and what happened to the man who'd disturbed it. I followed the tracks we'd seen the night before. Hours later, I smelled blood and decay.

"A man slept up a tree, dirty and dressed in rags, also covered with dried blood and flesh, with a belt of cured ears on a leather strip doubled around his waist. He clutched a bag damp with fresh blood. I remembered how my brother had been missing his ears.

"If I'd known how to kill the Feral, I might have tried.

Instead, I went back to Hrafin and, when the sun set, told him what I'd found. He set off at an alarming pace. I followed as fast as I could until I came to that foul tree.

"No one was there. After a while, Hrafin returned, saying he'd already found the Feral's trail. We followed it to a gully with a stream at the bottom. There was old blood on the rocks.

"Hrafin walked along the edge, trying to find where the creature had gone. At first, I watched, but tired of that and looked back at the trees. Something moved, and my leg slipped out from under me. I tumbled down the gully, bumping and scraping. When I hit bottom, I couldn't feel anything below my waist.

"I heard a laugh like a dog's bark from the top, and then Hrafin was beside me. He bit his wrist, and there was a scent like— But you already know what Changed blood smells like. A few drops fell in my mouth. All the breaks and bruises healed, and I felt my legs again. Before I could rise, Hrafin was gone again.

"I climbed out of the gully to wait. But, somehow, I could smell and see the footprints in the dark. Hrafin's blood made me better at what I already knew, so I followed the monster's trail faster than I'd ever tracked anything before.

"It was near dawn again when I came close to a Skraeling camp. I met Hrafin up a tree. He said that if I found the creature sleeping again, I could stun it. He pulled one of his own teeth then stabbed his wrist so its tip was coated in his blood. I could stab the creature with it, but from as great a distance as I could. Before he could say more, the sun rose, and he slept.

"The Feral was in some bushes beside a stream where some Skraeling women bathed. I hid, waiting for them to leave, but one didn't. She was an older woman, with hair gone mostly silver, staying to rest and warm herself in the sun by the water. As quietly as I could, I tried to go around so she wouldn't see me. I was almost to a place where I could cross the stream quietly when she opened her eyes and spoke.

"The old woman said, 'Take what I leave, and make a weapon to use against the creature you hunt.' She spoke in my own tongue, and to this night I don't understand how she knew our language or what I was doing there. There is Wisdom beyond human or even Changed senses, and that was the first I'd of seen it. But that's a story for another time.

"The old woman got up and hobbled slowly away, leaving a walking stick behind. I waited until she'd gone to go look at it. There was a groove in the wood at the top. It had been a spear at some point.

"I took Hrafin's tooth and bound it against that groove, with sap from a pine tree to make it stronger. I came to where the Feral slept just before sunset.

"There wasn't much time. I thrust the spear at the Feral's head. It jumped up, and the spear missed. As I got my balance, the creature lunged at my gut. Something tore and broke, I smelled blood and offal. I stepped to the side, saw an opening at the Feral's armpit. I hit but only made a scratch. It wasn't enough.

"The sun was down now. The Feral left me, headed for the Skraeling camp. I was too tired to follow and laid on the ground to rest for a moment. I'd failed my family and Hrafin, even that old wise woman. I was dying.

"I felt colder than a winter morning, though it was the end of summer. Then Hrafin was with me. He said I was too wounded to heal this time, but we could stop the Feral together if I Changed to be like him. I said yes, took his blood like a tonic, and death took me. And that is how I came to be as you see me tonight.

"The Feral couldn't evade us both. I wasn't fast or quiet like Hrafin, but my noise distracted the Feral until it stopped listening for Hrafin. We cornered and killed it before dawn.

"After that, I had a terrible blood-thirst and knew my people wouldn't be safe with me nearby. We went south and west. For a long time, we lived near here, and Hrafin taught me all I know of this life like Oguina teaches you now. The Skraelings she came from were our neighbors; they thought we were animal spirits. We played that part, tried to avoid them. Sometimes one of them would see us or find a kill, but only by accident. They were wiser than my own people. They stayed away.

"When the British settlers came to Plymouth, Hrafin and I went northwest. But I missed our old home and left Hrafin for a short visit without telling him. That's when Oguina came to me. She wanted to be a spirit to defeat her enemies. I thought there'd be no harm in Changing a small woman, that her strength and appetite would also be small. But she Changed stronger and hungrier than even I had. I taught her each night she came to me. She was stoic and attentive and learned fast. A week later, Hrafin came. Another Feral threatened our new home, and he needed my help again.

"I thought Oguina knew enough." Bersi's hung his head, rubbed his eyes. "I thought she'd help her people and come find us, but she didn't. I wondered whether she'd been burned in a fire or, perhaps, won her battle and gone into hiding. I didn't expect to find her when I returned."

"But you said you came back to meet me." Leo gathered his legs into a crouch. "How did you get here so fast from Canada or wherever?"

"That was only part of the truth, Leo." Bersi sighed the tension out of his body. "I knew about your Change because I was close enough to feel it. I didn't lie about that. But I was already in Plymouth by then. I've looked everywhere I've been since my own Change, and now I need help. Hrafin has been missing for the better part of a year. I haven't been able to find him."

Oguina perched in an oak tree shaped like an owl. Flying gave her time away from the others and left no traces in the snow. She had no business teaching anyone how to be Changed. She shouldn't have Changed Leo, but it was too late now.

She'd promised to prepare him to fight Bianco. Incompetent or not, it was her duty to teach him. Oguina might know next to nothing, but it was still more than Leo. She'd help him as best she could. She'd just have to learn more herself.

Was she overcautious? Bianco was just a buck, a delicate creature that bled easily. He was powerful in human terms, but what hope did he have against even an undisciplined cub? What was stopping her from having a look at the crime lord?

Oguina extended her wings, gliding from the branch to catch an updraft, then turning toward the city. Soon she soared over mills and tenements instead of trees and farmland. She decided to check the speakeasies. The human authorities had been foolish to prohibit drinking. All it did was help criminals. They'd have had more success outlawing the rain.

An owl in a speakeasy was as foolish as the law, so

Oguina scanned tenements for open windows. She spotted one and flew inside. Incredible luck, a doe's bedroom. The closet was a riot of colorful clothes, shoes, hats and jewelry. She returned to human shape, gathered items of the same color, and put them on. She glanced at a large looking glass, wishing she could see herself.

Oguina opened the door, then remembered paper money. Better to have some and not need it than be stuck without any. Oguina checked the wardrobe, drawers, a steamer chest. She scoffed, shaking her foolish head. Money had a particular scent to it, like hundreds of hands co-mingled. Oguina followed her nose and found some under the mattress. She looked at the numbers. Many had a 1, and a few had a 5. The rest were coins in a linen bag, mostly tiny and silver.

The bright blue drop-waist garment she wore glittered with beads and spangles but had no pockets. She spied a small container on a chain shaped something like a clamshell. She'd marveled at the impracticality of handbags, now here she was using one. It smelled like hands, money, oil, rubber and tobacco. She opened it.

Inside was half a packet of cigarettes, a metal tube full of bright red oily paste, and a scatter of coins. There was also a mysterious rubber-scented round thing wrapped in gleaming foil. She stuffed the paper money in, closed the case, and slung the chain across her body. She'd blend in at a speakeasy now.

Oguina stepped into a hallway. There were three other doors in the hall, and a room for bathing at the end. She found stairs opposite from the bathroom. She went downstairs, passing three floors like the one she'd come from. The ground floor was all open space with brightly colored sofas and chairs. The door to the street had a pane of pink frosted glass embedded in the wall beside it, where a gilded coat tree and umbrella rest stood sentinel. Was this a rooming house?

Just as she reached for the door latch, a voice called from behind her. "Oh, you're the new girl. Did you want dinner before your tussle, dearie?'

"No, thank you," Oguina spoke without turning around. "I'll be dining out."

"Well, that's a generous gentleman then." Footsteps carried the voice closer behind her. "Let's have a look at you, dearie. We wouldn't want the gent to say we send substandard girls on a dinner date, would we?" Puzzled by the words, Oguina turned to face the speaker.

"Well, you're a pretty little thing." The voice belonged to a garishly dressed middle-aged woman. Her blouse revealed the tops of breasts like risen loaves. Oguina smelled peroxide in her hair. This was no typical rooming house. She'd raided a brothel.

"You ought to go by Tiger Lily, like the character in the Barrie story," said the woman, "but of course, they don't care what name you give them as long as you show them a good time."

Oguina smirked and nodded politely, swallowing a laugh.

"Take an umbrella, dearie." The woman took one from the stand by the door and handed it to the monster. "The snow will probably stop, but better safe than sorry."

Oguina turned toward the door before speaking. "Thank you, Madam. Good evening." She pressed the latch and stepped out, hearing a muffled exclamation of *"bonjour"* as she pulled the door shut.

She lifted the umbrella because she'd never used one before. It opened as easily as the door, but it caught the wind, so she left it at the end of the brothel's walk. Oguina didn't have to ask for directions. It was easy to find speakeasies by following the scent of alcohol.

One of the buildings was where she'd met Leo. Oguina found three more secret drinking establishments in other parts of town. She stood across the street from the last one, watching people go in and out. How would she find one of Bianco's men?

The other night, when Leo lost control, they'd smelled cologne. The cloying smell wasn't here, so she tracked booze again. This one was more popular than the last, with twice as many heartbeats inside. She got close enough to find a trace of cologne in the air. This was the place.

She headed toward the side of the building, listening. Someone asked the man ahead of her for a password. "Jenkins," he whispered. If she hadn't been Changed, she wouldn't have heard it. At the door, she repeated the word. She entered a haze of dry, dusty tobacco smoke. It dulled other scents, but not enough to confuse her.

A long, gleaming bar was to one side, with people sitting along it like beads on a string. A stage held a man at a table above a crowd of swaying people. The table was black, except for the edge where the man sat. White and black pieces of wood stood out like teeth and spaces. When he touched them with his fingers. Music tumbled out the other side. She'd heard this sound before outside of buildings through the years but hadn't seen how it was made. The musical table was novel, like the time she'd seen a guitar. She shook off that memory. A doorway was no place for a fugue. Everyone else was either sitting or dancing. She'd want to blend in.

Oguina scanned the room and saw a small empty table. She went toward it as quickly as she could without bumping into anyone, then sat down. The man on the stage finished making his music. He stood up and bowed. People slapped their hands together. She imitated them, watching the man smile and bow some more. Was the slapping noise making him happy? Indeed it was. How strange.

"What can I get ya?" A young woman with bright red lips stood by the table, holding a small tray. Oguina should have expected this. She grabbed the tiny handbag and opened it, but the woman shook her head. "That big-timer over there wants to buy you a drink." She pointed at a man in the corner. "What'll it be, doll?" A drink? She hadn't had any such thing in centuries.

Oguina tried to buy time by looking bashful. What could she ask for, and how would she talk without showing her teeth? She rummaged through the items in the clamshell container until her hand fell on the tube of red greasepaint. She opened it and rubbed it across her lips as she spoke, using the motion to hide her mouth. "Gin and tonic." She mimicked another order from across the room. The woman smiled and went away, so she must have done it right. She hoped she'd be able to drink the gin and tonic, or at least pretend. People were watching her.

Oguina looked back at corner. She wanted to see who had bought the gin and tonic concoction. He had dark hair and bronze skin, wore a blue and red striped suit. The cologne smell came from him. He also had an oily metal smell, which meant he carried a firearm. He saw her looking so he waved and smiled. She waved back. He winked. The buck she'd been looking for had found her first.

The waitress set a glass in front of her with juniper-scented fluid inside. Oguina held the glass up to her mouth. Bubbles wiggled up the side through the clear liquid, like corn fermenting in a jar. This drink smelled nothing like corn. She tasted it.

It tasted the way pine smelled and was ice cold. The bubbles made her nose tingle and carried the pine taste from her tongue into her breath. She swallowed it and kept on breathing even though she didn't need to. Her stomach made a noise like a yawning cat. The man who'd bought the drink sauntered toward her. He was Leo's enemy, but now she owed him a courtesy for the thoroughly entertaining beverage.

"I haven't seen you here before, dollface." The man leaned over to smile at her from the side of the table. "I'm Jimmy. What say we go cut a rug so you can show off those glad rags?" He nodded in the direction of the area in front of the stage and held out one hand. Oguina steeled her resolve, smirked at him, and nodded taking his hand. She wasn't sure how rags could be happy, but obviously, he wanted to dance.

His pulse was fast and warm, but not enough to indicate fear. He was either mildly excited or had a fever.

Oguina let him lead her. The other people were doing a variety of strange movements she wouldn't consider dancing. Many of them were positioned near each other without much touching. This was the style she would copy.

Her inhuman reflexes helped. She was able to mimic movements she'd just seen and still keep time with the music. The man on stage was playing at a fast tempo. He changed tunes three times until he stopped for a break. Surprisingly, she was disappointed.

The bucks and does repeated their hand slapping. This time, Oguina joined in eagerly. She wanted to hear more. A doe came on to the stage with the man from behind a curtain. Her clothes were even fancier than Oguina's, but somehow less garish. This woman leaned against the musical table, and the man sat down again. He started making slower music this time. After a few moments, the woman started singing.

The bucks and does were dancing in pairs again closely, holding each others' hands. Some of them sat down. Oguina decided it would be better to head back to the table instead of trying this sort of dancing. It involved more prolonged contact than she thought she could handle.

"What's the rush, doll?" He followed her back to the table despite his protest. She wasn't sure what to do. She couldn't pretend to apply cosmetic to her lips for a whole conversation. Out of the corner of her eye, another couple gave her a socially acceptable escape route.

Oguina swooped down on her barely-tasted gin and tonic. She put the glass to her lips, gulped its contents, then picked up a napkin. "Let's go somewhere else." She blotted her lips to hide her teeth. Oguina went toward the door she had come in through.

"You sure don't punch the bag, do you, doll?" The man kept smiling at her. She liked his smile, was even a little jealous. Humans had such benign smiles it was hard to believe they could take each other's lives. She glanced back at the musicians with regret. Perhaps she could come back sometime just to listen.

This time, she took the lead. Oguina had a good idea of what this man had in mind, so she went to an alley. She'd decide what to do with him after she got information. In the shadows, she let him put his arms around her waist and leaned against the wall. His blood and breath piqued her hunger, but she pushed it down. She let him rest his head on her shoulder before saying, "You work for Bianco."

"Yeah, doll, I do imports." He reached up and touched her hair more gently than she expected.

"Good." Oguina paused. The man's neck was against her cheek. She could turn her head and tear his throat. She didn't want to. "Tell me where Bianco spends his evenings."

His hand stopped stroking her hair. "What are you, some kind of gold digger? Bianco ain't the sugar daddy type, doll."

"Perhaps I'd like to work for him." She had no idea if women worked for crime lords, but had to say something. "I'd rather make a living with my wits, perhaps even in imports like yourself."

"Wow! You're one ambitious dame." He pulled his

head back from her shoulder to look her in the eyes. She regained her control. "A stunner like you wants to be a snakecharmer?" She saw admiration where she'd expected skepticism. An old memory caught her like a rip-tide.

It was midday in late summer hundreds of years ago, and she was walking back from bathing in the river. Her teeth were still blunt, and her heart was still beating. A familiar whistle came from up ahead. She stopped and waited, smiling.

She knew where Ahanu would step out on the path before she saw him. It made no sense, but he grew more attractive the more they spent time together. Oguina watched him smile with his eyes before the expression overtook the rest of his face.

Ahanu was her betrothed. At first, Oguina hadn't been pleased about the arrangement, hadn't wanted to marry anyone at all. But once she got to know Ahanu, her reservations vanished like fog on a sunny morning.

"I think there's something in one of your snares." This was one reason she loved him. Ahanu admired her trapping, encouraged her when other men might have told her to stop. He extended his hand, and she took it. Then they walked down a deer trail to the trap he'd mentioned.

The snare had a rabbit in it, so Oguina climbed the tree to get it down. As she worked, Ahanu gazed up at her from the ground. When she got back, he put his hands on her shoulders and kissed her. She would be a happy woman at the end of autumn when they were wed.

The echo of that sunlit day fell away from her. Instead of sun and pine, Oguina's nose wrinkled at gin and cologne. She opened her eyes. Jimmy's lips still touched hers. She panicked, not wanting to lose control and kill this buck.

Oguina pushed Jimmy, breaking their embrace and sending him flying against the alley's opposite wall. She rushed to him, taking one of his arms in her hands. Then she twisted.

"Ow," said Jimmy, "what'd I do?"

"Bianco. Where does he spend his evenings?" He'd been looking down when she spoke so he hadn't seen her teeth.

"What are you doing? Trying to horn in on Bianco's operation or something?" This Jimmy had quick wits. She took some pressure off his arm. He looked up at her, then she smiled.

Jimmy froze with fear. He was barely moving enough to breathe, but his heart raced. He'd take this seriously now.

"Holy Mary, Mother of God. You're one of the monsters! Are you taking me for a ride?" How did this man already know creatures like her existed? She hadn't met this Jimmy before. What could it be? His face married despair to resignation. He'd asked a question she hadn't answered. She wasn't sure what "taking a ride" meant, but whatever it was, he wanted to avoid it.

"I will take you for a ride if you don't tell me where Bianco spends his evenings." She glared at his face steadily while waiting for his response. He mumbled something under his breath about the valley of the shadow of death, then nodded.

"Okay, I'll tell ya. The Boss stays in most nights, except when he goes to Saint Anne's. Lives outside town, in Assonet. I'm getting a pen, not my piece." Jimmy opened his coat, reaching into a pocket. He produced a pen and matchbook, scribbled an address inside its cover. "If he asks, I never said nothing. Go ahead and rough me up a bit. It'll make a good show for your Boss, too."

She wondered what he meant by her boss, but it wasn't important now. Jimmy had met her conditions and didn't want to harm him unless she had to. But she couldn't have him follow her, either. Would it be better to kill him anyway? He knew about Changed, though and if he died, she'd never know how much he knew or who he'd learned it from.

"Thank you for a thoroughly diverting evening." It was a genuine sentiment. Confusion and relief washed over his features. "I promise I shall make this quick, though I am afraid it will be painful." She leaned in, put her arms around his neck, then pulled down quickly while lifting her leg. His head met her knee with a dull thunk. Gently, she lowered him to the pavement.

Oguina made her way to the roof. Even in the shape of an owl, she could still taste juniper and smell traces of cologne.

"Tell me again what happened." Howard watched Jimmy Delaqua wince as he rubbed the goose egg disrupting his hairline.

"It's like I already told you." Jimmy left his head alone and poured himself two fingers of whiskey. "I was in the juke joint over on third, all done with business for the evening. This stunner of a came walks in, a real tomato. Hotter looking ticket than that torch singer up Plymouth way. I mean, she was stacked and dressed to the nines."

This was going nowhere. "Okay, Jimmy. Listen. You want me to ID her for you, you gotta get more specific. Hair and eye color, how tall she is, what did she sound like. That kind of stuff."

"Oh." Jimmy kicked the whiskey back and poured himself another. "Long, shiny black hair with big brown eyes. A little thing, maybe five foot. Small on top, but all wiggle in the hips, if you know what I mean. Smooth skin, darker than mine, more coppery. Talked all formal, like she had a real straight-laced mother. Oh, and those teeth. Never seen those up close before." Instead of grimacing or shuddering, Jimmy gazed wistfully into his whiskey glass before taking a sip.

"Hmm." Howard was stumped. He hadn't heard of or seen a small, dark monster. And he'd never heard of any monster going into a speakeasy. If they dressed up, it was to hunt, not dance and drink. "You sure she was a monster? Not just a regular gal who put up a fight and got one over on you?"

"I swear, Fallon, she had those teeth. Also, she felt colder than other people." Jimmy sipped more whiskey. "Look, I know what you're thinking. Jimmy got clocked by a dame, and he knows there're monsters in town, so he tells a story to save face. But that ain't it at all."

"Okay, so you saw teeth and her hands were cold…."

"Her lips, too." Jimmy dashed down the rest of his drink and poured another.

"Excuse me?" Howard had to shut his mouth before it started catching flies. "Wait. You slapped the make on a monster?

"Not a monster." Jimmy rolled his eyes. "A monster dame. We all know those exist. And like I said before, she was a hot ticket. I bet any red blooded male would've wanted to lay one on her. Until they saw the teeth, I mean."

"Um."

"Well, of course, you wouldn't. You can pick a monster out of a crowd from 500 feet." Jimmy didn't drink his whiskey. This time, he just rolled the glass between his hands.

"You have a point." Howard put his hands flat on the table and looked Jimmy in the eye. "I gotta ask, just because I'd ask anyone. How many drinks did you have before you met this monster dame?"

"About half a G and T. I wasn't there that long before she showed up." Howard glanced at the clock on the mantel. Jimmy must have caught him doing it because he smirked. The clock jived with this story.

"But then you had another drink with her." Howard held his eyebrow down, trying not to look as skeptical as he felt.

"No, I just sent the waitress to her table. Then we danced. She could really cut a rug, too." Jimmy sighed, looking into his whiskey again.

"A dancing monster dame. Right." Howard thought of something. "Wait. You sent her a drink. Did she drink it?" He hadn't heard of monsters drinking gin before.

"You know, I thought it was funny at the time." Jimmy stared at the wall just to the right of Howard's head. "She just gave it a little sip at first. Made a face like it was the cat's meow, but something she'd never done. Most dames gussied up like that kick back half their hooch before hitting the dance floor. Liquid courage, you know." Jimmy look at directly at Howard now. "She drank the rest of it before asking if we could go somewhere else."

"She did?"

"Yeah, she drank it all."

"I mean, it was her idea to leave with you?"

"Well, yeah." Jimmy shifted his weight in the chair. "You're wondering why that wasn't some kind of red flag. Sorry, Fallon, but you seem like a bit of a prude. It ain't that uncommon for a dame to do that. Especially one who's, um, working."

"So you thought she was a lady of the evening." This

made more sense. He'd seen Bess pose as a prostitute before, just in an alley, not a night club.

"Yeah. And I thought, so what? I make tons of cabbage. I ain't married, don't even got a goomah right now. And then, when we got outside, she asked about my work. She knew what I was into, running hooch. I thought she was looking for a sugar daddy, to get out of picking up randoms." Jimmy drank half the whiskey.

"Well, Jimmy, I don't know what to tell you. She wasn't hunting, or else I'd be checking your bones for tooth marks instead of talking to you." Howard lowered his voice. "She was after something, they always are. So either she asked you a question, or she stole something." Howard cleared his throat and let his volume go back to normal levels. "You're lucky you got off with that goose egg."

"Don't I know it." Jimmy looked at the door, then checked his shoulder holster and put his hands in every pocket. "She didn't take nothing," he murmured, hefting his full billfold before putting it back in his jacket. Jimmy shrugged. Howard felt familiar instinct knot his stomach. Jimmy must have dropped some information the monster wanted. Howard could either give him an out or sell him out.

"Oh, man," Howard spoke slightly louder than normal. "She pinched your dough?" He winked. Jimmy seemed smart enough to know a good cover story when he saw one.

"Damn," Jimmy smirked. "A monster dame who drinks hooch, cuts rugs, and picks pockets. What's a monster need money for anyway?"

"Dunno." Howard thought about what to say in case someone was listening. "They don't need to buy food, but they need clothes. Most of the time, they steal that kind of thing." He was starting to think Jimmy's dame wasn't with Daniel's group. He shouldn't trust anyone with that information just yet. "She was wearing a real fancy get-up, though, right?"

"Yeah. More beads and spangles than a Vaudeville show." Jimmy sighed. He seemed hung up on this kitten, monster or not.

"Well, then, she's got expensive tastes. If she made a habit of stealing things like that, she'd attract loads of attention." Howard nodded. "She could buy a couple of dresses legit with what you had on you. And guys who get mugged by hookers don't go to the police."

"Ain't that the truth." Jimmy drank the rest of his whiskey. This time, he put the glass down without refilling it. He stood up. "Thanks for answering my questions and everything, Fallon. I owe you one."

Jimmy left the room, closing the door behind him. Howard stared at Jimmy's empty highball glass. He took a clean one from the tray in the middle of the table and sloshed a dollop from the half-empty decanter for himself. Jimmy's dame could be a lone wolf, but that kind of thing almost never happened. There had to be a second pack of them in town. But why? And if they had nothing to do with Daniel, what would they care about Jimmy's business? Unless they were the little bastard's rivals. And there was that knot of instinct in his guts again.

Howard wished Jack hadn't had that accident. He'd

need more loyal allies than he could find in Bianco's little corner of the Mafia. From the feeling Howard got, he'd need them soon.

When Bersi woke up, Leo was still asleep. The older he got, the earlier he woke, though direct sunlight would put him back to sleep. A hint of sunlight clung in the west outside, a sight he'd grown used to seeing over the last fifty years or so. Hrafin said he could force wakefulness when the sun was still halfway above the horizon and Bersi was inclined to believe it, especially now that he'd seen Leo push some of their boundaries.

Hrafin also said he couldn't see the likeness of anyone Changed. Last night, Leo had proved that wrong, at least for the three of them. Leo questioned things Bersi had held as fact. Oguina's continued existence proved that solitude didn't automatically equal insanity. Either Hrafin was wrong, or his knowledge was limited to the Changed he'd met. Bersi knew for sure Hrafin wouldn't intentionally lie to an ally. That was a trait they didn't share.

The light faded from the sky. Where had Oguina had gone last night and where was she now? He'd wanted her to leave for an hour, not a night and day. He scanned the trees but found no sleeping owl without a heartbeat. Bersi wasn't worried about Oguina's physical safety. She was too cunning to get trapped in a burning building. He worried that she might have decided to leave him with Leo and go off alone again.

He looked at the snow. Patches had thawed and

vanished during the day. That was good. If they wanted, they'd be able to continue training Leo. Last night, Bersi had an idea for a way to get Leo past crowds on the streets. If only he knew where to go, they could try it tonight; he had no reason to think either of them would have trouble killing Bianco once he was found.

He heard Leo behind him, let the youngster think he could sneak up unnoticed. He had confidence, but Bersi wanted to break him of moping every time he was only decent at something. Hrafin was like that but too experienced for small mistakes on familiar ground. That only made his disappearance more troubling. Hrafin wouldn't have been gone this long without reason. He'd gone on memory trips before when he sat still and mentally revisited the places he'd been. But on Bersi's first night in Fall River, he'd found a clue. Bersi took out the small stone carving, dangling it on a leather thong that Hrafin usually wore around his neck.

"Nice cat." Leo sat next to him. "What's it for?"

"This belonged to Hrafin." Bersi turned the carving over in his hands. There was an engraving on the base, XIII. "This is how I know he's missing. I found it in town, just before we met."

"Oh." The youngster seemed unsure what to say next. "Well. Oguina, she's not back yet? She missing now, too?"

An owl landed in a tree across the clearing, and they watched as it changed shape. "I'm not missing. I was in town, scouting." She dropped from the tree, the modern dress she wore sparkling like fish scales in the moonlight.

"Scouting for what?" Leo stood up.

"Bianco." Oguina took a small case on a chain from over her shoulder. "I have money if we need it. Also some of these." She tossed a deflated pack of cigarettes at Leo. "And this. I have no idea what it is." She flicked the round item wrapped in foil at him as well. Bersi raised his eyebrows at Leo.

"Um." Leo hung his head, clearing his throat several times through his explanation. "That's what they call a rubber. We, um. People use it so they don't catch diseases when they, uh, have relations."

"Relations? What does rubber have to do with your family?" Bersi was glad she asked. He found the question as confusing as she did.

"Relations is. Oh God, why do I have to explain this?" Leo shrank more than a violet. "It's when people, uh, mate with each other."

"Wouldn't something like that defeat the point of getting a child?"

"Well, yeah." Leo took a deep breath. He looked like a man with seasickness. "It does. But people who use these aren't trying to have babies, they're trying to have fun. Or make money."

"That explains things." Oguina jerked her chin once in a nod. He'd have to hear the story of how she got the dress and its accessories. Oguina took off a pair of shiny shoes. "I discovered his address. Bianco's."

"What? How?" Leo hovered at her elbow like a hummingbird.

"I found the man from Highland Avenue who smelled of cologne." She smirked. "I got him alone, and I convinced him to help."

"Why did you do that? He'll tell his boss we're coming!"

Oguina smiled, teeth glowing wicked as the moon. She held Leo by the throat off the ground. "Don't make such assumptions, cub. A woman defeated him in combat. How much do you think he'll want to say about that?"

Oguina released Leo, who landed lightly on his feet. Bersi watched, waiting to see what Leo would do next. He just rubbed his neck, looking ashamed.

Bersi cracked his knuckles to break the silence before speaking. "So? Where is Bianco?"

"I said I have his address," Oguina spoke quietly now. "But Leo is not ready yet."

"So get me ready already." Leo sighed. "Look, I want him and the men who did the hit on my family dead. Sooner the better. And anyway, when we're done with Bianco, we can help Bersi with his problem."

Oguina turned her glare on Bersi. He wondered why she looked so angry. "Bersadottir. I need help. It's one reason I came here."

"I'm sorry to hear that." She shook her head. "I figured as much. But we have something to do first." Oguina narrowed her eyes. "And I know from experience Leo shouldn't have to do it alone, or wait for you."

"Bianco's only a human." Bersi tried not to let his voice tremble. "Whatever got to Hrafin is still out there. Anything that could harm him puts us in extreme danger."

"Extreme danger?" Leo raised an eyebrow. "If we go off looking for Hrafin, we might not be in shape to get Bianco ever." He looked at Oguina. "That's not what I signed up for. I won't go look for Hrafin until we at least have a plan for Bianco."

"The Cub has a point, Bersi." Oguina put a hand on his shoulder. "If we go now, he'll be too distracted to focus. Also, dealing with Bianco will give Leo some experience. You said yourself he needs it."

"We'll do it your way, Bersadottir." Bersi put on a smile like a mask. "Let's get this youngster into shape, get him his kill."

He watched as Oguina went into the cave, probably to change clothes. There was little he could do besides what they wanted. He'd wait and keep his reservations to himself. Changed had all the time in the world.

Leo was sick of walking with the endless stream of people leaving the mills and factories. Every night it got easier, so when would he be ready to take on Bianco? Oguina may have been alone for hundreds of years, but she'd gone out on the town. Leo was jealous. Drinking and dancing were things he'd never done, but that wasn't all.

She'd gotten the dirt on Bianco. Oguina's dance partner had been Jimmy "the Hooch" Delaqua. Jimmy rivaled Rhode Island's own Danny Walsh, the most infamous rum runner in New England. He was also one of the wiseguys outside Leo's burning house.

Leo went under the Brightman Street Bridge to wait. It was still raining when Oguina and Bersi met him. She held a large sack, and he had three umbrellas. An unkempt hobo peered under the bridge but kept walking.

"Here." Oguina handed him a bundle of fabric. "Put these on." The clothing turned out to be a stylish blue pinstripe suit. Bersi had its close relative in a shade of gray. Oguina opened her overcoat to reveal a deep blue dress. "This will hide blood better than the one I took last time."

Bersi struggled with the knot on his necktie. "I hate this tie, like a noose! Do I have to wear it?"

"Here, let me." Leo tugged out the twisted knot. "This suit would look all wrong without a tie. You'll see." Now they'd fit in. Oguina opened her umbrella and led the way. The rain let up as they went. Leo tried to see his reflection in shop windows. There were only watery versions of Bersi and Oguina. After a few more blocks, they walked up to a building that surrounded muffled music.

"This isn't the one I went to before." They'd stepped under an awning, so Oguina closed her umbrella, grinning. "We don't want that kind of attention. Let's wait for someone to go in. That's how to get the password."

Oguina made adaptation look effortless. She'd either been sharper than diamond or had done centuries of work. He would have tried to bribe his way in instead of waiting to listen. His new hearing wasn't second nature to him yet, so he didn't think to rely on that. When he was good at something, Leo could tell right away. Leo thought he must only be a mediocre monster, trying not to bother with the hard stuff. He wanted the skills without practice, just like drawing.

"It's the Queen of Hearts." Oguina faced the wall as she whispered. Right, the password. The three of them went to the door in intervals. Leo walked up, said the password, went inside.

It was early for nightlife, several tables stood empty. Leo picked one near the dance floor where all the action would be. A man lazily tickled a baby grand on stage next to a sign billing him as Irving Ivory. A bona fide stage name, for sure. Lone men sat at the bar while couples and groups of girls stuck to the tables. He tried to scan the room without looking obvious, but couldn't see anyone behind him. Not such a great seating choice, after all. Yup, mediocre monster Leo at work.

He considered moving to the bar, but Oguina arrived. She took a table with a better view, of course. She watched the pianist for a few seconds when a waitress appeared at her side. What was that about? He'd been ignored for five whole minutes. The waitress pointed at a barfly and shook her head when Oguina tried to pay. Leo couldn't get a good look at the guy from where he was sitting.

Bersi looked slightly bewildered when he came in. He went right up to the bar. Bersi must have gone to bars before, lucky old bird. The man Leo couldn't see was only three seats down from Bersi. Too bad he'd missed the thing with buying the drink.

How could he get a better look at the mystery drink-buyer? She'd ordered another gin and tonic. Predictable. There was something off, not quite right, something to do with that man. He had a severe case of the heebie-jeebies now. Maybe this was a bad idea.

"Hey, fella, what can I get ya?" The waitress, finally. She shivered slightly, poor thing.

"Tom Collins." His father's drink. Leo rubbed his nose as if he had an itch. The waitress nodded and left, thank God. He'd have to be careful talking, use his glass or a napkin to hide his teeth.

He'd get a clear view of the bar from the dance floor,

but he'd need a dance partner. He scanned the room for a likely-looking gal. Bingo. A table with three flappers. He forgot about his Tom Collins and strode over, trying to look confident without smiling.

None of them remotely attractive. Was this another consequence of being a monster? That was probably a good thing. He didn't want a massacre on the dance floor. None of the girls were looking at him.

"Hey, smartie, let's dance." Leo held out one hand. The girl he asked wore a pink dress with fringe. Right. Definitely there to dance.

"Sure thing, big six." She popped out of her chair and made a beeline for the parquet floor without touching him.

He followed her, and they danced. At least that was easy. He tried to Charleston toward the bar. He managed that but lost focus on the tempo. Oguina's admirer was a powerfully built heavyset man. Patches of gray clung to his temples, and his suit was an older style that had seen better days. He shifted in his seat. Leo saw a wicked old scar under his ear on the left side. Something tried to rip his throat out years ago. Could a Changed have done that? How had he survived? Who was this neck-scar guy, anyway?

Bersi smirked at him from the bar, so Leo flicked his gaze at neck-scar. Bersi moved casually, pretending to scratch his chin to turn toward the man. Neck-scar glanced at Oguina.

"Hey, square!" The flapper slapped him on the shoulder. "You're a lousy heeler. Get lost!" She shooed him away, all for the best anyway. He left the mostly empty dance floor, stopping at his table to exchange the Tom Collins for a couple of Oguina's stolen greenbacks. He passed Oguina's table, tipping his drink to her. She mimicked the gesture. Up at the bar, neck-scar watched him. Leo sat between Bersi and the big guy.

His rear end barely touched the seat before neck-scar spoke. "Hey buddy, you wanna stay away from that one. That dame's the baddest of bad news."

"What does she got, some kind of social disease?" Leo spoke into his drink to hide his teeth.

"Something like that." Neck-scar tugged his shirt collar, probably to hide his neck scar. Leo stifled a rogue giggle.

"Maybe you don't like competition." Leo hid his teeth with his glass again.

"I mean it, back off from her." Neck-scar sat up straight, squaring his shoulders. He would have been scary before Leo's Change. "Big trouble for you if you don't."

"Yeah, you gonna stop me?" Leo tried goading the guy, but neck-scar was a cool cucumber.

"Nah. I won't stop you. Young bucks are supposed to do dumb things." Leo started when the guy said the word buck. Did he know? "Just don't say I didn't warn you." Neck-scar got up and approached Oguina. He walked like a cop, not a guy about to pitch a woo. Neck-scar murmured, and Oguina nodded. He spoke again, then extended his hand. She took it. They went to the exit.

The door was closing behind Bersi before Oguina and neck-scar crossed the room. Good. Leo hurried after them, so they'd be flanked. Why did neck-scar have him so on edge? One guy, even a big one, should be a cakewalk for three Changed.

The empty street echoed. Oguina linked arms with neck-scar for a few blocks and took a right down an alley, a red dog slinking after them. Leo caught up a few moments later and turned to peer down the space between buildings.

Neck-scar stood over Oguina, an empty syringe in one hand and a full one in the other. She slumped against the wall, sliding down to rest in a heap at his feet.

"I told you to leave her alone." The big man didn't look up. "Scram."

"Who the hell are you?" Leo strode forward in sudden outrage, pushing neck-scar away. The liquid in that syringe knocked out Changed. Neck-scar brandished the full syringe dangerously. Leo didn't give a bucket of damns. The man arched an eyebrow. Neck-scar's heart thundered in his chest. He'd seen Leo's teeth.

"Just a guy you should have listened to before." The man smiled. "Guess you did something dumb after all. Maybe I can help you fix it." The man walked toward him, but Leo leaped back. If he only had a gun. Neck-scar broke into a flat sprint.

Leo waited until the last second, then leaped straight up like he was trying to crash wild bat party. He landed, turned. Neck-scar was out at the curb, facing the street. The red dog transformed into Bersi, who hoisted Oguina over his shoulder. He jumped like a flea to the fire escape and the roof. Leo should leave too, but he needed a better look at that syringe.

Speaking of syringes, neck-scar was back, holding one in a ready-to-jab kind of way. Leo leaped to the end of the alley. A human couldn't see back there.

"Where'd she go?" Neck-scar probably thought Oguina pulled a Houdini. Good. The man started advancing again. Not good. "At least you're still here."

Leo sniffed, trying to figure out what was in the syringe. It smelled horribly familiar. He didn't have time for a memory bomb; he had to get out of here. Leo could just follow Bersi over the rooftops, but shouldn't assume neck-scar was alone. He'd need to do something to make Mr. Neck-scar retreat and take his buddies with him.

Leo knocked the burly man down with a trash can, then jogged past on the man's left side to avoid the syringe. Leo went slow, hoping neck-scar would get up. He did. Leo turned on a dime, then caught him under the arms and pulled up. Neck-scar wavered. Leo clocked his head against the wall, syringes clattering on cobblestone.

"Why?" Leo pulled back on the man's arms again.

"You—you're a monster—didn't you know that? This ain't the dark ages—you ain't the only ones with teeth anymore." The man's voice was slurred. Too dazed to follow, but he could get to his pal or whatever. Leo bumped his head against the wall again, like a threat this time.

"How'd you hear about us monsters, neck-scar?" Leo couldn't help it. This time, he chuckled. He sounded like a door-to-door salesman.

"From her—when she bit me—nine years ago."

"Bullshit." It was. Oguina hadn't bitten this man. His scar was on the wrong side of his neck. "Why wait nine years? It's not like she's hard to find. I should know."

"You want to keep this paper like I said before." Neck-scar wasn't dazed anymore. "Kill me already if you're gonna."

"Not gonna." Leo hit the man's head against the wall again and tossed him out to the sidewalk. Ouch, right on his face. Something white fluttered against neck-scar's lapel like one of Oguina's moths. Leo picked up along the full syringe. He stuck the business end of the thing in an apple core from the scattered trash before pocketing it.

Leo caught movement from the head of the alley and looked back. Neck-scar was up already, clutching the paper and waving at a sedan. Leo saw the car's door open. He hit the rooftops and escaped.

"What is that?" Bersi leaned away from the liquid-filled glass tube. He hadn't been this scared since his last human day.

"It's just a syringe." Leo moved to the lamp, held it up to the light. "People use it to give medicine, or take blood."

"Well." Bersi stayed where he was. "Then is that medicine?"

"That's what I'm trying to figure out." Leo glanced back at Oguina. "She's been asleep this whole time?"

"Yes." And she'd slept through the entire trip back, even while Bersi dressed her in the trousers she favored.

Leo left the syringe and went over to Oguina. He rolled up her sleeves, moved her hair away from her neck, looking for something.

"What are you doing?"

"Looking for a mark."

"No, there's not. I checked for that already." Bersi peered again at the syringe. "Something's strange. Whatever's in there smells familiar, but at the same time, I can't entirely recall any scent like it. How can that be? We remember everything, even from before."

"Not really," Leo answered quickly, implying he must

have thought about this before. "We don't remember our days. Maybe it's something that's only around then."

"But what would we smell in the daytime that wouldn't be around at night?" Bersi shook his head. "All I can think of is sunlight. That can't be held in a glass tube."

"We smell it through the glass. What if it's the glass and not the stuff inside that stinks? We should let the liquid out of the syringe." Leo was probably right, but Bersi didn't like it. He pushed aside his dread.

"Let's do it outside," said Bersi, making a compromise with his fear.

Leo picked up the syringe again, and they went all the way to the clearing. Leo hesitated, then kept on walking. He stopped in a stand of trees they seldom used, then pointed the tip of the syringe down over a tree stump, then pushed the plunger. Blue-black liquid made ropy spatters on gnarled wood.

Now Bersi knew what it was. "Dead blood. This is blood from one of us like we'd use to Change someone. But it's blank. It wasn't given freely or with purpose." Bersi bit his wrist and sniffed, breathing in a rich loamy smell. He held his arm out to Leo, who copied him and nodded. "That's what it smelled like the night I Changed. But what do you mean by blank?"

"Whoever it came from gave it thoughtlessly. Our blood can Change or harm or heal. But without our will to do those things, it's foul." Bersi stared at the dark stain on the old tree stump.

"How so, though?" Leo nudged Bersi with an elbow. When he looked up, he saw the youngster's eyebrows had climbed halfway up his forehead.

"I'm not entirely sure." Bersi shrugged. "I only know what Hrafin told me. Dead blood like that, either a Changed lets it deliberately, or someone takes it from them. The idea of humans out there who can just take blood from us should frighten you."

"It does. But the way to get past fear is to think around it." Leo shrugged. "So, who did neck-scar get it from?"

"Hrafin?"

"Do you think they could catch Hrafin without using something like this in the first place?" Leo turned the syringe point-up, peering at the tip. "This needle is one of our teeth. I bet they caught someone Changed pretty recently, probably someone who doesn't think when he hunts." That made more sense, but it still didn't feel right.

"None of us has Changed anyone." Bersi stroked his beard. "We'd know."

"Then it has to be another family of Changed." Leo gave up looking at the syringe out here. It was too dark. They headed back to the cave and the lamps. "That Feral you hunted with Hrafin way back had to come from somewhere."

"That's not so important now. We must figure out how to wake Oguina." Bersi clapped Leo on the shoulder.

"Bersi, what happens if we don't hunt for a while?" Leo asked the question like he already knew the answer, but wanted to hear someone else say it.

"After about a month, we don't wake up after day-sleep." The cub had figured it out. "That might be how a human captured a Changed. But if we starve ourselves to sleep, someone has to bring us..." He'd figured both things out. "Someone has to bring blood. Fresh blood. And that's how we'll wake Oguina."

Bersi went back out and returned with a rabbit. He cut it so it would bleed while Leo held Oguina's mouth open. They only bloodied her face. He went out again and caught a badger. That didn't work either. The third time, he brought a bobcat, thinking a predator's blood would be stronger. Still nothing. Dawn was coming, and they were running out of ideas.

"A deer," said Leo, "how about that? That's what she usually hunts at any rate. It can't hurt to try." Bersi heard one stripping bark from a tree just on the other side of the rock. He brought it back.

But again, nothing happened. Dawn saw them no closer to a solution. There were humans out there with tools and dead blood to paralyze them. If the man with the scar was one of Bianco's fighters, Leo's revenge could be more dangerous than anything Bersi had ever done.

"I don't understand it." Howard sat up on the cot, shook his head with a grimace. "Your dame was out cold. She shouldn't have got away."

Jimmy held the rubber bag of ice out. Howard took it, tough old bird. "And the kid didn't take her." He sat across from the monster hunter in the boat's only below-deck chair.

"Nope. She was gone before he did the shot-put with

me out of the alley." Howard winced as he put the ice on top of his head. "Two goose-eggs. I'm one up on you."

"Are you sure she got the dose? Could she have faked it?" Jimmy hoped he wasn't asking a dunce question. He wasn't sure how all the monster stuff worked.

"Do monsters fake being hurt?" Howard leaned against the hull, letting the ice bag balance on his head. "Yeah. I've seen that before. But did this one, probably not. I got the drop on her for sure. She was dosed, the syringe was empty."

"So she's immune?" Jimmy got a tin cup from a hook over the little galley counter.

"That shouldn't be possible, not if she's the same kind of monster as the little bastard and his pack." Howard adjusted the ice bag so it covered both bumps on his head. He shut his eyes.

"You think she is? Different, I mean?" Jimmy shook Bromo-Seltzer from a blue bottle into the cup.

"No." Howard shook his head, making the bag slip. He sighed and adjusted it again. "All the monsters are different from each other, but not like that."

"Then what's the story? How'd she get away?" Jimmy poured water over the powder, watching the concoction fizz up the side of the cup.

"Dunno for sure, but that kid was running a distraction. He's sneaky. I talked to him for at least two minutes back at the bar, had no clue he was a monster. He's new. That's probably why."

"Here, drink this for your head. Headache powder, not hooch." Jimmy handed the Bromo-Seltzer to Howard. "How'd you know he's new?"

The cup nearly disappeared in Howard's hands. "Because he's the Riley kid. The one your Boss is so bothered about."

"Oh boy. Why didn't that kid just beat it up to Boston? Jeez, no wonder no one's caught him. The Boss'll cast a truckload of kittens when he finds that out. We're gonna have to tell him." There was a seasick silence.

Howard gulped down his medicine, wrinkling his nose. "Really?" The ice bag fell off his head. He rolled his eyes and put it back over his lumps.

"The Riley kid's a monster and has at least six reasons for revenge. Loyal guys can't just ignore that kind of threat."

"Are we?"

"Huh?" Jimmy listened to water slap against the outside of the hull. Usually, that sound was a comfort. Not tonight.

"Loyal guys? We're not Italian. The only reason he deals with an Irish guy like me is the monsters. If they leave town, he'd have a hit out on me before you could say potato. He hates Puerto Ricans even more than Irish. You have your imports, but what happens if they repeal Prohibition?"

Jimmy read the papers, he knew it could happen. "I'll just have to convince the Boss I can smuggle something else."

"Did you know Niccolo keeps telling me to teach you hunting, get you out of town?"

"Niccolo wouldn't do that. We worked together since we were half-pints. He likes having me around."

Jimmy's gut told him he was wrong right after he spoke.

"Yeah, he likes knowing you're alive even more, I'd bet." Howard stared into the empty cup. "Don't you think it's odd for Giacomo Bianco, dealing with monsters all of a sudden?"

"It ain't for me to question the Boss."

Howard held the tin cup out toward Jimmy. "Then don't. Just listen for a minute. You've been working for him, what, more than ten years now. Monsters have been around hundreds of years, maybe more. You grew up here, so you know the stories. The little bastard or something like him has been in this town before. Bianco only hired me last summer. Why now? What's different?"

Jimmy took the cup, walked it over to the galley. "Something was different before that. Couldn't put my finger on it, though. Thought it had to do with his cousin's operation up in Plymouth. That almost went sideways fifteen years ago. You hear about that?"

"Yeah. Cavalcante was the cousin, right? He and some Tucci fellow died in a local dispute. The guys still talk about it when they play poker. It's a big deal because Cavalcante's wife took over his business." Howard adjusted the ice bag again and frowned.

"You only got it half right." Jimmy dunked the cup in a basin of soapy water. "Cavalcante married the cousin, Esmeralda. She picked that supper club right up and ran with it after her husband died." He scrubbed the inside of the cup with a rag, then pulled it out of the suds and rinsed it from the canteen. "I'm up there all the time to supply the place. She runs a tight ship. The guys all think he goes easy on her because they were close growing up, like brother and sister. But the truth is, she makes bank without much help."

"So that's why you think Bianco might let your pedigree ride. He made an exception for his cousin, and she makes money. So you thought you'd get a pass?" Howard took the ice bag off his head and shook it. It sloshed instead of clinking.

"Well, yeah. I did." Jimmy dried the cup and put it back on its hook. "But we ain't related at all. And you got a point about Prohibition. And yeah. Something's been different for about a year. Can't put my finger on it, though. So I can't do nothing about it."

"One of the smartest people I know would say, if you keep your eye on something, you can put your finger on it later." Howard took the lid off the ice bag.

"Yeah. Sounds like a smart guy."

"Smart dame, she was. Brains come in all shapes and sizes." Howard peered into the ice bag and sighed. "Nothing but water."

"Give it here. There's plenty of ice outside." Jimmy dumped the water in the galley basin to make more suds, then took the rubber bag up the steps to the deck.

Above deck, Jimmy used the butt of his pocket knife to chip a couple of icicles off the roof of the wheelhouse. When he set them down to break them into smaller pieces, he saw the big cat perched in the bow. It had fluffy brindle fur and blinked at him thoughtfully with yellow eyes.

"Scat!" Something about the cat gave Jimmy the heebie-jeebies. "Go on. Shoo!" Jimmy stomped a foot in the cat's direction. It got up, stretched, and walked casually down the gangplank to the dock. It sat again and looked over its shoulder. Jimmy broke the ice and put it in the bag. When he was done, the cat was still on the dock.

"What do you want from me?" The cat blinked again, then glanced at the pail of bait fish Jimmy kept on board. "Fine. But I give you a smelt, that means you get lost. *Capisce*?" The cat purred.

Jimmy uncovered the bucket and tossed a wriggling fish in the cat's general direction. It jumped up higher than Jimmy would have expected, twisting in the air to catch the smelt. The cat landed neatly on the ground as if the impact didn't bother it one bit. It purred again as it trotted away, its fluffy tail puffed out behind it like smoke from a factory smokestack.

Jimmy shook his head and headed back downstairs to find Howard asleep on the cot, snoring like a buzz saw. He tossed the ice bag back upstairs so it wouldn't melt and sat down in the chair. He had a lot to think about.

This time, when blood passed her lips, Oguina stirred. She reached out, grasping soft feathers. Her eyelids felt like bits of slate. She managed to open them long enough to see that she held an owl. Eersi peered at her, a cautious grin tugging his lips. Her head felt heavier than her eyelids, so she let it lie. The light in the cave got brighter. It was dawn. She went back to sleep.

When Oguina woke again, she was stiff and ached all over. It was inconvenient but novel; she'd barely felt physical pain since her human days. She opened her eyes to see Leo look up from a sketch. She also felt something soft in her hands, wondered what that could be. Then she remembered. The owl from last night.

"Bersadottir. We were worried you might never wake up."

"Can you sit up?" Leo dropped his charcoal, extending a smudgy hand. "Do you need help?" She wasn't sure. She put aside the owl carcass and tried. It was slow, difficult and painful, but she managed. She must have winced. "That hurts?" Leo's forehead wrinkled.

"Yes." Her voice creaked like two tree branches rubbing together. "Everything hurts. What happened? I remember the alley and that man."

"He had this syringe." Bersi held up a glass tube with a sharp pointy end. "He used it to give you, how do you say, an injection?" Bersi looked at Leo for confirmation, eliciting a nod.

"But how did that pierce my hide?"

Leo took the syringe from Bersi, held it up in the light from the cave's deer-fat lanterns. She sniffed the air. "I can't smell anything, not even the lamps. What is it?"

"This needle isn't metal." Leo pointed at it. "That's why it worked. This is one crazy contraption. Whoever made it got some Changed teeth, then found a way to make them hollow. Anyway, neck-scar dosed you with dead blood, and it knocked you right out. We tried to wake you so many times before we thought of your owl shape."

"Leo, if this happens to you, we won't be able to help." Oguina's voice sounded like she'd spoken into a seashell.

"You're right, Bersadottir. He shouldn't go anywhere until he knows his other shape. I'll hunt." Bersi looked at Leo. "You stay here until you learn." Bersi got up and left the cave.

"I have no idea what to even try changing into." Leo looked annoyed. "You made it look so easy."

"Easy?" Oguina tried to chuckle, but something like a cough came out instead. "Nothing is. Effort expended increases worth. If we only do what's quick and easy, we'd do nothing important at all."

"I just don't have time for this." Leo tapped his fingers against his knee.

"Is there time to fail in front of Bianco? Complain about time and it's wasted." She stared at his eyes like she'd done his first night.

Instead of blinking or looking away, Leo nodded. In the middle of the cave, he closed his eyes. His efforts made slight shifts in his form like ripples on a pond. Here, his fingers merged. There his nose flattened. "I can't do it." He opened his eyes, sighing and shaking his head. He'd tried for less than a minute.

"Don't give up, cub. Something happend to your hands and face. Try again."

"But this isn't how I learn things." Leo raised his voice slightly. "I learn in the moment, when something's coming at me. I grow when the straits are dire. I know the risk if I don't learn this, but that's not doing it for me. I need to feel danger."

"I understand." She didn't. Saying so wouldn't help Leo. "You're good at believing in things. Why not imagine a danger for yourself? Can you make yourself believe a threat is present?"

"Okay. I'll try that." Leo sighed, slumping his shoulders. How did all the cleverness coexist with this laziness? He closed his eyes again, but opened them almost immediately. "Um, Oguina? Could you please turn around? It's hard to imagine imminent danger with you watching."

"Very well, cub." She turned her back. After a moment, she glanced over her shoulder.

This time his forehead smoothed and his jaw set itself in a determined clench. Orange hair grew on the back of his hands. Then, his fingers grew shorter until they resembled paws. She looked up, noticed his hair shorten and grow down to cover his face. His nose had turned pink and elongated slightly, stretching his jaws. His ears grew points and migrated to the top of his head.

Leo's legs were shorter now, shifting his weight to hands and feet more like paws now. The fur springing up all over his body combined the tawny color of his hair with orange in patterns of stripes and spots. He opened bright green eyes with vertical pupils. The cub's transformation was finished. Oguina had expected a cat, though less domestic than this.

Leo opened his mouth in a caterwaul that made him jump up and glance around. He looked at Oguina quizzically. "You're a cat." Leo mewed softly this time, shook his head, and sat on his hind legs. His long sleek tail curled around his feet. She watched him grow in height and lose the fur as he returned to human shape.

"That's almost as hinky as the Change. Thank God it doesn't hurt as much." Leo rubbed behind one ear with the back of his hand. He noticed the gesture and the cave echoed with the sound of mingled laughter.

"And what is so funny?" Bersi dragged a large wriggling burlap sack into the cave. Oguina heard several small hearts beating. She was hungrier than the first night of her Change. Bersi dragged the sack next to Oguina. "Don't let them get out," he said.

The bag contained several ducks and a goose. She wrung their necks and plucked feathers into another bag, starting with the goose. They should talk more about the man with the syringe. Leo was too excited to listen, so she let him tell Bersi about his new cat shape.

While she listened, she ate all the flesh from the goose and three of the ducks.

Oguina dumped bones into the bag with the feathers and reached for another duck. "Why did the man with the neck scar only have two syringes when there are three of us?"

"I don't think he knew there were three of us." Leo looked at the remaining ducks and licked his lips. "He figured out what I am when I confronted him, but looked surprised about it. He didn't see Bersi at all. He kept asking how you got up again, so maybe he thinks dead blood doesn't work on us for long. I fought him until he was too hurt to follow us. He wasn't alone. Someone was in a car across the street."

"This is terrible." Bersi ran a hand over the top of his head. "This neck-scar man knows enough about us to make weapons from dead blood. He must have a Changed captive."

"What if Hrafin came here to track this guy down?" Leo reached for one of the ducks, but stopped and clenched his hands. "Neck-scar could catch him if he found Hrafin during the day. If only we knew who he was and how many friends he has."

Oguina tossed a duck to Leo. "The waitress who brought the drink said it was from the man with the scar, compliments of Bianco. We should scout at the house, all things considered."

"Yes." Bersi stroked his beard. "We'll need to know how many of Bianco's people are armed with syringes."

Leo's voice was garbled by a mouthful of gizzard. "I have a better idea." Leo swallowed and cleared his throat before continuing. "We find the captive and rescue him. Or them, if there's more than one. If we take their dead blood away, they can't use it. Worst case, we limit their arsenal. Best case, we wake the captive up and get more numbers on our side."

"So let's plan this." Bersi slapped his hands together once and stood up.

"Not until I eat something besides a bag of waterfowl." Oguina dropped the last of the bones in the bag.

"It's warm enough for the cows to be out at the farm." Leo smirked. "Who wants hamburgers?"

Oguina rode the drafts over and around Bianco's house. It was the size of most tenements in the city that housed three or more families, though far more ornate in design. It sat in the middle of a yard, which was surrounded by a high stone wall topped with wrought iron spikes. At first, Oguina thought the ornate front gate was the only entrance, but on her third pass over the back of the property, she noticed an ivy-covered gate the size of a regular door.

Flying in for a closer look, she skimmed over a hedge maze Bersi's height. The rear gate was at the far end of the maze from the house, at the back of a little clearing with a stone bench beside a dry fountain. She perched on a small cherry tree next to the bench, turning her head all the way around. She smelled a warm and earthy draft from the water pipes, so she fluttered across to perch on its top tier. The draft came from the fountain's base. She took off, spiraling up then taking a direct line back to the house. The warm earthy air came up at intervals from under the maze and the rest of the yard, making a trail back to the house.

Turning back toward the house, Oguina saw a garage with six doors, separate from the house. There was a kennel attached to the back of the house at its back door. Bianco kept guard dogs, with sleek black and brown fur. She saw them in the yard that night and could tell by their scent they hadn't been fed since morning. Oguina noticed a light on in the window at the west side of the attic. She perched outside and peered in, seeing a pale blonde woman in bed.

Oguina thought the woman was asleep at first. She was dressed in a nightgown, so perhaps she was a guest or relative. But why would Bianco house a guest in this room? It was tiny, had no radiator, and the furniture was shabby and worn. Oguina focused on listening. The woman's blood and breath were as still as her body. So she wasn't a guest, but a corpse. Why keep a corpse in the attic? Did Bianco not believe in covering the faces of the dead like other humans? Oguina didn't get an answer until she came back the next night.

On her second night scouting, Oguina saw the man with the neck scar in the room with the dead woman. He set a big black bag down on the crooked bedside table and opened it. He removed a struggling rat, pressed it against the woman's mouth. The rat bled into her mouth, its struggles weakening as it died. "Neck-scar," as Leo and Bersi called him, shook his head as he wrapped the rat in a handkerchief and put it in his pocket. He rubbed his eyes with hands that came away wet, then wiped them on his trousers.

The man rolled up the woman's sleeve, then took a syringe from the bag. It looked just like the one Leo had. He put the hollowed-out tooth to her arm and pushed, forearms bulging and brow furrowed with effort. Once the needle was in her arm, the man pulled back on the top of the syringe. Oguina watched as the glass tube attached to the needle filled with a thick black substance. Here was the prisoner they meant to rescue, Bianco's supply of dead blood. She went back immediately to tell the others.

She left out the utterly confusing fact that the man had been weeping.

Howard Fallon got in his car and drove away from the mansion. When he and Jack first started tracking Daniel, Jack had been nineteen and Howard sixteen. They'd been full to the brim with confidence, blindly chasing someone they thought was their own age. Every time he thought of the truth he choked down a bitter laugh or maybe a scream. He didn't know because none of those sounds had escaped before.

Pearl had been Daniel's prisoner. Now she was in a worse predicament than before. At least with Daniel, Pearl had been able to walk, talk, and think. But then again, if Howard tracked down and burnt Daniel's lair, at least he'd be sure his sister wasn't in it. The sound threatened again, but this time he let it out. He'd been wrong. Not a laugh or a scream. More like a battle cry.

Howard still wasn't sure why Bianco wanted the monsters or their teeth so badly. Jimmy might have some idea, but Howard might not ever get the information out of him. Every day that passed since he put Pearl up in the attic room on Oak Street was worse than the last. Howard was under the pressure of fear. He could barely handle taking his sister's blood. What if Bianco wanted him to tear out her teeth or worse? His hand stung as he slapped the steering wheel.

As a hunter, Howard's life depended on getting all the information he could before acting. Bianco kept too much secret for Howard's comfort. If he didn't need Bianco's money to care for Jack and his ailing mother, he'd take Pearl and run somewhere. Maybe Canada. Were there monsters in Canada? So what if there weren't, he was sure Canadians played poker. But how would he live with a monster for a sister? He couldn't escape what she was no matter where he ran. He cried out again, reminding himself of the other double amputee at the hospital with Jack. That little old guy used the Rebel Yell to call the nurses.

Howard was the best hunter on the eastern seaboard and had a monster for a sister. Well, maybe something like that wasn't so unusual. He wouldn't have been a hunter at all if she hadn't been a monster. He'd go all in on a bet that had happened before, though he doubted both siblings survived nineteen years of that kind of luck. Could he really call what Pearl was doing surviving, though? He slapped the steering wheel again. It wasn't as satisfying as before.

He found it hard to believe Bianco's thugs, with all their brutal experience, didn't have the patience to do the legwork required to hunt monsters. Bianco might want to enslave more monsters as he'd done with Pearl, but Howard's gut told him something else was going on. He was a boss, but a small fry compared to Boston and Providence. He'd need big muscle to expand his territory.

What if the mafioso wanted to change his own people? But Bianco was a devout Catholic. He went to Mass at least twice a week, and confession even more often than that. Making people into monsters had to be some kind of sin. But so was murder. That didn't stop Bianco. This time, Howard punched the dashboard. He saw right away the chrome was dented, so he pulled over to get a look at what he'd done to his hand.

Howard couldn't see because his eyes were blurry like they'd been up in Pearl's room. He blinked a few times, then saw blood on his knuckles. Howard reached into his pocket for a handkerchief but remembered it was wrapped around the dead rat he'd fed to his sister. He yelled again. She was a monster. He shouldn't think of her as his sister anymore, shouldn't care. But it was like Jimmy and that dame. What did they say about first impressions? Whoever they were, they had it right. He just couldn't see Pearl any other way. Did monsters he'd killed have little brothers? They all had mothers, regardless. Had he been wrong all this time?

Howard got a rag out of the glove box to wrap around his bloody fist. He wished Jimmy would come around already. Howard didn't like the way Bianco looked at him, and Niccolo's hints only inflated his suspicions. The rumrunner couldn't replace Jack but was the only help Howard had a snowball's chance of getting. If only there were a way to get Jack walking again. Monsters existed, why not miracles? Maybe it was time Howard went to Saint Anne's.

D.R. Perry

"We can't wake her up to get her out of there." Leo managed to keep from tapping his fingers on his knee. "We don't know her shape change. We'll have to carry her out." He waited for one of them to object, but he knew he was right. They did too.

"I can't get in by guile." Oguina tucked a stray strand of hair behind her ear. "They know what I am. Leo, too."

"Hrafin always said I was the worst kind of liar." Bersi stroked his beard. "You could give me something to say, but they probably won't believe it."

"What's our goal here?" Leo's fingers were tapping away again. Even as a monster, he couldn't escape nervous habits.

"To get Bianco's dead blood away from him," Oguina said. Bersi nodded.

Leo took a deep breath before spouting off his possibly revolutionary or probably ignorant idea. "It would only take one of us to break in and destroy her."

Oguina hissed. Bersi was at his side in half an instant. Leo didn't even feel the air of his passage before the fist slammed into his jaw and knocked him to the ground.

"Say nothing like that ever again in my presence, or I'll put you to sleep for a thousand years."

Leo stayed on the ground, baring his throat and cutting his eyes away from Bersi. "I'll never bring that up again, promise."

Oguina helped him up. "All we must do is get her down to the basement. There's a tunnel I don't think Bianco knows about. It leads almost to a gate in the back wall."

Leo brushed dirt off his trousers, then his hands. At least Changed didn't bruise. "How many people were in there? Was there a time we'd be less likely to get caught?"

"They have guard dogs at night that might sense our presence." Oguina glanced at his fingers. Dammit, he was tapping them again. "If you approach as animals, they'll only see a cat and a dog. I heard eight heartbeats, that means six bodyguards. If there were more Changed, I didn't see them or hear them moving around."

"Oh boy." Leo sat down. "What if they have more than just that girl? Can you go back and look in some more windows, Oguina?"

"I tried." She shook her head. "Most windows have curtains. The ones who didn't had no Changed or other prisoners."

"Then the night we break her out I go in as a cat. They'll chase me for sure, maybe try and shoot me, but they'll have no idea what I am. I'll make sure I'm on the other side of the house from you."

Bersi was stroking his beard again. "Could they have a way of detecting us? Neck-scar knew Oguina was Changed."

"He must have talked to Jimmy Delaqua." Oguina sat

down, tucking her legs under her. "I hit him, but not hard enough for him to forget I wasn't human."

Bersi guffawed, slapping both his knees. Oguina joined in, covering her mouth with her hands.

"I just thought of something that's not funny." Leo was still angry about getting decked for a stupid mistake. "You have to wonder how Bianco found out we exist in the first place. Someone could have taken a photo of either of you. How would you even know it? We really have to hope none of us ends up in a newspaper."

That stopped them laughing. They blinked like he'd just flashed a Daylo in their eyes. Didn't they understand? But why would they? Leo knew these times were dangerous in a way Oguina and Bersi couldn't. Photography wasn't even a twinkle in humanity's eye when they were born. He'd need to get them more familiar with modern technology, stay up to date on it himself. At least that was some kind of goal he could set that wasn't limited to revenge.

"Do you think Bianco heard the same stories you did when he was growing up?" It was Bersi's turn for finger tapping. He did it on his cheek instead of his knees.

"Maybe." Leo nodded. "Probably. My grandfather told me those stories. He learned them from the altar boys when he was a Deacon at Saint Anne's. Bianco was one. He must have heard them."

"So that explains why his men know about us." Oguina nodded. "He knows."

"But it's not just Bianco." Why didn't they get it? To Leo, it was so obvious that Changed weren't as secret as they'd like to be. "What about neck-scar? Where do you think he got that, um, neck scar? He's been attacked by one of us before, years back too. That scar looks older than I am."

"That's impossible," Bersi smirked. Leo really hoped he wouldn't laugh again. "That man was alive. If one of us did that, he'd be dead."

"We have hospitals now, and the doctors can do plenty of things for people with injuries like that. They can take blood from one person and put it in someone else, you know."

"So what are you saying?" Oguina's eyebrows got closer together. At least one of them was listening. "Mortally injured men can be cured if a doctor helps in time?"

"Yes."

"So we need to kill everyone who might have seen us." Oguina's face went slack, and she slumped her shoulders.

"Or we hunt animals instead of people." Bersi stroked his beard.

"We can figure out the best way to avoid having our photos taken later. It doesn't really matter how Bianco found out we exist. What's important is how we fix this."

"We almost had a plan." Bersi leaned an elbow on his knee. "Something about a cat distraction?"

Leo nodded. "You two can use the tunnel Oguina found. We go and get the prisoner out. If you smell any stashes of blood on the way, get those. I'll be busy running the wiseguys around the house. Maybe the dogs will get into it too, cause a hell of a mess if they do. Then we go back another night to kill Bianco, hopefully after we wake the prisoner up. Bet she'll be plenty angry at him."

"But what if he gets another prisoner in the meanwhile?" Bersi stroked his beard.

"He'd have to find one of us." Oguina seemed to perk up a little. "I hope he tries."

"Where did the prisoner they have come from, though?" Leo put one hand over the other to keep from tapping his knee. "There have to be some other Changed around."

"Maybe they got her from some other city," said Oguina. "This city is small. There might be more Changed in bigger cities. More hunting there. It's what I'd do if there were more of us."

"Oguina, you're an odd creature," Bersi said this as gently as he could. "Our kind weren't meant to hunt people in cities. It's poisonous for the mind, Hrafin says."

Oguina and Bersi were staring off into space now, lost in their little individual worlds. Could this be part of that perfect memory distraction he'd noticed? Being a monster had some unforeseen drawbacks. Was he in more danger as a monster than he'd been as a kid on the run? Bersi and Oguina seemed to snap into it. Finally.

"Leo," said Oguina, "your idea is good. We ought to try it. After the rescue, I'll just check the house every night for more prisoners."

"Good idea," said Leo. "You can wear these, for when you're in human shape." Leo gave them one of the balaclavas he'd liberated from a shop in town. Oguina turned hers over and over in her hands, poking her fingers through the eye holes. Bersi just sat, watching Oguina figure out the shape size and function of the item. "Bersi? Do you have any ideas?"

Bersi stared at him for nearly a full minute before speaking. "We should revive the prisoner, no matter how long it takes. Someone Changed her, and we'll want to know who. She might be a powerful ally. We don't know what to feed her, but if one of us brings something different each night, we'll find her animal. If she's anything like Hrafin, she might even have a clue on her."

Had there been some point in the past when humans knew about dead blood? Leo couldn't think of a reason monsters would wear or carry that sort of thing besides superstition. He wished he'd thought of it before getting the balaclavas. They should all have something to identify their shapes. What if they were all asleep and some other monster came to their aid? Now he was the one spacing out. Leo focused back on planning.

"So." Leo stood up, stretching even though he didn't need to. "We'll make the rescue tomorrow. We all hunt deer right after we wake up. Oguina will fly in, while Bersi and I cat and dog it on to the premises. Bersi can go through the kennel as a dog. Oguina can get in the window, bring the prisoner down the stairs to meet Bersi. Then, you all go out through the tunnel. I'll try and keep Bianco's men away from the back stairs and the basement. We meet up at that back gate. Sound okay?"

Bersi laughed again. This time, Leo didn't mind. "Dog fighting and sneaking a woman out of a house. This is almost like the days of my youth."

"It's nothing like mine." Oguina's eyes twinkled. "This

might be diverting enough to rival that first speakeasy."
She smiled and, for once, her teeth didn't give Leo the
heebie-jeebies.

Neither of them seemed nervous, which was a good
thing. Leo had enough anxiety for all three of them and
the girl in the attic.

Oguina perched on a lamp behind the door, trying to preen soot out of her feathers. The window had been closed, so Oguina had flown down the chimney. Then she'd had a difficult climb up a quilt rack to get the height she needed to glide to the lamp. She heard the man with the black bag on the stairs. Last time, he'd left the door open as he used his syringe. The lamp behind the door seemed like the best hiding place. Under the bed would have hidden her better, but she'd be grounded. At this height, she'd have freedom to attack or escape if she had to.

The door opened, revealing the man with the scarred neck. He didn't have the black bag this time, so what was he doing here? She froze as he shut the door. He hadn't seen her. He turned toward the woman in the bed and knelt, brushing a few stray hairs away from the monster's cheek. He leaned over and kissed her forehead. It was only then that Oguina noticed that she'd been dressed in a fresh nightgown. The man held her hand to his cheek.

"Hello, Pearl." His voice was raspy. "Do you like the nightgown? It just like the one I got our Mother. She's been in a bad way lately, thinks we're still schoolkids. I wish I could bring you to see her, visit Father's grave too. I used to think you wouldn't care about that now that you're… what you are." He paused, cocking his head as though listening for something. "Yeah, maybe I was wrong. One of these nights, I'll get that little bastard. Who knows? That might even cure you."

Oguina's mind raced with thoughts and questions she didn't have time for. The man placed his sister's hand gently beside her on the coverlet, got up, then walked to the door. He paused with his hand on the knob, frowning. She could tell by his heartbeat that he'd gotten nervous about something. If she could have held herself more still, she would have.

The man turned back, leaned across the bed and pulled the window shade. He switched off the lamp on her bedside table, then pulled something from his pocket. Oguina tensed, ready to fly at his face, but when he turned she saw he held a handkerchief. He dabbed the tears gathering under his eyes. He never looked up as he left the room.

Oguina listened to his footsteps descend both flights of stairs. She waited until she heard him cross to the front of the house. Only then did she dare swoop down and change to human shape. She checked the drawer on the bedside table for anything that might belong to the woman. There was nothing but extra handkerchiefs, dusty and starting to yellow at the edges. If this creature had a trinket revealing an animal shape, it wasn't here.

The girl in the bed had a young appearance, perhaps she'd been eighteen when she got Changed. Oguina looked around for shoes or a coat or anything else that might harder to spot than the pastel pink nightgown Pearl was wearing. A large green blanket hung on the quilt rack. That would have to do. Using skills she hadn't needed in centuries, Oguina wrapped the blanket, so it functioned as a garment.

Once she was finished, Oguina hoisted Pearl over her shoulder and opened the door, revealing the back stairs. She heard barking outside, then whining that cut off after a moment. The dog door in the kennel clattered downstairs. On the other side of the house, she heard a feline caterwaul, a crashing of breaking glass, and stomping human footsteps. All clear. She could go.

Bersi leaped the west wall. No matter how many times he landed on four feet, he still felt strangely content to be a dog. The first time he'd shapeshifted, he expected a bear shape. The dog disappointed him at first, but he'd come to know that a bear shape wouldn't be useful. He couldn't have tracked Hrafin here as a bear, and he'd have been useless tonight.

He encountered the first dog just outside the kennel. It barked at him, frothy drool flying from its mouth. He recognized its breed as a Doberman, remembered they had a reputation for a tenacious bite. He'd seen them before, but only from a distance. It raced toward him and clamped its teeth down on his throat. This dog deserved its job as a guard, but it was completely ineffective against Bersi.

A moment later, the dog opened its jaws. It crept backward whining with its tail between its legs. Blood dripped from its mouth, taking bits of teeth with it. Bersi caught it by the throat and shook as hard as he could. Its neck snapped, ending its whining and its pain. He made his way to the kennel and through a hole with a rubber flap over it.

The darkness in the kennel didn't bother Bersi. He changed to human shape when he reached the door. He knew the footsteps on the stairs were Oguina's even though they fell with twice her weight. Good. That meant she had the prisoner. He went inside, shutting the door behind him. Bersi stood in the kitchen.

The lights were on. Dirty pots and pans made a leaning tower in the sink, topped with a few china plates. Bersi saw two doors, one to his left and the other to his right. Oguina's footsteps came from the left. There wasn't a knob, so he pushed through. It swung shut behind him.

Bersi filled most of the dimly lit hall. A flight of stairs ended right in front of him, and on his left were two doors. He smelled the dust and oil soap behind one door. A broom closet, then. A scent of earth and coal wafted under the other. He had to twist and press against the wall to get the door open. Oguina came down the stairs balancing the prisoner on one shoulder. She squeezed past him across the threshold. He followed, cramping his shoulder to close the door behind him.

The basement stairs were steep and narrow. Was this house built by fae folk? Bersi smelled the tunnel entrance in the wall behind the stairs.

"There must be a hidden latch somewhere." Oguina

planted her feet, steadying the weight of the prisoner.

"We need a light." Something brushed Bersi's shoulder. He reached up and pulled. A light came on above his head. The basement had been a wine cellar. Most of the racks were full of empty bottles.

Bersi went to the racks, jiggling them. Nothing happened. Leo's commotion upstairs had gone from one end of the house to the other and back again. Meows and hisses mingled with breaking glass, pounding feet, and thuds of heavy objects falling to the floor. Bersi chuckled softly under his breath.

He turned in a slow circle, scanning the wall for anything he might have missed. And there it was, under the stairs. A delicate wrought iron sconce clung to the wall. It was so out of place it had to be the latch. He reached for it. The sight of his hand on the sconce brought back a memory that rocked him like a left hook to the nose.

Bersi was back at the settlement in Vinland, fifty years after his Change. The church there had sconces just like this one. He stood in the vestibule, gazing down the aisle between pews like a sailor gazes at the shore. The pale pine box gazed back at him across that candle-lit abyss. His little sister was in that box, the last of his family to grow old and die while he stayed exactly the same. He was the only one left who knew that she didn't belong this church or the Christian burial ground beside it.

Because they were so close in age, they'd been confidants. She never believed in the Church or its

Father and Son and Holy Spirit. His sister had prayed to Freya when she crossed the ocean of girlhood for the land of womanhood. And when their littlest brother was stillborn she prayed for Hel to watch over the unborn child, not the Virgin Mary.

He'd come here to rescue her remains from a fate that her spirit was surely kicking and screaming about. He walked the length of the church, lifted the lid of the box and looked at his sister for the first time in half a century. Her only resemblance to the girl she'd been was her slenderness. Her hair had gone from a color like strawberries dipped in honey to the dingy white of ice on the beach. Her cheeks were like storehouse potatoes at the end of winter instead of spring apples showing their first hint of red. He knew her anyway. He'd never forget someone he loved so much, with or without the Change.

Gently he lifted her, cradling her corpse against his chest. She weighed less than goose down, but the fact of her death was so heavy it could have crushed him. He resisted an urge to stop and weep, he hadn't much time, so he turned and carried her out of the church.

The place he'd prepared wasn't far. Bersi remembered every step of that walk, every twig that snapped underfoot, every stone that turned on his path. He remembered the smell of the fishermen's nets, the sound of the sea taking the land apart bit by bit. He remembered the whisper of her shroud as he lowered her into the boat, the fear he swallowed as he set fire to the boat and sent it on its way.

"Is that it?" Oguina's voice knocked Bersi out the memory fugue like a fist knocks out a tooth. He could only nod and move the sconce to disengage the latch from it. Something clicked, then creaked. He felt the air of the hidden door opening behind him. All noise from upstairs had stopped. He heard floorboards creak at the top of the cellar stairs. Bersi hustled Oguina through the hidden door, following closely. He made sure the door closed and latched behind them.

The tunnel was completely dark, with dust and cobwebs adding a dry aspect to the earthy root-cellar smell. That was good; it meant no one had walked here for several years. Bianco and his people might not even know about the tunnel. It went in a straight line and was paved in some kind of stone. The walls must be earth since their footsteps made only a little noise.

A clattering came from the cellar, as though someone searched the room. Their plan had been to close all the doors, and that's what he'd done. How would the men in the house have known they went into the basement? Humans didn't have a keen enough sense of smell to find them. Then he heard a sniffing and the scratch of dog claws back in the basement. They'd brought a Doberman inside, probably to catch Leo. The dog probably heard them as they were leaving.

The hidden door stayed shut behind them. Whoever was in charge of the dog must not know about it. The dog would point them at the wine rack, of course, but they wouldn't be able to open it. But what if the dog pointed at everything Bersi had touched? They might find the sconce. He was about to tell Oguina to hurry but found they were facing what smelled like a stone wall with metal in it.

"A ladder." Oguina nudged him with an elbow. "You will need to hand her up to me." She slowly transferred the prisoner from her shoulder to his arms. Bersi might be older, stronger, and less timid than Oguina, but she was nearly as canny as Hrafin. He followed her suggestion. After handing the prisoner up the ladder, he followed her.

Leo crouched in a juniper bush by the empty fountain where the tunnel let out. He had been there for more than a minute, his fur standing on end as he thought about the dogs finding him. Doberman dogs had good noses, surely they'd be able to smell him through the piney scent of the shrubbery. Something moved somewhere under the fountain. Was it his friends?

Stone scraped on stone. A piece of granite with a decorative plaque next to the fountain moved aside, revealing a hole in the ground. Oguina hoisted herself out, so she sat at the edge of the hole. She reached down and lifted back up again, slinging a light haired woman wrapped in green woolen fabric over her shoulder. She stood up carefully.

Leo read the words on the plaque. "You are loosed from your moorings and are free. –Frederick Douglass." This house must have been part of the Underground Railroad, the tunnel used to free slaves, not for some booze smuggling operation. It was actually nice to be wrong about that. It meant they used the tunnel for its intended purpose. He watched Bersi come up from the tunnel and move the rock back over the hole. He did that so fast, Leo almost missed it.

Leo stretched himself out of his curled up position, untangling himself out of the juniper. Oguina stood by the vine-covered gate in the wall; Bersi headed toward her to open it. Leo followed, sticking to the shadows. He'd rather not to be spotted near them if he could help it. From afar, an observer might think the male figure with Oguina was him. He wanted Bianco and neck-scar to go on thinking they were a two-monster squad. He waited until they were both through the gate before running at full speed through it. Anyone who might be looking would see a pale streak against the wall for a second. As the metal gate clanged shut behind them, Leo pushed down all his memories from four weeks ago, before his paranoia was born.

"Bless me, Father, for I have sinned." The kneeler in the reconciliation booth made Howard feel like a clumsy oaf. "It's been six months since my last confession."

It was quiet, but Howard thought he'd heard the priest go in and sit down. "Father? You okay in there?"

"Yes, child. I'm listening." Howard heard a match strike. The heady scent of myrrh wafted through the screen from the other side of the booth.

"I don't mean to be a pest, but should I come back in the morning?" The last thing he needed after the day he'd had was the priest falling asleep during a sacrament. Howard tried to picture Father Francis dozing off in there, but that didn't seem right.

"The hour may be late, but you have my full attention, child." The Father took a long, wheezing breath. "For whatever reason, you've come here."

"Uh, thanks, Father." Howard cleared his throat. Was Father Francis afraid? "So, I guess I'm here tonight because I saw things most people wouldn't believe. I spent years and years fighting. I thought it was the right thing, that I was fighting evil." He closed his eyes, took a deep breath. Howard was sick of his sight getting blurry when he thought about this. "But it's not that simple.

I've been wrong. I don't know what to do."

"This kind of problem is more common than you might think. I've even had a dilemma like this myself." Fabric rustled and wood creaked as the Father leaned forward, his shape faintly outlined by ember-light from the censer. "Tell me, why did you start fighting?"

"Some people took my sister almost twenty years ago. I've followed them ever since, fought them when they attacked. Someone here hired me to go on the offensive against them, steal their weapons." Howard's face was wet again. All that incense must be irritating his eyes. He pulled a fresh hankie from his pocket to wipe his face.

Father Francis coughed dryly. "So, you've been fighting. What would happen if you stopped?"

"If I just quit, people I love would suffer. I'd never find my sister. I got a friend in the hospital and my mother with a nurse at home. My job takes care of their bills." Howard unfolded his hands and put one across his forehead to rub his temples. "But it's worse than that. The guy paying me, he's the type that might hurt them if I quit."

"Those are heavy consequences." The Father took another long breath, less wheezy this time. "What would happen if you kept fighting for this man?"

"If I keep working for him I'm giving him weapons. I fight these people to help him, not my sister." Howard tapped his swollen knuckles against the top of the kneeler. He wanted to punch something, but not here. "I'm scared that one of these days he'll order me to hurt her. He's just getting stronger. And I'm just angrier at myself for being such a rube. Father, that anger scares me. I could fly off the handle, do anything to anyone."

"Let compassion guide you instead of this man. You'll find your anger replaced with conviction. You've come to a fork in the road with enough strength to walk either path. Both are thorny, but your conscience can only flourish on one. I know it seems like an impossible choice but remember King Solomon. He advised a heinous course, but revealed the right answer." That dry cough came from the other side of the screen again.

"Father, Solomon was one of the wisest men who lived, a king. I'm just a lug with a sick mom, a crippled friend, and a mon—" Howard cleared his throat. He'd almost spilled the beans about Pearl being a monster. The Father would just think he was bonkers, but still, it was unlucky to say. Last time he said it out loud, Jack lost his legs. "Uh, and a money problem." It wasn't a lie, at least not technically. What was he doing, telling lies in here? Howard genuflected. "I should say a rosary right now, Father." He reached under all the handkerchiefs, pulling the beads from his pocket.

Father Francis wheezed again before he spoke. "Why?" Something rattled, then hissed. The myrrh smell got stronger.

"I just lied to you, right here in Reconciliation. The truth is Father, my sister's mixed up with some bad people. Monsters, some might say. The man I work for thinks they're all evil. I used to agree. But father, my sister's one. I can't believe she's evil. So how can I agree with a guy like Gia-"

"Please. Don't name him. I know who you work for. I've known him since his Christening." He heard a sniffle and the rustle of fabric. Even through the screen, he saw something white move up into the shadows the Father's voice came from. Was the priest crying?

Howard turned his head up to the ceiling. His face was wet again. Too much smoke, or maybe a leak in the roof. "My mother used to say something before she went senile. She said you got to question beliefs you share with sinful people. If you think like them, you'll end up like them. And here I am, agreeing with this guy. Don't matter that it's something I'd done for years before I met him. It just don't sit right with me anymore."

"So you've been comparing yourself to this other man." The Father leaned forward to take another deep breath of incense. Did he have asthma or something? "What do you have in common?"

"We both have a temper. Those people my sister got mixed up with? He knew all about them. He told me they're animals not people, that he hates them. I realized I hated them too. All those years, I didn't even think they were real people except my sister. I might as well hate myself, as far as he's concerned. I'm Irish. You know he hates the Irish, right?"

"I know that well." The Father took another breath, another wheeze.

"Well, he hates more than the Irish. He hates pretty much anyone who ain't Italian." Howard stared at his hands, even though he could only see a twilit outline in the booth's darkness. "I cut up my knuckles punching things just to let some of the fire out of my belly."

"And you're different from this man." Another rattle and hiss. "How?" This time, he smelled frankincense as the Father leaned over the censer.

"I didn't think I could be, at least about those people. And then last week, a guy I work with met one of them. He acted like she was just a regular gal. A couple days later, I met her. She wanted to go talk about how my boss hates my people. I got her alone, then didn't even let her get a word out. I hurt her. But that kind of thing's my job now, right?" Howard curled his hands into fists, pulling the skin of his knuckles taut. It bled and stung. He deserved it. "Then another one came, risked himself so she could get away. He had me over a barrel, but he let me go. These people I hated so much showed me mercy. I didn't think they were capable of that." Howard hung his head, ashamed. Something dripped from his cheek to his bloody hands. "My boss ordered a guy to murder some kids because they looked at him funny. So who's evil? Him or them? And what am I if I work for that kind of man?"

"Those are good questions. You're still having trouble answering them because you're at a crossroads. This man you work for inspired a moral dilemma. All I can tell you is, he's done it to others. Watch the people around this man. Someone else might have your answer, like the baby's mother had Solomon's. You're not the only one trying to do good in a bad situation."

"Thanks, Father."

"Now, let's say the Act of Contrition."

"Oh my God, I am sorry for my sin with all my heart." The familiar words gave Howard comfort if not peace. At least that was a start. As Howard finished the prayer, the Father took a long slow breath.

"God the Father of Mercies through the death and resurrection of His Son has brought forgiveness of sin to the world." Only the faintest hint of a wheeze was left in the priest's voice. "Through the ministry of the Church, I grant you pardon and absolution for your sin in the Name of the Father, and of the Son, and of the Holy Ghost. Amen. You may go."

"Father, thank you." Howard wiped his face and wrapped his bleeding knuckles before standing. He was about to put the rosary away but didn't. He unwrapped his left hand, then grasped the beads and did up the binding again.

Howard was looking down as he left the booth. That's why he was halfway up the aisle before seeing the hobo. He turned his head to get a better look. Something about the size and stance of the figure was familiar. Howard couldn't see the vagrant's face or any exposed skin for that matter. The man was large, wore a tattered coat, a ragged scarf and a hat that looked like it had been sat on several times.

The hobo headed toward the booth Howard had just vacated. Why was he suddenly so alert? Howard had seen street people in Saint Anne's before, but this one wasn't hunched or shaky or dragging his feet like the rest. He walked upright, not confident but with purpose. Howard felt the flutter in his gut that usually came when he saw a monster.

Monsters couldn't go to church. Daniel couldn't even walk on the property, as far as he knew. This raggedy man couldn't be a monster. But why the gut feeling? The hobo moved the curtain aside and went into the reconciliation booth. Monsters wouldn't go to church. But monsters wouldn't go to speakeasies either. Howard turned, heading back toward the booth as quickly and quietly as he could.

"Forgive me, Father. I've sinned. I stood by. I let others sin when I could have stopped them. It's been, oh God. I need help, Father, and she's gone. It's been fifty years since my last confession." The hobo's breath hitched between sentences punctuated by sniffles.

Heat filled Howard's cheeks as shame changed the flutter in his gut to nausea. He sprinted out of the church, leaning with his hands on his thighs as he pitched a retch on the steps. The rosary beads pressed painfully between his hand and thigh, clearing his head.

Monsters didn't go to confession. They didn't cry. They didn't smile or laugh unless they were trying to scare the pants off their victims. They didn't ask for help from elderly priests with such desperation. They couldn't. If they did, Howard was a murderer with a body count to rival Bianco's. Howard took a few steps to the side, away from the mess he'd made. He sat down, put his head in his hands.

Something brushed against his calves. He opened his eyes to a big fluffy brindled cat. It sat by his right foot, head tilted up and to one side. It blinked, gave him an inquisitive "brrt" and flicked its tail three times against the heel of his shoe.

"You don't want nothing to do with me, pal." Howard curled his left hand around the rosary. "I'm not a good guy."

The cat sniffed primly, then blinked again. The tail

flicked his heel twice this time. It looked at the door of the church, then back at his face. Howard glanced over his shoulder, but there was nothing at the door. Maybe Father Francis fed the strays, and all the late night confessions were holding him up tonight.

"I got no food if that's what you're after."

The cat's ears flicked. It tilted its head from side to side a couple of times. There was that tail against his heel again, two taps. It looked at the puddle of sick at the edge of the steps, then back to Howard.

"Yeah. That's my fault. Sorry if I made a mess where you like to hang out. Epiphanies ain't all they're cracked up to be, know what I mean?"

The cat's tail tapped his heel again, only once this time. The whiskers around its eyes lifted, giving its gaze an almost sympathetic feel. A sympathetic cat? That was impossible. But so were monsters.

"Listen, thanks." What was he doing, thanking a cat? "I'll be okay. Been through worse than sicking up in the street. I gotta scram." Howard started to stand, but the cat twined around his feet. He didn't want to trip and hurt the critter. He lowered his rear back to the still-warm step.

"Told ya, I don't got any food." The cat didn't seem to care. It just rubbed its fluffy self all over Howard's right leg, shedding tufts of fur all over his trousers. It bumped its head against his wrist, purring loudly.

"Oh, fine. You want attention? That I can do." He picked up his hand and rubbed the cat under its chin and then behind the ears. Its eyes closed as it purred louder. The tip of its tail tapped Howard's shoe once, paused and tapped once again. Howard didn't get the tapping thing. His mother kept cats for as long as he could remember, but none of them had ever done that. What was he going to do, ask? Well, why not?

"Are you tapping me for a reason, pal?" The cat stopped its rubbing and purring, looking back up at him. It tapped his foot once.

"Did someone train you to do that?" Two taps. He still wasn't sure.

"Are you a dog?" Two taps again. Did two taps mean no?

"Are you trying to talk to me?" One tap and the purring started up again.

Before Howard could continue the conversation or his line of thought, the door behind him creaked open. Steps on the stairs and a hint of warm, incense-infused air compelled him to glance up. He finally saw the face of the raggedly dressed hobo from inside the church. It was Sampson, his dark brow furrowed and his face wet with tears.

Howard got his feet under him, ready to jump up for an attack. Movement at the edge of his vision stopped him. Two people crouched on the roof of the hospital across the street like they were ready to pounce. One was a tall woman, a corona of red outlining her head as the moon shone behind her. Bloody Bess. And the other figure had the slender build of a youth. Daniel Denton. He thought they were looking down at him, waiting for Sampson to drag him off the steps, but he was wrong.

Sampson passed him by without even a glance. He came off the church steps, wiping his eyes with his sleeve, turned left toward Forest Street. Howard looked back at the hospital roof. Bess and Daniel were gone. He looked up and saw them in mid-leap, flying through the air clear across Middle Street. They landed on the roof of a tenement, pacing Sampson. He couldn't imagine Daniel Denton would be happy to find out his lieutenant went to church.

Howard remembered Sampson's weakness was tunnel vision. He'd never see Daniel and Bess coming. What had the monster been saying in the booth? Something about standing by while others sinned. Howard took a deep breath and stood up.

That breath came out of him in a wordless shout as he found himself falling down the granite steps. He came to a stop near the bottom. Howard Fallon had just enough time to realize the cat tripped him before he could leave Holy Ground. Then he blacked out.

Hrafin trotted down the steps and up the street, following the other Changed. Daniel had crossed a nightmarish line which all Changed should fear. He'd transitioned from Haunted to Feral. Worse, he'd taken the tall woman with him. It seemed to be deliberate. The Moor, Sampson, was Haunted but fighting it. One too many atrocities and he'd be the next Feral.

Hrafin turned the corner. The Haunted fellow was only halfway down the street. He caught up enough to pace him at a reasonable distance. If he was defiant enough to seek spiritual help, he might help Hrafin fight the Ferals. He'd need it. He'd never taken on more than one Feral alone. If only he had time to go back to Mount Washington for Bersi.

Hrafin glanced at the rooftops. Daniel leaped from one roof to the next, pacing Sampson. Unlike Hrafin, Daniel was making some noise. Sampson didn't look up but walked faster. He must have known he was being followed. He turned a corner, heading west toward the waterfront.

Someone in this town hunted Changed. Daniel's followers occasionally wandered away, secluding and starving themselves into a millennial sleep. That wasn't unusual, but a few months ago he started to find remains instead of sleepers. He would have used the revivification ritual to ask some questions, but there was a problem. Each set of remains was missing all its teeth. A revival wasn't possible unless all the pieces were there.

Daniel wouldn't care if he knew. Even a capable hunter would have little chance alone against Ferals like Daniel and Bess. The hunter might even be inadvertently helping Daniel by culling potential rebels from his pack. Pearl might have overthrown him if she'd had enough support. Sampson was a warrior, but Pearl wasn't.

As Sampson left the tenements behind, Hrafin noticed Bess and Daniel separate. They still pursued from the rooftops, but now they appeared to be driving Sampson away from the factories where there would be people. Hrafin wondered whether they were steering him to a particular location. It wasn't the warehouse where he'd fought Daniel before. They'd passed that a few blocks back. Bess and Daniel had something in store for Sampson tonight.

Ferals were canny. They lost their moral balance, not their wits. Hrafin followed Sampson all the way to the waterfront. He paused and Hrafin heard Bess laugh, an inhuman sound which was more like the yapping of a dog than anything else. Sampson looked over his shoulder, then walked stiffly onto the dock. Hrafin couldn't follow him, there was no cover. The slips were all empty for the winter except the one at the end. He'd have to hide and follow Daniel and Bess.

Sampson approached the boat. It was bigger than the

last boat Hrafin had visited in this marina, but not my much. Hrafin tilted his head, trying to get a look at the name of the vessel. He saw it after Sampson stepped from the dock to the slip, "Niña." Something about the way the boat moved in the water bothered Hrafin. He scented the air. People were on board. Living people, and several of them. Sampson walked past the gangplank. He stood at the edge of the slip, shuddering as he stared wide-eyed at the water. Hrafin would have jumped in and made his escape at that point. Was the Moor unable to swim?

Light footsteps knocked hollow on the dock as Daniel approached the slip where Sampson stood. The youth stopped, blocking the way back. Sampson was cornered, surrounded by deep water and a boat full of frightened people.

"You're not even Catholic." Daniel put his hands on his hips. Sampson's shoulders flinched with each syllable, as though someone whipped him. "What were you doing in there, eating that bony old priest?" Daniel chuckled. "I know you didn't. I haven't smelled blood on your breath in weeks. Did you think you could hide it from me, the fact that you haven't killed?"

"I only went in to see what it was like." Sampson turned, fists clenched, facing Daniel. "If I end up like you, I'll never see the inside of anything like a church again."

"If?" Daniel shook his head. "When. Your time is almost here, old friend." Then Daniel smiled. Hrafin's tail stood up along with all the fur on his back.

"No. You didn't get better, Dan. You got worse, went

bad. If I end up like you, I'll be no better than the men who owned me. I won't be your slave." Sampson glanced to his right. Hrafin thought he'd take to the water anyway, fear or no.

Something emerged from the water with a splash. That yapping, inhuman laughter echoed off the slip and the surface of the water. "Jump in if you like, lovey. I'm here to catch you."

"Bess won't let you leave, Sampson. And really, it's bad form for the guest of honor to desert his own party before it's even started." Daniel took a step toward Sampson. Even though the Feral was half his size, the Moor flinched. "We've got a banquet in there for you. Even that little weakling Pearl would have been hard-pressed to refuse."

"Pearl." Sampson blinked a few times rapidly. He looked at the top of the wheelhouse, then the dock. Hrafin nodded. The angle was good. If Sampson timed his jump just right, he might get away. "I'm going to find her. And we'll stop you one of these nights."

"The only thing Pearl's stopping now is a chimney. Do you think I'd leave her asleep in that awful pine box? I put her out of that misery weeks ago. Remember the night I sent you to scout the edge of the forest?"

Sampson hung his head, dropped to his knees. A single quiet sob heaved up from his chest, carrying any trace of defiance or hope away from his large frame. Hrafin steeled himself, trotting toward the edges of the shadows he'd been hiding in. It was almost time to act if he was going to stop this.

He could hear voices crying now inside the boat, then

a high-pitched wail. He hadn't heard mortals with that particular pitch and timbre to their voices for a long time. He started to remember something; a pair of clasped hands smaller than his own, and a small smooth forehead bowed over them. He blinked, trying to chase the memory away, but it halted him like an anchor stops a boat....

The child had sought sanctuary in the church, in days when the depth and breadth of Faith deterred more than Ferals. Hrafin watched the child through a narrow window, and he clung to the outside of the building. His vocation as Ranger of Rome and his vow to shield the innocent offered him extra protection from the pains that the building and its grounds could cause Haunted Changed.

The Feral outside the wall around the building glared up at him, its teeth bared distorting its face. Hrafin couldn't tell who it had been before its Change. This Feral was so far gone its only identity was the desire to kill as swiftly and brutally as possible.

Hrafin heard the footsteps just a second later than the Feral. A mortal was approaching the Church. Hrafin leaped off the roof of the building, but the Feral moved out of the way just in time. He was left holding a scrap of fabric that had once been part of the creature's shirt. It bounded toward the helpless mortal on all fours. Now Hrafin could see that this was another child, though older than the one already inside the Church. The children smelled enough alike. They were related, perhaps siblings.

He acted swiftly, jumping over the Feral to put his

body in between it and the child. The Feral slammed into him. They tumbled over each other in the dusty gravel path.

"Run." The child followed Hrafin's command immediately and swiftly, like a loyal soldier on a battlefield.

The Feral's teeth clamped on his shoulder, tearing at his flesh. It had enough presence of mind not to drink and be paralyzed. The feral unhinged its jaw to spit out the dead blood. Hrafin had time to turn the tactic to his own advantage. He rolled over, pinning the Feral under him. He pushed up on its lower jaw with the top of his head. Now the Feral couldn't bite.

As Hrafin chewed away flesh and bone from the Feral's neck, he heard the Priest open the door. The child was safe. The feral died beneath his teeth. Haunting weighed heavier on Hrafin than ever before. He wouldn't be able to approach any Holy Ground again until he'd gone to the Cloister on retreat....

When Hrafin's mind came back to the present, the moon was setting, and the boat was silent. He lifted his head and perked his ears forward, sniffing the air. Blood in the air and in footprints on the dock. Daniel had passed him without even noticing. Did he know nothing of shape-shifting? The old Haunted part of him insisted he walk away, leave and spare himself the sight of what might be on the Niña.

But the part of him that was still a Knight objected. He'd let a memory fugue keep him from his duty. The consequences would weigh more if he left than if he saw this through. Hrafin padded softly down the dock and up the slip on cat feet. In near perfect silence, he stepped up the gangplank and down into the hold. Moonlight shone down through round windows and the door behind him. The sight that met his eyes birthed an outrage he hadn't felt for centuries.

The broken bodies of at least seven children lay on the floor. They'd been discarded like tools used carelessly until they were beyond repair. Hrafin's bones, skin, and hair shifted, as he took the form that could shed tears. He wept for the children whose already brief lives had been cut short. He wept for Sampson, a creature who should be a guardian of memory now turned into a Feral killer. He wept for Pearl, who'd tried to do the right thing.

Hrafin couldn't walk away from this. Daniel wasn't just bloodthirsty, he was power-hungry. He was deliberately building a pack of Ferals and murdering innocents to do it. Hrafin couldn't stop him alone. He'd been errant from his order so long, Hrafin wasn't sure how to locate other Knights or even if they existed anymore.

How long had it been since he'd left Bersi in the woods outside of Worcester? And hadn't he felt a new Changed created only a short while ago? He'd need to find them and convince them to help before Daniel's Ferals outnumbered them.

When Oguina told the others how she'd watched Pearl's brother at her bedside, Bersi got still and quiet and gruffly excused himself. She didn't know why this detail disturbed him. She was frustrated by how little about Bersi's life before her Change. Leo went after him but returned only a few minutes later. He held a terrified squirrel, which he carried to the unconscious girl. He kept his back to Oguina, but she still smelled fresh blood.

"Pearl doesn't turn into a squirrel." Leo's lighthearted words were delivered in a deadpan tone. He kept his back to Oguina as he spoke. "That's probably a good thing. Oguina, now that we know her brother is Neck-scar, what should we do? He might have acted like an old softie up there in the attic, but he hunts Changed. It can't be a good idea to get on his bad side if you know what I mean."

"Pearl's not human anymore. Her brother won't accept it. None of that's our fault, but that won't make a difference. What's important is what she wants, not her brother." Oguina went to Leo's side. His hands and Pearl's face were messy with squirrel blood. "We know nothing about her except that her brother's devoted all his energy to helping her. Either he's obsessed, or she's remarkable." She took a rag from her sleeve and wiped the blood from Pearl's face. Blood was still on her lips, reminding Oguina of the tube of greasepaint in the gaudy handbag. "I'm curious to know which is true. The brother seems simple enough. I'd guess he wants revenge against whoever Changed her. You understand that, of course." She handed the tattered cloth to Leo.

Leo took the rag and nodded, looking thoughtful. "You know, Bianco wasn't there. I wrecked every room of that house making a distraction for the two of you, and I didn't see him." He clenched his fist around the rag instead of cleaning his hands. "Smelled him, though, so at least I know he goes there."

"If you had seen him, would you have killed him?"

"No." His voice was dry and brittle. If he'd been younger before his Change, it might have cracked. "No, I wouldn't have. This is bigger now than my revenge. Bianco has dangerous information and at least one powerful weapon against us. I'd bet diamonds to dollars he has proof Changed exist. For all we know, he's told everyone in the syndicate here and the neighboring towns. His cousin runs things in Plymouth. So, he can't die until we find out how far this goes." Leo looked at the squirrel's bloody corpse in his left hand. The rag left his right hand and fluttered to the floor. "I don't feel as bad about that as I thought I might."

"You have learned some wisdom, Cub Leo." Oguina picked up the rag and eyed the squirrel. She was hungry, but the flesh on the carcass would only sharpen it. "Was the lesson easy?"

"Easy?" asked Leo laughed, an ironic short burst. "No

way. It's the hardest thing I've had to learn so far."

"Was this new wisdom worth the effort?"

"I don't know. And I don't feel as bad about this either." Leo studied the squirrel, then wiped the corner of his mouth with the back of his hand. A trail of red highlighted his right cheekbone like a Madam's rouge.

Now it was Oguina's turn to laugh until she remembered something she had to tell him. "I have found that nothing worth keeping is easy to gain. But some things we make an effort to get should be thrown away. It's dangerous to keep things that have lost their value just because they were hard to get. Sometimes, valuable things turn to poison when we hold them for too long."

"Like our memories." Leo sounded so confident she'd been talking about that. She let him change the subject even though it wasn't. "I notice when you remember something, it's as if you go away for a moment. Sometimes a bunch of moments. It happens to Bersi too. I had to stop it from happening to me a few times already. Bum deal if it happens at the wrong time, huh?"

"Yes. If we get too lost in our memories, we forget about anything else." Oguina didn't add that she'd been lost in the fugue for days at a time in the decades after her brother died. She didn't want to scare him. "There were a few moments in the basement last night when Bersi's mind was on something else. The first time you saw it was the night of your Change. You reminded me of someone, and I remembered."

Oguina carried the rag to the kindling pile, dropping it on top. She asked the question she'd had since they met. "Leo, when you were still human and came to find me, did you see my teeth?"

Leo blinked at her from under a furrowed brow. Then he smiled as if he was finally truly seeing her. "Yes, I did, Oguina. Yes, I saw your teeth. But only for a moment, and only because I was looking for them so I'd know for certain you were real."

They came back to the cave later, flush with fat geese. Neither of them noticed Bersi sitting under a tree, holding a proper dress and shoes for Pearl, adrift again in the memory of his sister's funeral pyre. His eyes ached, and his face felt tight and gritty, as though he'd washed his face with seawater. He went into the cave to greet the others and let Oguina put the dress on Pearl, but already they slept. The sun stabbed through the trees to the east. Bersi slumped unconscious on the bare earth.

It was full dark when Leo woke up, finding Oguina out and Bersi sitting next to Pearl. The burly man was staring off into space, holding a dress that was a bit nicer than the ones he usually brought back for Oguina. There was a pair of shoes on the floor next to him.

"Nice dress." Leo stretched even though he didn't need to. "Her name's Pearl."

"I know." Bersi blinked. "She's also neck-scar's sister."

"Hey." Leo stood up. "Maybe she's the one who got him to a hospital after that neck bite. Wish I could ask her. That and who Changed her. Had to have been during or right after The Great War. She looks younger than me, and neck-scar seems twenty-odd years older."

"Hrafin and I were in Canada then." Bersi still hadn't moved. Was he depressed or something? "Oguina says she has not seen any others. This is what you call a dead end, no?"

"Just because she didn't see any doesn't mean there weren't any." Leo squatted in front of Bersi. "They could have come from some other city or town anyway."

"I know." Bersi's eyes pointed in Leo's direction but seemed to look right through him. "She can't tell us until she's awake."

"And there's no way at all to figure out her animal?" Leo moved, so his eyes were directly in Bersi's line of sight. "That's lamer than a no-legged man."

Bersi opened his mouth, and the grouchy maiden aunt of a chuckle came out. "Why should anything about us make sense? Humans make little sense of their lives without time or gods and temples and churches."

"There's science now, Bersi." Leo was in no mood for a heavy conversation. "Maybe our answers will come out of a lab someday."

"That's interesting." Oguina stood in the mouth of the cave. "Last night you said humans shouldn't have those answers."

"Bersadottir." Bersi sighed as he stood up. "Sneaking up on us again. Come, put this dress on Pearl."

She arched an eyebrow. "Is there some reason not to do that task yourself? Surely you're strong enough to lift her, and there's no shame in being unclothed for Changed." Leo's ideas about that were in China compared to Oguina's, but he held his tongue hoping this would snap Bersi out of his funk.

Bersi stood there blinking, just holding the dress and staring at nothing. Something about Pearl must be knocking Bersi into the fugue. Leo didn't care whether the memories were good or bad. Bersi's frequent trips down memory lane made him the next step up from useless. He hadn't even hunted yet.

"Hey, Bersi." Leo snapped his fingers in front of Bersi's face. "Look, I'll take care of Pearl's dress. Go out and hunt something, keep your strength up. Maybe bring something new back. No squirrels, though, we tried that last night."

Bersi blinked, then nodded and handed the dress to Leo. He turned and left the cave. Leo tried to figure out how to take the green woolen blanket off of Pearl. It had knots a sailor would have envied. He tried just pulling it over her head. No dice. Some Houdini-esque contortion attached it to her nightgown. Oguina leaned against the cave wall, her hand over her mouth like a giggling schoolgirl.

She came to his rescue. "Here. I'll remove those. Then you can put the dress on."

He didn't feel right, looking at a complete stranger in the altogether. For all he knew, she'd been a nun. Leo asked Oguina a question to distract himself from his unease. "What's wrong with Bersi?"

"He's lost in his memories." Oguina tugged the blanket back in place over Pearl. "As we discussed last night, they can be a hazard."

"Whatever it is, can't we do something for him?" Leo watched Oguina find a tiny corner the of wool fabric. "Would it help him to talk about the memories?"

"I don't know. It might." Oguina pulled the corner and the front of the blanket. Knots fell apart like an overcooked brisket. "More likely, reason will win if we wake her. He'll stop being triggered when he understands she's not part of that memory." Oguina pulled the blanket from under Pearl, then chucked the bundle of fabric into a corner. Houdini, absotively.

"Is that how it was with you on my first night?" Leo undid buttons on the back of the dress. "Once you got to know me better, I stopped reminding you of whoever you were remembering, right?"

"Something like that." Oguina turned Pearl, so she was on her stomach. "I do not think Bersi's had this sort of problem. He has lived in nature, with little chance to see people."

"The more I think about it, the more it makes sense." Leo pulled the dress over Pearl's feet and up her legs, keeping it under the nightgown. "If we stayed around people, made friends, we'd be tempted to Change them. Eventually, we'd start to outnumber them. Finding food would be a problem."

"You may be correct." Oguina took Pearl's arms out of the nightgown's sleeves. "But I hope we never find out. I don't know what force of nature or spirit is behind our Change. What I do know is that the hunting of living creatures is part of our nature. The progress humans make is part of theirs."

"Yeah, okay. That's true." Leo put the dress sleeves over Pearl's arms, then did up the buttons.

Oguina pulled the nightgown over Pearl's head. "I have watched the humans change the earth as profoundly as Bersi Changed me. Eventually, they'll start to outgrow the earth itself. Growing crops and raising livestock would be a problem."

Leo pulled Pearl's hair to one side and turned her over. "Also true. Your point?"

"Consider those parallel dangers. Is it part of the natural order for us to exist alongside them, or apart?"

Leo smoothed Pearl's hair. He went to the corner where the blanket lay crumpled and picked it up. He couldn't answer Oguina's question. Instead, he covered Pearl's feet with the blanket, a homey, humane gesture.

Oguina was filling lamps when Bersi returned holding a swaying a burlap sack. He walked to Pearl, passing Leo and Oguina without looking at them. He knelt slack-faced at Pearl's side. Oguina could tell his mind was somewhere else. Leo was right about Bersi's memories, but now wasn't the time. She took some rags from the pile and eased the sack from his loosely curled fist.

Oguina peered in the bag. A pair of bright eyes glittered and the animal made a chittering sound. She grabbed a scruff of fur and dropped the sack, revealing a raccoon. It stared at her, then blinked once. It chittered again in distress. Bersi was so still he could have been sleeping. Leo frowned.

"Come on, Bersi." Leo tapped him on the shoulder. "Let's give Oguina some room. Maybe this'll do the trick and wake her up."

"She'll never wake." Bersi's voice was monotone. "This is the long sleep. We must give her a proper funeral, take her to the boat."

Oguina shouldered Bersi further away, not the easiest thing while holding a squirming raccoon. She put rags over Pearl's chest to catch any blood, then took out a knife. She held the animal over Pearl's head, stabbing under its left fore-paw where the skin was thin. Blood dripped into Pearl's mouth. Oguina started to take the raccoon away, but something pulled it back. A pale hand grasped the creature's tail like a lifeline. Pearl was awake.

Oguina lowered the raccoon into reaching hands. Pearl drank neatly, getting little on her face and none on her hands. She opened her eyes. Deep brown, not blue as Oguina expected. She stood still, watching the girl's gaze move over her and around the cave. She showed no sign of fear, but swallowed and wrinkled her nose.

"Is my brother here?" Oguina heard hope she hadn't expected in that voice.

Bersi immediately turned toward her and Oguina glanced at him. Pearl followed her gaze. Leo stepped between her and Bersi.

Pearl looked at the raccoon, raising her eyebrows. "Who are you? And where am I?"

"Hello, I'm Leo." The cub's voice was warm and friendly. "That's Bersi and she's Oguina. We're Changed, like you. Some people had you as a prisoner, so we got you away from them and brought you here. You probably feel pretty lousy right now. The rest of that raccoon is yours, but don't worry. We're in the woods. There's plenty more where that came from."

"Thank you for the...um, food, I guess." Pearl sat up. She looked at the raccoon, then put her hand over her mouth. The gesture had a sadness to it. "But please. Don't bring me any people." Pearl shuddered.

"We don't generally harm them unless we have to. I'll

be back soon." Oguina put the knife away and turned to leave.

"Wait, Oguina." Pearl's voice sounded strained. Was she afraid? "Couldn't they go instead? I'd like to ask you some questions."

"Come on, Bersi." Leo slapped Bersi on the shoulder. "Let the ladies talk." Leo led Bersi from the cave like a farm boy might bring a cow to a barn.

Oguina went back to filling and lighting lamps. "What would you ask me?"

"I don't know how long I was asleep. Have you seen my brother?" She held the raccoon gingerly, glanced around like she was looking for something. "I dreamed he spoke to me. I'm afraid that means he's dead."

"If he's a large graying man with a scar on his neck, he was alive two nights ago." Oguina lifted the rock where they hid some items. "He's strong and cunning, formidable for a human. He hunts our kind successfully, judging by this." She handed the hunter's syringe to Pearl.

Pearl's face twitched with emotion too varied for Oguina to identify. "No wonder he hunts Changed. I gave him that scar when Daniel tried to force me to kill him. You're sure Daniel didn't feed him to me while I slept, like you did with this raccoon?" Pearl poked the syringe at the raccoon.

"I do not know who Daniel is." Oguina handed her the knife. "You were in a house that belongs to a man named Bianco. There were no other Changed there. I saw your brother tending you. He took your blood with a syringe like that one. You couldn't have attacked him.

You were paralyzed, not asleep."

Pearl held the knife, looking from it to the raccoon. Her brow crunched up like Leo's did when he was puzzled. "How do I do this? I've plucked chickens before. Before my Change. But I never skinned anything, never hunted animals. I wasn't sure we could."

"You could eat the skin." Oguina sat across from Pearl and took the knife and raccoon. "We can digest all that, but anything furry is unpleasant going down. You start by cutting here." Oguina turned the animal belly-up and made the first cut near the tail. "Make it shallow. We don't need to clean the entrails. We can digest those, too."

Pearl looked a little green. "Can we clean it anyway? I'm not sure I can. Um. Look, I don't do this kind of thing."

Oguina stopped cutting. "You don't hunt?"

"Well, no. Not really." Pearl looked everywhere but at Oguina's hands. Oguina just waited, let her speak in her own time. "Daniel says we can only live off people. He tells us to ambush and kill them. But when I'm hungry, I go to hospitals, drink breath from people who're dying."

"I have heard of that." Oguina nodded. "I've also heard it gives us barely more strength than before the Change. Animal blood and flesh would make you much stronger."

"That's true. But I don't care about being stronger than humans. I was the odd duck in the group I'm from." Pearl relaxed a bit. "You three must be from somewhere else, or you wouldn't have been told about drinking breath."

"So this pack you come from, they value strength and cruelty above all else?"

"Yes."

"I mean no disrespect, but why would they Change someone like you?"

"The pack wasn't always like that. They used to be about Changing people who wanted out of a bad situation. Daniel offered me a choice. I was trying to escape getting married." Pearl wrinkled her nose.

"You didn't desire the man chosen for you?"

"I didn't desire any man at all. I wanted to be on my own. Make something of merit that's all mine, like the Brontë sisters."

"That's something I can understand, though you'll have to tell me about these sisters some other time."

Pearl smiled. It was natural, spontaneous. "They were schoolteachers and writers. Early suffragettes. You ought to read their work sometime."

"Perhaps someday." Oguina changed the subject. "How did you end up as a prisoner?"

"I've been working against Daniel for years." Pearl twirled a strand of hair around one finger. "A stranger came and challenged him. I thought it was an opportunity to make my resistance public, but Daniel cheated. The stranger lost the duel. He got away, but I wasn't fast enough. Daniel made me drink his blood. That's the last thing I remember."

"As Leo said, we found you in a house full of armed humans, including your brother." Oguina's voice lowered. "The men in that house are feared in this city, competent in battle. Is it possible they eliminated

Daniel's pack and took you as spoils?"

"You're talking about Giacomo Bianco's gang?" Pearl let go of her hair. "No. They couldn't have."

"You don't think that many humans, assisted by a hunter like your brother, could fight them?"

"No. Daniel's gone bad and it made him extremely powerful. He could kill maybe ten Changed by himself. But Bess went bad, too. The both of them could probably wipe out twenty or thirty Changed. Bianco's men would be like chickens in a fox's den." Pearl sighed. "What's worse, my friend Sampson was pretty close to going over. If he did, there's worse things to worry about than illegal drinking and protection scams."

"What do you mean by 'went bad,' Pearl?"

"I'm sure you'd know what I'm talking about if I had the right name for it. It's something that can happen to us. You know how we get hopeless sometimes, stuck in bad memories? When a Changed like that does something really terrible, he goes bad."

"I haven't heard about this. Do you know more?"

"All I can do is describe it. Is that okay?" Oguina nodded and Pearl continued. "It happened to Daniel after he killed a bunch of sailors in Boston. He'd been moody before, but since then he's just cruel. I saw it happen to Bess not long after that. She spent most of her time in a corner thinking. Daniel sent her to a brothel to steal some clothes. She came back covered in blood. She's been more like a jackal than a woman since then. Daniel would lock me up until I was too hungry to think straight, then put me next to a human. Most of the time, I could just run away, get to the nearest morgue. But sometimes…" Pearl sighed, shook her head and crossed herself. "I wasn't broody like they were. I think going bad has something to do with that."

"I haven't seen anything like that." Oguina shifted her weight, suddenly uncomfortable. Broodiness? Dwelling on the past? That sounded unnervingly like herself just before she'd met Leo. "I spent hundreds of years alone in the woods, Pearl. I'm not the best person to ask about things like this."

"Maybe whoever Changed you?"

"Perhaps. Bersi should be back soon. He's the one that Changed me."

"Wait. You're hundreds of years old, Bersi's even older, and neither of you went bad? Or did you at some point, and then come back from it?"

"I haven't gone bad like you described. If Bersi doesn't know, you'll have to wait and ask the one who Changed him. You might wait quite a while. Hrafin's been missing for months."

"Wait. Hrafin?" The pitch of Pearl's voice heightened and she clapped her hands. "Hrafin's the Changed who challenged Daniel. He got away, so he's out there, in or around the city. If Hrafin changed Bersi, then he's sort of like a grandfather to you, right?" Pearl smiled again.

"Something like that." The corners of Oguina's mouth tipped up. She hadn't intended to smile, but Pearl's good mood wasn't just infectious, it was downright virulent.

"Hey!" Leo snapped his fingers. "What's wrong with you? You're stuck in the past half the time. It's dangerous." He took a deep breath before saying the one word that might set Bersi off. "Weak."

"You don't know what danger is, whelp." Bersi glared down at Leo's eyes. "Call me weak again, and you'll soon find out."

"Good. I've got your attention." Leo blinked, ending the little staring contest. "Oguina thinks it might help if you talk about what's got you distracted."

Bersi said nothing, but he walked more quietly now. He'd ignored his woodcraft skills so much he'd scared off four deer, two rabbits, and a badger. It must have been some kind of miracle that Bersi caught the raccoon. Maybe it was half tame or had rabies or whatever.

"We should go to the dairy farm first. We're too hungry to bring anything back. Come on, let me take you out for a hamburger." Leo saw Bersi's mouth twitch slightly at the joke. "But seriously, you should talk about it. We have some real problems and need our heads clear."

Bersi changed course, taking a deer path that led to the dairy pasture. "It started in the basement. I was supposed to open that secret door. I remembered my little sister, her death, and funeral as an old woman. That memory plagues me." Bersi stroked his beard, eyes on the path instead of Leo. "This Pearl looks much like my sister as a young woman. Hildr was a year younger than I. We were almost like twins. When Hrafin asked for help, she was the reason I hesitated, also the reason I accepted. I went to protect her."

Leo walked with Bersi in silence. They reached the edge of the pasture. "Maybe Pearl looks like Hildr because they're related. Hildr would have married and had children while you were gone. If there's even a tiny chance Pearl's some kind of umpteenth great-grandniece of yours, shouldn't you watch out for her? I can only wish one of my siblings was still around to protect. You're lucky you didn't have to Change for revenge like me."

"Wisdom from the mouths of cubs." Bersi stopped his beard stroking. He squared his shoulders, walking with sure steps to one of the sleeping cows. Leo smelled fox near the chicken coop. Perfect cover. He'd bring some of those back. It was getting too late for hunting.

"You'll have to replace the blood we were taking from her, Mr. Denton." Giacomo Bianco stared at the monster leaning in his doorway like a regular kid. He sat behind the mahogany desk, palms flat on its surface. Bianco was sometimes referred to as *volto di pietra*, the face of stone. No one knew that face was just another symptom of his Parkinson's.

"Have to?" The kid laughed. "I only have to do what I want." Daniel Denton smiled, showing those oh-so-valuable-teeth. In the corner near the door, Jimmy stopped clinking the ice in his whiskey and visibly paled. Niccolo stopped chewing on his toothpick and put his hand on the gun in his coat. Bianco didn't stop anything. He'd have to show this monster punk what it meant to be Boss.

"Go ahead. Do what you want, as long as it means we get more dead blood." That little bastard threw back his head, laughing like he was attending some kind of garden party. The damned little shit reminded him of Peter Pan. Bianco couldn't believe people read that Barrie story to kids. Peter Pan was a selfish punk with an old-fashioned press gang. Daniel fit that description, besides also being a monster with heart attack-inducing teeth.

"That's funny." Daniel enunciated the "F" carefully, showing his teeth to maximum effect. "I gave you trash I was going to throw out anyway. You shouldn't have lost it. What makes you think anything else I have is so disposable?"

"Because we have a deal." Bianco was more excited by the teeth than spooked. "You give us a source of blood, my people don't light your people on fire at high noon."

"I did give you a source of blood. You lost her. My end of the deal was satisfied; yours not so much." Daniel shifted his weight to lean on the other side of the doorway. "You have a choice now. Make a new deal, or we go our separate ways." What a conniving son of a bitch.

"What else could your kind possibly want from us besides silence or blood?" Bianco easily kept his face straight. His face was the only thing that didn't threaten to twitch lately.

"I want numbers. Soldiers." Daniel's eyes were on Niccolo like Jimmy's would be on a burlesque dancer. "You have plenty of trained fighters, killers who enjoy what they do. I want half of them. Once I've Changed them, I'll give you one back."

Bianco had to pause for a moment to keep the outrage out of his voice. "You'll want to be able to choose which ones you get, I'd imagine."

"That's the thing I think you'll find most amenable." Daniel stepped out of the doorway. "I need people with a desire to become stronger and faster. It's hard to find good help. Power-hungry fellows make much better monsters, as I'm sure you know."

Giacomo Bianco knew no such thing. The men in his organization weren't monsters. Business was business. Daniel was inhuman; the moldy old book he'd stashed in Plymouth said so. What the book didn't say was that these Changed must have been dreamed up by the Devil himself. He nodded in as patronizing a fashion as he could at the little monster. "And what if only a handful of my people are willing?" He might be able to agree to this if he could pick his most loyal soldiers. That way, he'd have allies in Daniel's camp. He saw Niccolo glance at Jimmy out of the corner of his eye. He was right to be concerned. If that half-breed spic screwed up again, he'd be the next guest in the attic.

"I'd take them. Even as few as five would be sufficiently dangerous. The one you want back could be anybody, though." Daniel winked. "Bosses like us know the best way to dispose of broken tools." The monster glanced at Jimmy this time, then smiled. Bianco thought again about what he could do with those teeth. He'd pull them all out someday, one by one. Howard Fallon shouldn't get to have all the fun.

Without warning, Daniel was gone. Bianco couldn't track something moving so fast. All of a sudden, a dazed-looking Howard sat in a chair facing the desk. Daniel stood behind him with his hands on his shoulders.

A vial of dead blood clinked to the floor from one of Howard's sleeves. Jimmy dropped his drink. The toothpick fell from Niccolo's mouth, sticking in his buttonhole. Daniel's hands flexed, and a creaking sound came from the vicinity of Howard's shoulders. The man's face wore surprise and pain. Bianco sent a silent prayer to the Blessed Virgin that Daniel wouldn't kill or maim Howard too badly; without Howard, Bianco would lose his source of teeth.

"Giacomo, Giacomo, Giacomo." Daniel tsked and shook his head. "Don't your people know they can't sneak up on creatures who hear heartbeats?" Daniel leaned close to the scar on Howard's neck, sniffing. That was fucking disturbing. "This one's been a bad boy at some point in the past. Smells like cabbage, too. I'm surprised you hired him." Bianco blinked once but kept the rest of his face still. His hands still rested palms-down on the desk.

"True, he's not one of my best and brightest." Bianco played as cool as he could in this situation. "He's got a knack for stitches and bandages, so I've kept him around." He'd need to double up on his Hail Marys after this meeting. Bianco wondered whether lying to a monster was even a sin. He couldn't ask Father Francis without telling him he'd stolen that book when he was a kid.

"He needs both his hands for that kind of work, but not both his eyes." Daniel moved his hands to Howard's head. "Which shall I put out?"

"Neither." Bianco's left pinkie finger twitched, he'd been unable to stop it. This was a bad night for his shakes. He needed Daniel to leave already so he could get that vial off the floor. He glanced up as Niccolo stared at Daniel while Jimmy gazed sadly at the remains of his dearly departed whiskey glass.

The monster chuckled. "He can keep both eyes if we have a new deal, Giacomo." The little shit had him over a barrel, and he knew it. Bianco said another prayer, this time to Saint Jude that Daniel didn't know how big that barrel was.

"All right. I'll give you any of my men who want to be Changed, plus one piece of trash to turn into treasure. The previous deal is null and void."

"Not quite." Daniel's boyish voice lilted mischievously. Bianco hated that pretentious British accent. "You still keep your end of the previous bargain. I honored it and so will you." Slippery little bastard.

"I'd say that's fair, but one other thing." Bianco took a big risk and stood up, knowing his adult height would let him loom over Daniel. "You keep your people off my boat. I'm used to cleaning messes, but that's above and beyond what I'd do even for a Consigliere."

Daniel's eyes narrowed slightly, though his smile widened. "A mess on your boat? How awful. Why would you think any of mine were part of something like that?"

"I had one of you as a guest, remember?" It was Bianco's turn to grin, though stretching those muscles was a battle against the Parkinson's contractures. "You think I didn't take a look at her teeth? And then you come in here flashing that smile. Those kids were ripped to shreds, not much left on the bones except marks from teeth just like yours. Keep that kind of thing off my boat, out of my clubs, and off my property."

"My boat, too." Jimmy was so pale he almost looked full-blood Italian. He cleared his throat. "Messing with that means no booze in the clubs."

Bianco's belly flared with anger, but he kept focus on Daniel. "You want my continued good-will? Do unto others, Mr. Denton. Quid pro quo. That's my final offer."

"I suppose that's acceptable." Daniel made a face that could have been on a kid whose beach day got rained out.

"I'll start talking to my men tonight. I'll have a list after Christmas." He stared at Daniel, unblinking. The monster-boy stared back. Were his mask-like face and lack of expression the reason Daniel tolerated his business? How ironic, if that were true.

"I'll be back the night after Christmas, then."

Bianco's eyes couldn't track Daniel's exit from the room. He nodded to Niccolo. He wanted to know for sure that the monster had left the building. Niccolo left the office, closing the door behind him.

The little bastard never said what time he'd arrive, which was obnoxiously smart. Bianco hadn't set up an ambush good enough to capture Daniel. With these new developments, he'd pray to God the monster made a mistake soon. Whoever had Changed a kid barely out of childhood had to be a sicko, but he'd bet diamonds to doorknobs Daniel was worse than whoever made him.

Howard's face was a double feature of relief and fear. Sure, Howard had screwed up, but Bianco needed teeth and blood more than money right now. He and Jimmy had been in the same leaky boat since the Riley massacre fiasco. The scales were tipping to micks over spics.

"I should execute you myself right here and now." Bianco let his left eye twitch, a relief that looked like impending apoplexy to his least favorite underlings. "If you weren't an expert monster hunter…." Bianco loomed until Howard got whiter than most Irish, then Bianco sat. He blinked and removed his hands from the desk's surface, trying to fold them in his lap. It was difficult, but he managed.

"I'm sorry, Boss." Howard gulped and hung his head. One point in Howard's favor: he didn't make excuses.

"Why did you come up here when you know they can hear you coming?" Bianco looked from Howard to Jimmy and back again. "I'd expect that from this ignorant sap, but not you. You know better."

"Someone took Pearl, probably him. I hoped to find out for sure, but no dice." Fallon was right on the money. Bianco had thought of that himself. "Also, I was flustered. Daniel even gives me the creeps, and I've seen more monsters than you and your guys."

"Well, the bright side to all that is, you heard the deal." Bianco would make the hunter earn his keep. "He won't mess with our stuff again. What do you think he wants with more monsters?"

"I can think of a couple of things." Howard leaned back in the chair, more at ease about monsters than his boss. He stuck one finger up. "Number one, he's nervous that we have some dead blood. It's a paralytic to them all. Sure, we can't sneak up on him, but we can arm people he's never seen, have them pose as hobos or whoever he eats. But he didn't know about our tooth-tipped syringes until tonight, so maybe that's not it." Howard put up another finger. "Two, he wants to fight the Riley kid and the dame. No way they're his allies.

That kid's got a grudge against you the size of Narragansett Bay."

"Leo was supposed to take a ride last month. So, he's a monster now. And that redskin's the one who gave you the TKO, Jimmy." Bianco winked. Jimmy blushed but didn't say anything for once. "You told me they got away because dead blood didn't work on the dame." Bianco looked back to Howard. "Describe how that happened for Jimmy, in case he wants to make a habit of chasing monster skirts."

"Like I told you before, the blood dropped the dame, but then the kid came around the corner and got in my face." Howard sighed. "When I looked again she was just gone. She could have been faking when she dropped, but it seemed real. No one's seen them since then. So you think Daniel took our monster in the attic?"

"Doubtful." Bianco shook his head slowly. "Something about it doesn't sit right. He could have forced this new deal without taking her. The little guy's a bastard, but he's got some kind of limey honor code, always talking about good form. He came right out and said he didn't take her."

"Makes sense." Howard folded his hands and tapped his thumbs together. "Makes a world of sense. Whatever code you think he has, though, be careful. He's twisting the truth for sure."

"At least we know they can be killed by burning and beheading. How'd you learn about that anyway?" Bianco managed to raise an eyebrow. "It's not like there's a school for monster hunters."

"Me and my buddy Jack got jumped by one down in

New Jersey. We took off, hid from it in the Art Metal Works building." Howard rubbed the ugly scar on his neck. "It found us of course. It wouldn't come near us when we got to the furnaces, scared of the fire, they are. You know Ronson lighters? Came out a few years back?" Howard looked up at him, so Bianco nodded. "Well, they were making those in that factory. We each took one, made torches, chased it into one of those big sheet-metal cutters. The monster didn't know what that was until we took its head off."

"Don't you know anything you didn't learn by accident?" The sourness in his voice startled Bianco. He shouldn't enjoy hearing the exploits of two bindle-punk cabbage eaters.

"Not much." Howard rubbed his eyes. "These monsters pop up in spooky stories, but not much else. I got the idea they used to be pretty rare until recently. But maybe not. Maybe it's just harder for them to hide now. People are up and out all times of the night. Streetlights and cameras get better all the time. Someone will catch them on film. Sooner later, someone's going to have to take drastic measures. Us or them."

"Drastic measures. I like that." Bianco laughed. "You can give them a run for their money on that front." Bianco wouldn't tell Howard or Jimmy how drastic he intended things to get. "You go do whatever it is you do, track them down."

Jimmy took out a cologne-reeking handkerchief to mop up the whiskey, then picked up the remains of his glass. Howard stood up and then bent to pick up the vial of blood.

"Leave it. I'll put it away." Howard hesitated, then did as he was told. The mick walked out of the room, the spic followed with his eyes on the broken glass. "Shut the door, for God's sake, Jimmy."

Once the latch clicked, Giacomo Bianco rolled up his right sleeve. His arm was pale, skinny, and covered with track marks. He stood shakily on stiff legs, holding on to the desk as he shuffled around to pick up the vial. He shuffled back, sat down again.

Bianco opened the slim top desk drawer, sliding it all the way out and placing it on the desk's surface. He used a letter opener to lift the drawer's false bottom and removed the small metal lockbox. He fished his keys from his vest pocket and opened it. A couple of empty vials rattled around with a leather strap and a plain old syringe. He cinched his arm with the strap and drew up the dead blood in the syringe.

Bianco leaned back in the chair, jabbed his arm and pushed the plunger home. The smell of spilled whiskey, leather and old books sharpened in his nose. The whole room brightened. He heard the garage door open and close, and music on the other side of the house where a few thugs played poker. He held his hands out in front of him, hands that didn't shake. The dead blood was a big fuck you to Parkinson and his damned disease. Prohibition might be ending, but he was in an excellent position to make that bank and more in pharmaceuticals.

Bianco pulled the strap off his arm, put it in the lockbox with the syringe and the empty vial. He leaned over the box, inhaling the lingering smell of the old parchment book that used to share space with the syringe. He'd had been an altar boy when he'd taken it from Father Francis's office at St. Anne's. Bianco wished he hadn't sent it off to Cousin Esmeralda in Plymouth. His hand hovered over the phone.

Bianco knew his Latin, so he'd been able to read the slim volume. He'd thought the story about Changed monster Crusaders was the work of a lunatic. Then, when he was ten, he'd seen the Wampanoag dame smiling at him and Esmeralda through the window one night. Bianco wanted to keep the most interesting facts about their blood to himself. He had to keep that info from Fallon. The big guy was lucky as a leprechaun. If the book were here, he'd find it eventually. Even worse, Daniel would be able to smell it from inside the box.

Bianco took his hand away from the phone. The last thing he needed was the mick or the little bastard to find out exactly how much he knew about the Changed. Bianco would leave the book with Esmeralda for now. She hadn't bothered to learn Latin, and wouldn't dare ask any questions. He could always go up for a visit and have a look in the book once he had a few vials of blood for the trip. He put the box back, put the drawer together and shut it.

He needed to get to work on that list immediately before the edge came off the injection. Bianco wrote the names of five of his most loyal, single up-and-comers on a piece of paper, marveling at how neat his penmanship was. He wrote "Jimmy Delaqua" as the sixth name on the list, and "to be returned" next to it. He folded it, then sealed it with a wax stamp. Jimmy wouldn't know what hit him until he was in the room upstairs.

"Out with the old, in with the new." Bianco waved the list in the air until the wax cooled. He stood up as he slid it in his vest pocket. How amazing, being able to do two things at once. At the door, he picked up the cane he wouldn't need for the next twenty-four hours. He'd need to keep up appearances downstairs, where three of the five on the good list would hear some interesting news.

They stood around in front of the garage of the house on Elm Street, smoking cheroots. The Boss didn't want cigars in the house, so Jimmy and Niccolo indulged in those outside. The garage was full of cars. Bianco favored the Graham-Paige, Niccolo liked the Pierce Arrow and the Rickenbacker, but Jimmy wished he was up in Plymouth driving the beat-up Model A packed with hooch for the operation up there. Things were getting hairy here.

"Look." Jimmy reached into the open window of the Rickenbacker and turned on the radio. "All I'm saying is, I'm in imports and exports. When I fight, it's in self-defense."

Al Jolson's voice lilted, echoing through the garage, pleading with his Little Pal to be good while Daddy's away. Niccolo couldn't keep his expression neutral. His eye twitched like it always did when he was nervous. Even if they hadn't known each other for twenty years, Jimmy had a nose for that kind of thing.

"And I'm saying we had orders." Niccolo leaned against the Rickenbacker and took a deep drag off his cigar. "It would've been us getting whacked if we didn't do it." The little shake in his voice and the tension in those boulder-sized shoulders let Jimmy know he was getting his point across.

"Okay, so it was the Boss's orders." Smoke puffed out of Jimmy's mouth with his words. "But this was a family, what did they do? I know the Boss said they're just some half-breed Micks, but they had bibles and school books all over the house. No guns, no hooch, no connection to Boston. There's no way this was business, and nobody does personal since last Valentine's Day. Something's wrong, Niccolo. Since when does the Boss send a rumrunner out whacking random people?"

Niccolo blew smoke out of his nose. "Since he gives the order, Jimmy. It's definitely hinky-di-di that he gave it to you, though. You ain't button-man material, and you'll never be." Niccolo's eyebrows nearly merged. He took another drag. "If you were full blood Italian, I'd think this was the test before he made you."

"Well, I'm not, and that's that. It's you that's gonna get made. We've been talking about that since we dropped out of High School." The taste of the cigar in Jimmy's mouth suddenly made him feel green around the gills. "I got no problem takin' orders, you know that. But we whacked an old grandpa, a factory worker, a teenage girl and her mom. You couldn't even finish the job. We had to call Father Francis."

Niccolo just puffed his cigar for a couple of minutes. Jimmy didn't sweat it because that meant Niccolo was burning the brain cells on this one. Niccolo wasn't much of a thinker, no matter how good an enforcer he was. Maybe it just took time for everything to get around that massive skull of his.

"Yeah, you're right. It didn't feel like any business we've done before. But all this monster stuff ain't regular business either. If we just treat everything the Boss orders us to do like it's business, does our opinion of what's business matter?" Niccolo still didn't get it about the monsters. If the Riley hit was such a big deal, Bianco could have hired someone from Providence to take that contract. Anyone with Niccolo's experience should know that.

"It matters because we got a code, Niccolo." Jimmy tamped out his cigar on the heel of his shoe. "We're loyal. We do our jobs, we don't squeal when we get pinched, we pay the Boss on time. In return for that, a rumrunner and an enforcer don't get ordered to whack little old men and kids in diapers. That's something those monsters do. You saw that mess on the Boss's boat. Tell me he's not acting more like the little bastard than his usual self, and I'll give it up and agree with you."

"Jimmy, I've known you since we were kids buttlegging around the neighborhood." Niccolo's cigar dropped to the cement next to his right foot. "No one else in this town's got a nose for business like you do. I don't wanna see you get broken or worse. Drop this. Giacomo Bianco is our Boss, no matter how he treats us. We owe him everything, even our lives. You feel bad about your conscience, tell it to the Father and leave me out of it. Agreeing with him isn't important." Niccolo put his left hand behind his back, over where he kept his knife. At least he hadn't gone for his gun.

"Okay, okay. I'll drop it." Jimmy put the cigar behind his ear instead of in his pocket. The last thing he needed was a tussle with Niccolo. "I'll go to Saint Anne's, do contrition. I'll also pray to Saint Jude that the Boss orders some hooch. He hasn't sent me on a rum run in weeks." Niccolo took his hand from behind his back and let it hang at his side like a ham shank in a meat locker. His head hung too. The dig about Church must have stung his old friend. The big enforcer stepped on his cigar and walked past Jimmy. He paused, glancing at Jimmy. He leaned in and shut the Rickenbacker's radio off, cutting Jolson's voice off before he could ask his son to pray for him. Niccolo didn't look back, just went into the house through the garage.

Jimmy decided to walk around the garage to the front door. He nearly ran into Howard Fallon where the walkway met the driveway. He wondered what a guy who killed monsters for a living would think if he heard a couple of his co-workers arguing about killing regular folks. Jimmy already knew Howard's opinion of the Boss. Would he start thinking Jimmy and Niccolo were like monsters too?

Jimmy nodded and smiled at Howard, who returned the gesture. For a second, he thought Howard might have heard something. He couldn't tell for sure, the man always seemed on his guard here. The guy was a survivor. At least Jimmy was sure Howard wouldn't say anything about it if he had. Smart fellow.

Howard eased his foot off the gas and let the car coast along the narrow road. Driving in the dark out here was dangerous, especially with the temperature below freezing. He'd have to be careful of deer, too. This road bordered the woods, so headlamps didn't catch everything.

Howard was almost sure the Riley kid and the dame had taken Pearl. But why? And why wouldn't the dame have killed the Riley kid anyway? She'd turned him; that was the only thing that made sense. She could be building a group, setting herself up to become as dangerous as Daniel. But why would she leave a house full of gangsters alive? Riley must want revenge, but that still made no sense.

He'd have to go looking at some point if he wanted to find his sister. He'd do it on his own time. He wanted to talk to her, the Riley kid, and the dame, too. They must have wanted to parlay with him the night they fought in the alley. He couldn't think of any other reason they'd try and lure him out there except kill him, and the kid said that wasn't gonna happen. He didn't know where to begin looking for them, though. Howard's eye itched. He took a hand off the wheel, just for a second.

The headlights glinted on a dog with glossy red fur. Howard pushed in the clutch and feathered the brakes, but he wouldn't be able to stop in time. He pulled the wheel to the right, hoping to pass the dog on the road's shoulder.

He smelled burnt rubber and heard a screech. The right wheel caught gravel, then he felt it lose purchase. Howard couldn't turn the wheel, so he turned his head. Ice, all along the side of the road. He heard a thump and canine whine at the left fender, the shatter of glass. Branches hairy with dark green needles loomed then screeched against his windshield.

Howard relaxed his arms so they wouldn't break. He'd smelled pine sap and antifreeze before his head hit the wheel and everything went dark.

Neck-scar's knuckles dragged along the ground. Howard. The man's name was Howard, and he had an angry sister.

"That's going to leave a trail. Not to mention scrapes all over his hands. Come on, let me help."

"No." Pearl huffed out a breath, strands of hair flying up from her forehead.

"Look, I'm sorry. It's just, Howard never introduced himself. We didn't know his name. And that scar's a doozie. Really stands out."

"There's no point in apologizing if you're just going to make a bunch of excuses for yourself right after. No." Pearl shook her head. "I'm strong enough. I don't need help from you, Mister Riley."

"Holy crow. What's next? You're going to bid me a good day and la-di-da?"

"You're awfully rude for a man who wants to help."

"Still, he's already got a hell of a goose-egg on his noggin. You want to do something about his hands, or he'll have trouble using them after he wakes up. Ow!" Something cold and wet fell on Leo's head. Old snow.

"Oh!" Pearl stared somewhere above and behind Leo. She put her hands up to her cheeks, almost dropping Howard. She reversed the gesture and caught him in time.

Hooting grew into throaty laughter. Leo didn't have to turn around. He knew Oguina must be changing out of her feathers behind him. He brushed snow out of his hair.

"You're almost to the barn now." Oguina dropped from the tree with a light thump, then trotted to Pearl's side. "I've got his hands."

Leo considered trying to apologize again but had to jog to keep up. In about a minute, the trees thinned, unveiling a barn that might have been bright red before the Great War. Now it was sort of mottled gray and pink, like knee-scrapes when he'd peeled the scabs off early. It had double doors, probably to let carts through. Pearl and Oguina hurried through a dark rectangle to the left. As he caught up, Leo realized it was a frame for a long-lost door. He followed them inside.

They'd sat Howard up against the wall on a trunk where Bersi patted him down. Leo blinked. Last month, he wouldn't have been able to see a damn thing in here.

"This, and these," Bersi smirked, handing a Bowie

knife and pistol over to Oguina. He ran a hand down Howard's legs, then up around the ankles. He passed her the holdout .22. "That's all, I think."

"No." Leo strode over, reached into the inside left pocket of Howard's jacket. He pulled his hand out, holding a tin can and something much more interesting. "You know what this is, Bersi?"

"A metal box with cotton inside?"

"Wrong. Smell." Leo held the shiny metal rectangle up, waving his hand to waft air in Bersi's direction.

"Smell what? It's wet, but not much else."

"Thorens fluid. It's for lighters. This is a Nassau push-button." Leo flipped the top and engaged the trigger."

"A fire-maker!" Oguina stared wide-eyed. "I've seen them use those in town. They usually smell much worse than that."

"It's the fluid he uses." Leo shook the can. "This burns like gasoline, but it's deodorized. Difficult to smell unless you're checking. Dangerous stuff for us." He looked at Pearl. "Your brother has good information. Suits up like he means business."

"Well he's doing it for money, isn't he?" Pearl didn't pout, but Leo thought it was a near thing. "That's Howard. One-hundred and ten percent effort and he still thinks he could do more."

"I suppose we've all got that in common with him, or we wouldn't be here." Oguina took a length of rope off the wall and began binding Howard's hands behind him. "Let's not underestimate him again."

"All the more reason we need him on our side." Leo put the lighter and fluid in his satchel. He'd brought the

Daylos, in the hope that the talk would lead to Howard leaving here with them. If he didn't come around, they'd leave him here until they were done at Bianco's then put him on a freight train to Ohio or something.

"All we need now is for him to wake up." Bersi tapped his foot, glanced at Pearl. "He's not a late sleeper?"

Pearl leaned over to whisper in his ear as if a bunch of Changed with super-human hearing wouldn't know what she'd said. "I forgive you, Tootles."

Before Leo could laugh, Bersi's hand was over his mouth. He almost punched him in the ear but remembered in time. Tootles was a character from that J.M. Barrie book about Peter Pan, the one who'd shot Wendy by mistake. Pearl probably read that book to her kid brother back in the day. That whisper was for Howard's sake, not theirs. He felt like a horse's ass. He'd have to thank Bersi later for stopping him looking like one.

"Howard." Pearl stepped back from her brother. "I know you're awake now. Listen, we only want to talk to you. That's it."

"We? What's we? We who?" Howard sounded a little groggy, but that could be an act. Sure enough, Leo heard the rope strain around Howard's wrists as he tested it. At least Leo had faith in Oguina's knots.

"Your sister, of course." Leo tried to talk straight, but the sarcasm crept into his voice like a fox in a hen-house. "And us. The night-shift folks from the speakeasy who you assaulted in the alley."

"You. You're the Riley kid. I still can't figure out why

you didn't kill me back there."

"Oh, that's easy," Leo smirked, not caring that Howard couldn't see it. "Didn't want to. Your name's not Giacomo Bianco. Good thing, too. Your sister Pearl here says you're a reasonable man, except when it comes to a little fella called Daniel. She says you might talk to us about him."

"Why should I talk to you about any of that?" Howard strained against the rope again, but no dice for the big guy.

"Because we know you've spent years hunting this Daniel." Oguina's voice carried the calculated calm Leo wished he had. "You know how he's a threat to you or any other human. He's making trouble for us as well."

"What, because he has a gang?" Howard scoffed. "You could make your own and take him out."

"What do you think we are trying to do?" Bersi's voice rumbled like a rock fall with the gravity of his words. "We have rules. Daniel breaks them."

"So why am I still breathing? Why haven't you made me like you?"

"That is one of our rules." Oguina hadn't moved anything but her mouth since she'd finished tying Howard up. Leo wasn't sure how she was doing it. "We Change only those who seek it out with worthy cause."

"Okay. Well, I don't want to be Changed. No offense, Pearl."

"None taken." Pearl sighed. "I didn't want that either. But it's what I am now, no going back. Daniel's horrible, a monster. However he got Changed, he decided to go in a monstrous direction with it. I didn't. Same thing with these three. That's why I'm here. They want to stop Bianco. I want to stop Daniel and so do you. Why not work together?" She took a deep breath. "Unless, are you loyal to Bianco?"

"No. He'll kill me the second I stopped being useful." Howard shifted his weight, moving his arms. Leo knew the knots were probably something spectacular; the rope not so much.

"Look." Leo knew the rope wasn't going to give them much more time. "You know my name, so you must have heard Bianco hit my whole family. We're trying to do something here for the greater good. We want Bianco gone, Daniel gone, and any Changed that will follow the rules to make their existences constructive."

"Oh come on, kid." Howard chuckled. "Greater good? Constructive? You Changed are built for killing. Seen that myself."

"You have the scar to prove we don't have to." Leo hadn't imagined Pearl could sound so stern. "There's got to be something else we're made for, and I won't stop until I find it. I've gone years without killing anyone. I'm as different from Daniel as you are from Bianco. These three are also. And there are more like them. You just never see or hear of them. We're different; that doesn't make us wrong. Sound familiar?"

"That's low, Pearl, bringing up Etta in all this." Howard hung his head. Leo didn't know what that was all about. Something from their childhood, probably.

"It's not. There's no difference, morally speaking." Pearl put a hand on Howard's shoulder. "Our parents were wrong about Henrietta. Don't repeat their mistake."

Leo smelled salt as Howard wept silently. At least he wasn't trying to break ropes anymore.

"What will you do with Daniel's people after this?" Howard's voice cracked a bit. "You know, the ones that won't go live up a mountain."

"We kill them if we have to." Bersi clenched his jaw. "If we give them dead blood, we can put them somewhere to sleep a while."

Howard couldn't have been able to see Bersi. He must have had good hearing, though, because he stared right at where he was standing.

"I'm in."

Pearl leaned toward Howard's back as if to untie the rope. Oguina waved her away. She moved her arm twice and old frayed hemp sloughed to the floor like shed snake skin.

"Now, what's the plan?" Howard glanced around expectantly, blinking into the dark.

"First off, take this." Leo pulled a Daylo from his satchel, flipped it on, handed it to Howard. "I'll give you that Nassau and Thorens after we leave the building. I don't have to tell you we don't like playing with fire."

"Thanks, buddy." Howard reached into his right jacket pocket. "And like I said that other night; you want to keep this."

Leo took the wrinkled yet neatly folded paper from Howard's hand. It smelled like carbon. He flipped it open, blinked down at red ink stamped across the United States Armed Forces application. It got a little blurry.

"Thought that was why you didn't kill me. Didn't turn you over to Bianco."

"No. I had no idea you had this." Leo looked at Oguina, struggling to stay in the present. "Why don't I remember that night like everything else?"

"I also had one day I don't remember clearly." Oguina studied the rejected application.

"Something has to knock it loose." Bersi clapped Leo on the shoulder. "This paper, is it putting you back there? If it is, you should let it."

"No. We don't have time." Leo looked up at Bersi, waiting for a challenge.

"I understand, Leo." Bersi shook his head. "Remember, there will be much to do later, but only you can decide whether now is better."

Leo started to put the paper in his satchel but put it in his breast pocket instead. Out of mind, but close to his chest. He'd have to pray nothing dragged him down memory fugue lane in the middle of battle. Oguina stared at the rectangle of moonlit night through the barn door. He'd pray for her, too.

D.R. Perry

On Christmas Eve, they always sat in the back pew so the Boss could be at the door before anyone left after Mass. Jimmy watched the handshakes, counting the amount of cash passed to each person. The tally in his head said five large.

Niccolo watched also, but Jimmy knew the big man focused on the hands not being shaken. While Jimmy looked for expenditures, Niccolo looked for weapons. Same as it ever was. On the surface, Niccolo and Jimmy hadn't changed much since they were kids just starting out working for the Boss.

What wasn't the same anymore was the Boss; somehow he'd gone all blooey. Jimmy never remembered him doing this kind of glad-handing at Saint's Days, let alone Midnight Mass on Christmas. Random Sundays, sure, but Christmas and Easter used to be strictly off-limits for business. Jimmy didn't know exactly what was different about the Boss, but it all started even before the monster malarkey.

The day after Valentine's Day in 1929, the Boss read the papers all about the massacre of the North Side Gang in Chicago. He'd been laughing, saying the Chicagoland Gang finally got what was coming to them after they hit

Patsy Lolordo. That wasn't so far out of the ordinary, for the Boss to laugh about a serious caper like in a city far away.

Something else had been off about the Boss that day, the way he held the paper and his face when he laughed. There'd been a sort of shake in his hands, the kind you'd see in a guy who hit the liquor too hard and had gotten a case of the *delerium tremens*. His face was like a rock; no smile to go with the laugh. And Jimmy also noticed that the Boss's gimp leg had gotten worse since Christmas. The Boss hadn't been completely healthy for a few years, but he never said nothing to nobody about it. Bianco was the Boss and Jimmy was a bootlegger, not a doctor.

By the end of February, the Boss's shakes stopped almost overnight. After that, he also got himself into a lather much easier. He'd get a phone call, not even bad news just no news, then he'd go on the warpath. By Easter, Jimmy had a feeling the Boss was hopped up most of the time, but he never found any dope.

What Jimmy did find was the Boss talking to the little bastard. Now that he thought of it, the anger problems and better health started after the Boss met Daniel. Bianco ordered more hits and busted his people down to thugs for tiny mistakes. And then he ordered the Riley family hit. Jimmy thought maybe the monsters were paying the Boss in dope, up close and personal. After recent developments with Fallon, he was almost sure of it.

It made no difference anymore whether Jimmy found dope or not. The Boss would either kick the habit or not. He was all done waiting for Niccolo to notice and do something. If anyone would see or find anything, it'd be him. But Niccolo was either blind or covering. He only ever made small talk or vague threats anymore.

Jimmy tried to keep things on the level for as long as he could, hoping to get some evidence to take up to Boston or down to Providence. The only thing he'd seen even remotely related to dope was the monster blood, and that was too big a whammy to lay on the higher-ups. Jimmy could get himself streeted talking about that, or maybe worse being a half-and-halfer. He couldn't be sure monster blood was like dope anyway. That was Fallon's area, and he hadn't had time to ask. Maybe tomorrow.

The cathedral was almost empty. Jimmy looked around. All he saw was Father Francis walking up the aisle toward them, and the priest looked like he had an avenging angel on his shoulder. He watched the Boss put a big fake smile on and say, "Merry Christmas, Father." The Boss extended his hand, but Father Francis didn't shake it.

"Before you go, don't you want to make Confession?" The Father crossed his arms over his chest.

The Boss's face and hand didn't move. This was bad news. Jimmy tried to catch Niccolo's eye, but the big man stared at the Father like a Priest could be a threat.

"I got nothing to confess tonight, Father." The Boss's voice had a sub-zero tone.

All Father Francis did was raise an eyebrow at the Boss's outstretched hand. Then he looked him right in the eye. Shit on a shingle. Father Francis knew about all the cash the Boss handed out.

"I think you do." The father smiled with his mouth, but his eyes were like the barrels of pistols. "Greed, pride, the lust you clearly have for more power. All of these are sins. Giacomo, can you tell me with total honesty that you came to Mass tonight to celebrate the birth of the Savior and not hand out money to my flock?"

Jimmy watched a twitch start at the left corner of the Boss's mouth. He should step in and say something: that the handouts were his idea; that he needed to go make Confession himself. Anything. But something moved outside the glass pane on the door of the vestibule. The Boss and then the Father said something else, but Jimmy didn't catch it.

He cut his eyes away from the Boss, saw a head of gorgeous, glossy, black hair just as it moved away from the window. There was only one head of hair like that in Fall River; the bearcat who'd strong-armed Bianco's address out of him. Another movement caught his eye. Niccolo had his hand on the butt of his gun.

"Say that again." Bianco's voice was a dangerous whisper.

"Fine." Father Francis paled, but his voice was like Sampson before Delilah shaved his head. "Confess your sins or leave. Don't come back to my Parish. You can go to St. Michael's or St. Anthony's for a little while if they'll let you, but not here. Never again. If you show your face in here again, I'll write a letter to Rome requesting your Excommunication."

"Ice him" Bianco's eyebrow twitched. His left heel lifted, tapping the floor three times. Niccolo drew slowly, hands reluctant, brow covered with droplets of sweat.

More movement caught Jimmy's eye, at the back, by the altar this time. The Deacon backed away through the door he'd been standing in. Jimmy heard another door close outside the cathedral. The Deacon had left the building, but the Boss hadn't even noticed anyone there.

"Boss, don't do this." Jimmy's face felt like there was a furnace in his head, but his hands and feet were like blocks of ice. His voice came out somewhere between a hiss and a croak.

"I said ice him, Niccolo." This was all wrong. The Boss wouldn't have done anything remotely like this even last year.

"Boss." Jimmy stepped between the man he'd grown up with and the priest who'd kept him as honest as possible. "Don't make him do this. We've been seen, fella's already left the building."

"He won't talk. He wouldn't dare."

"I think he will, Boss." Jimmy looked Bianco in the eye. "This ain't crossing a line; it's crossing the Great Wall of China. Boston and Providence ain't gonna stand with you on this; bumping off a Father ain't hunky-dory by any standard."

"Ice him." Bianco spat right there in the church. Where the hell did that come from? His eyes looked like a monster's, but his teeth were blunt as ever.

"Boss, Jimmy's right this time." Niccolo's gun went in its holster like a man coming home from war. "It's too dangerous." And then Niccolo put one of his hands on Bianco's shoulder. "Maybe the Father's right. But who am I to say? You're the Boss. I'm just a bambino off the boat from Sicily."

Niccolo never touched nobody unless the situation was seriously dangerous. He never touched the Boss unless it was life-or-death. Jimmy prayed to God that Niccolo's hand would snap this madness like he'd snap a rat's neck.

"Fine." Bianco's eyes were still wild, but more like a sleepy cougar's than a rampaging bear's. "Saint Anthony's will have the benefit of my membership in its coffers. I doubt anyone in Rome will approve a letter from a Franciscan like you. Pride's a sin too, Father. It goes before a fall. Falls can be fatal for a man your age." The Boss turned his back on the old priest and stalked out of the cathedral with Niccolo at his left shoulder. Jimmy started to follow.

"Jimmy." Father Francis put his hand on Jimmy's elbow. "I'll pray for you, son. If you ever need sanctuary like that boy..."

"Thanks, Father." Jimmy kept his back to the Father. If he turned to face him, he might not be able to leave the church. "I'll keep it in mind." His value to Giacomo Bianco as a rumrunner wasn't a factor anymore. Jimmy's time was limited, but he couldn't let Bianco keep running things. Not like this. Fallon had been right. He'd have to do something, but not directly. Providence and Boston wouldn't accept a half-and-halfer like Jimmy as Boss, but Niccolo was full blooded Italian. It was time to play Kingmaker.

Hrafin watched Daniel leave the big house on Maple Street. He'd known Daniel consorted with mortals since their first encounter. Now he knew where and who. But why? Ferals usually didn't have reason or restraint enough to tolerate humans.

It was uncommon in this age for The Changed to make arrangements even with individual humans, yet here was a Feral dealing with a large group of them. The last time he knew of Changed working with human groups was during the Crusades. There were rules for this, with good reason. Daniel Denton either didn't know those rules or didn't care, probably the latter. Rules on Daniel were like oil on water. Hrafin had to find out how far this went before acting to correct things.

The old familiar sensation of shifting joints, rearranging muscles, and shortening bone came over his entire body. Hrafin took the shape of a piebald long-haired cat. Thousands of memories of shape-shifting tried to claw their way out of the recesses of his recall. Hrafin honed his focus to the here-and-now, just as he had during the fight with Daniel. He wouldn't have long. If he didn't encounter physical and immediate danger, his focus could slip away, leaving him at the mercy of fate.

Hrafin steered his thoughts toward Daniel's apparent ignorance of shape-shifting. Either Daniel's maker had left him or been killed. Hrafin twitched his fluffy striped tail. Distraction was a third possibility. Wasn't distraction the bane of all Changed his age? Here he was, giving into it again. How long had he been tailing Daniel himself? Hrafin wasn't sure.

As Hrafin approached the house, he scented some other changed creatures. These weren't related to Daniel. He could also smell fresh wood putty and paint. A window had been repaired less than a week ago. As he headed over to investigate, he noticed a trap near a basement window sized for a cat or a raccoon. So, the occupants of this house had recently had trouble with a Changed shape-shifted into a small animal. That reminded Hrafin of the time in Constantinople when he and Lacertus stole fabric for Aelfwinn's gowns. Hrafin could almost smell the dyed linen. He had to stop this woolgathering. He blinked, sniffed, smelled old snow and paint again. He continued searching for a way inside the house.

Yelps and barks came from the other side of the house. Hrafin smelled kibble and meat; someone was feeding guard dogs. He turned the corner, finding a kennel attached to the back of the house. Hrafin scented another changed creature who'd come this way recently. He'd recognize that anywhere. Bersi was here, the night before the humans fixed the window.

This was an unexpected development. Bersi would have stayed in the wilderness until he'd been missing for more than a year. Had it been that long? Longer, perhaps? This was one of the troubles with being Changed, that sense of the passage of time wore away like a stone in the ocean until it dwindled to grains of sand. That poor woman Aelfwyrn kept at the Cloister gibbered fragments of memory held since before the Flood. He pictured her face, smooth ochre skin framed by tight black curls, amber eyes like beads made of sunset light. Hrafin heeled his focus firmly back to the present situation. He could think of his Lady and her curious guest later.

The dogs were quiet now, except for the tiny echoes of their chewing. Hrafin smelled stewed tomatoes, a sign that the door between kennel and house was still open. Perhaps the human was getting water for the dogs. Hrafin sidled up to the house, practically clinging to it as he made his way toward the kennel door. He focused on smelling how close the human was so he could decide how much time he had to sneak in without being seen.

A moment had passed before he realized his mistake. That focus on throwing his sense of smell forward had cost him in attention to where he was stepping. He heard a rattle, a click, and the jingle of a bell just before his whiskers sensed metal bars directly in front of him. He'd walked right into one of the cage traps.

At first, Hrafin thought this was barely an issue. Although he was in a cat's body, he still had a nearly impenetrable hide and ten times the strength of a mortal cat. He pushed with his head and his back against the sides of the cage, but couldn't reach the top. He tried catching the bars with his claws and pulling, trying to break the cage's hinges inward. Nothing worked. The cage was too big for him to get any leverage. He couldn't even turn around.

"Gotcha!" Hrafin looked up and saw a broad-shouldered man in a dark colored suit and necktie leaning over the cage.

"You cost us a lotta money, Puss." The man smirked. "The boss is gonna be glad you're out of the way." This man thought Hrafin was just a cat? Interesting. That meant the other Changed in a cat's body had kept his true nature a secret. He couldn't help feeling some respect despite the inconvenience this predicament posed.

The man picked the cage up by some sort of handle built into its top. Then he walked around to the front of the house and up to the door. It looked like Hrafin would get inside to make some observations after all.

Giacomo Bianco stared at the small cage on the credenza under the window of his office. The cat's eyes were a red-gold color and it blinked maybe twice. Uncanny. Niccolo said this was the cat who'd trashed the house the week before. Bianco thought Niccolo needed to go get his eyes checked. This cat was the same tawny color, and large, but its fur was piebald instead of striped, the coat long and thick. The cat from a few nights ago had been short-haired and that its eyes were green. He should bust Niccolo down a notch. Bianco sighed. None of his men got a decent look at it like he had. That short-haired cat had stopped right in the doorway of his office. It stared at him, fur standing on end, and hissed before running back down the stairs. This cat wasn't the same one. It only reminded him of that other cat, kind of like how Patriarca down in Providence reminded him of the guys from there.

"Now, why do you look familiar, fella?" Bianco didn't feel as ridiculous as he should, talking to a cat. "Do you belong to someone I've met before? Maybe I've just seen you around the neighborhood." The cat stared at him in response, blinking deliberately. Bianco peered at the cat's neck, trying to see if there was a collar hidden somewhere in all that fur, but nothing. Not even an indent. The cat let out a meow that sounded more like a noise a bird might make.

"Decided to talk now that we pinched you, huh?" Bianco toughed up his chatter. Old ladies talked to their cats, but not like this. "Are you a cat or a rat?" He reached up with one hand to run it through his hair, a habit he hadn't indulged since the Parkinson's had gotten bad enough to show off his tremors. A cat wouldn't care about that damned disease. He felt oddly comforted for a moment; even Niccolo didn't know. But the cat kept on staring at him, and any sense of contentment dried up like sweat on a hot tin roof. Bianco started to feel like the cat was judging him somehow. Ridiculous. God Almighty was the only one who could judge him or any other human on the planet. He was starting to feel like the fellow with raven troubles in that Poe story. Creepy.

There was a knock at the door. Bianco sat up straighter, placing his palms flat on the desk. "Come in," he said.

"Boss." Niccolo took up the whole doorway. "Howard Fallon is here, and he's got another hunter with him."

"What does he want?" Bianco managed not to roll his eyes.

"Says he made a kill. Says he has something for you." Niccolo glanced at the cat in the cage. Was that a shudder? Why would such a big guy be freaked out by a kitty cat? He ought to ask himself the same thing.

"Send him in." Bianco cleared his throat.

Niccolo nodded and left the room. He came back with Howard and another man about Howard's size. This other man was dressed in farmer's overalls, had muscles everywhere, and red hair with a full red beard. Great, another mick monster hunter. Just what he always wanted. The new guy stood at Howard's left shoulder. Right after he came in, he stared at that damned cat. The cat glanced once at the red-haired hunter, then went back to staring at Bianco. After that, the man directed his gaze from the cat back to Bianco himself, which was as it should be. The guy reminded him of something, but what?

"Boss, I brought you some teeth." Howard put a small metal box on the desk and opened it. The teeth were inside, along with a dusting of metal shavings and powder. A box made of wood or bag made of cloth would get holes ground in them, so they used metal. The teeth still scratched steel all to hell.

"Who's this?" Bianco nodded at the newcomer.

"His name's Bobby. A cousin from across the pond."

Bobby nodded at Bianco, and then smiled, revealing a

set of ill-fitting wooden dentures.

"You sure his name's not George Washington?" Bianco raised a skeptical eyebrow and waited for an explanation.

"He's mute, but he can hear. More important, he can hunt. He's got no papers, but wants to make more money than he can picking apples."

"So where'd you get these teeth?" Bianco could see inside the box from his seat. It looked like enough for a full set of teeth, pulled from a monster's skull. Something about them wasn't quite right, but he'd have to move his hands to examine them. He couldn't do that just now. A bad case of the shakes was coming on.

"The Riley kid." Howard dropped a smirk at Niccolo. Show-off. "He tried to jump us after I picked up Bobby last night."

"What about the broad? Wasn't she with him?" Bianco wasn't sure why the teeth in the box seemed off. Maybe younger monsters had baby-monster teeth. But the broad was more important. He didn't want her coming after his loyal guys before Daniel Changed them.

"No." A floorboard creaked as Howard shifted his weight. "My guess is, he came after me alone. Trying to finish what he started the night she got away."

"Too bad you only got the kid." Bianco thought about ordering the hunters to catch that broad. Maybe another night. He needed a rest. "At least you fixed what Jimmy botched. You micks work harder than those lazy PRs. Niccolo will pay you on the way out." Niccolo nodded and headed down the hall.

Howard turned, but Bobby didn't. He stood staring at

that cat, then looked at Howard and shrugged. Howard looked at the cat also, just one moment too long. Something was up. The hunter knew that hinky cat from somewhere, and Bianco didn't like it one bit. Still, Bianco needed more hunters. He was about to tell them to get lost and let it slide.

"Hey, boss? What's up with the cat? Thought you were a dog person." Howard stared at the desk instead of looking him in the eye. This he couldn't let go.

"We caught it in those traps we put out after Pearl went missing. It's not the same cat, so I was going to tell Niccolo to take it out of here." Bianco injected all the amiability he could muster into his voice. "Say, you're on your way out. Why don't you get rid of it for me?"

"No problem, Boss." Howard smiled, too big and too genuine for Bianco's tastes. He slapped Bobby on the shoulder. The big man picked up the cage, cat and all. Howard's smile got even bigger. A guy with a senile mother and a monster sister shouldn't be smiling so much about some damn cat.

"Before you go, did you find out who took Pearl? I need that info more than teeth with the little bastard showing up here tomorrow night."

Howard hesitated. He wiped that smile right off his lips, but it stuck in his eyes. He knew something. "I found the missing blanket near the docks. I think whoever took her got on a boat. She could be anywhere by now."

"The docks, huh?" Bianco smiled. "Bullshit. I've had guys down at the docks all week. All they saw was Jimmy, not you or your monster sister. You didn't pick this guy up last night, either. So, you and your friend are going to sit down in those chairs and tell me the truth. Now."

Oguina perched on a branch in the maple tree to the left of Bianco's house, hoping Daniel wouldn't notice her and Leo on the way up the walk. It helped that they were an owl and a cat. She looked in the office window again and saw Bersi turn to pick up the cat in the cage. She knew right away that the cat was a shape-shifted Changed, though she hadn't seen that cat before.

Leo watched Daniel like an actual cat might watch a dog; the hairs of his tail stood on end, his pupils round, eyes wide. Leo was still as the birds she'd find frozen on the coldest winter nights. Daniel prowled more than walked; so did one of the others with him— the female. The way the male walked reminded Oguina of the time she'd tied rocks to her feet and tried walking underwater. Both of his companions towered over Daniel's slim frame, though only the male had bulk comparable to Bersi's or Howard's. The female was pale with hair the color of autumn maple leaves. The male's skin was mahogany, his bald head gleaming in the moonlight.

All three smelled of human flesh and blood. They'd hunted recently then, would be faster and stronger after such a meal than her own allies. She and Bersi and Leo consumed every scrap of flesh from their cows, but it still wasn't as sustaining as human. Pearl would be even weaker, since all she'd had was blood and the parts humans used for steaks. Oguina found herself distracted by a familiar living scent down by the building with the automobiles.

Jimmy Delacqua peered around the side of that building but stepped back quickly. He'd seen Daniel arrive at the house. She scented fear rising from him in waves, heard his blood move faster even at this distance. Had Daniel come there unannounced? Perhaps Bianco simply hadn't told Jimmy of his visit. She'd heard their confrontation through the church doors. The rumrunner might be in danger.

Oguina looked back in the window again to see Howard wrinkling his forehead in Bianco's direction. Bersi glanced out the window at her, catching her eye. She hooted softly and nudged Leo with her beak. No need. He'd already seen the problem in the office. He looked inside, then back at her, then down at Daniel and his lackeys standing by the door. They hadn't rung the bell yet but were about to.

Things weren't going as expected. Pearl's signal still hadn't come, Howard and Bersi had a problem in Bianco's office, and Daniel was here when he wasn't supposed to be. Oguina peered to the back of the house, watching for signs that Pearl was ready. She hooted nervously, instinctively. They waited.

Shapeshifting hadn't come naturally for Pearl, but her animal form was integral to their plan. She couldn't offer any help besides being a doorman. She was worse at fighting than shifting. Pearl had always preferred not to touch other people. The whole mess with Jack had utterly disgusted her, but even before that his attempts to kiss her had been less exciting than doing embroidery. At least with embroidery, you had something to show for it. She'd be a liability in combat; Bianco's men were mortal, but they were seasoned fighters. She couldn't be seen in human shape because everyone would recognize her. She could do lots to help as a raccoon. Their paws were like hands. Add that to the better-than-average raccoon strength she'd have from being Changed, and she should be able to do everything she had to. If only it didn't take her so long to change into one.

Pearl had already ignored the big dog that tried to bite her tail. Bersi was right, the poor thing only hurt its own mouth. She had gone into the kennel via the dogs' door and climbed a canister of kibble. Now she was trying and failing over and over to grasp the door knob with the right leverage for her paws to engage the latch. Why couldn't Bianco like levers on his doors like her mother?

Had she been turning the knob counter clockwise all this time? Should she try turning clockwise? Maybe both paws? Should she try both or only one of those things? Pearl heard hooting on the other side of the house. Oguina. But what did the hoot mean? Was something wrong? Were they calling this off? She wondered why whatever it was that made them monsters didn't let them communicate with animal sounds. The doorbell rang out front.

Pearl swept those questions out the door of her mind, put both paws on the doorknob, and turned clockwise. She almost fell off the kibble canister and inside as the door swung open. Only one more task now, open the upstairs window. Pearl dropped down to the stoop and scampered inside. She smelled fresh air at the front door opening, then Daniel entering the house. She sniffed again and knew that Bersi and her brother were still in Bianco's office.

She scampered up one flight of the back stairs as quickly as she could, then directly to the window in the hall next to Bianco's office. There was a dry sink under it, and she climbed it, overturning a potted philodendron in the process. Pearl reached up and pulled on the window lock with one paw, relieved to find that it moved smoothly. Both paws on the bottom lip of the window, all ten pounds of her raccoon weight, and a little Changed strength lifted the sash.

The window was up just a quarter of the way. She wouldn't have the leverage to open it any further without going back to a human shape. Too late. Leo leap from the tree to the window sill and Oguina glide down from the branch. When they got to the sill, she saw they'd just fit. Pearl squeezed in between the dry sink and the wall. She crouched there, waiting for whatever would happen next.

Daniel smelled Pearl in the house somewhere. Giacomo was a lying bastard then. He must have moved the girl to get a second source of dead blood. The inglorious hunter was here too. Howard wouldn't be on Giacomo's list, but Daniel never intended to follow it anyway. They'd be Changing all the fighters and killing anyone else. It's why they were here a night early.

Daniel scented the air again, smelling whiskey and overactive muscles. Giacomo was in his office, having a bad night of it with his disease. Good. Weak prey was easy prey. He tried to get more, but a blast of cold fresh air muddled anything he could glean. Odd. Giacomo's men had strict orders to keep the upstairs windows closed. So, there were unknown forces at work here. Maybe the rumrunner had finally staged a mutiny. That was all right with Daniel. A challenge like that would just make this night more enjoyable.

Daniel glanced down the front hall. Six human guards sat at a round table playing cards. Daniel scoffed. They were only armed with pistols. He caught Sampson's eye, then nodded in the direction of the four. Sampson blinked instead of smiling as he should. The big man hesitated. If this venture didn't whip him into shape, Daniel would have to get rid of him. Pearl had stalled all his plans like the horse latitudes stalled Caribbean voyages.

"Change them." Daniel gave the order in a flat whisper.

Sampson bared his teeth in more of a grimace than a smile. He gashed his knuckles with his teeth, then moved with inhuman speed toward the quartet at the table. Daniel barely smelled the thick stench of dead blood on Sampson's fists. He punched each wiseguy in the mouth, ramming splashes of his blood down their throats. Each fell in turn to the highly polished floor, writhing in pain as blunt human teeth rattled out of their mouths. Daniel looked one of them in the eye, catching a gleam of anguished hunger there. Perfect.

Bess tapped him on the shoulder and pointed up the double staircase. More human guards came from the hall to the right of the stairs. Daniel smirked and nodded at Bess; no need to hold her hand with commands. She took the stairs in an instant, leaping forward and up over the steps and clearing the banister like it wasn't there. The man opened his mouth to call for help or raise the alarm or other such futile endeavor. Bess had bitten her tongue, and the blood she spat hit the human squarely in his open mouth. She took the other one in her arms and kissed him open-mouthed. Crass but effective; Bess all the way. She was the best monster he'd made so far.

Daniel pushed open the door to his right. A woman in a gray dress and white apron stood as still as she could. The feathers on the end of her dusting wand quivered. Daniel leaned close to her and took a good deep breath through his nose. No weapons.

"What a happy accident, us meeting this way." Daniel leaned across the doorway, blocking the woman's path to the front door. He smirked without parting his lips.

"Please." The woman's eyes carried an amusing twinkle of hope. "I have three children at home, all younger than you. I just clean the house, they don't tell me anything. If it were your mother here, wouldn't you want her spared?"

"I'm not after information, but I love mothers. It's been so long since I had one." He smiled and leaned toward her, moving like he imagined one of her children might, to give her a kiss on the cheek. Instead of planting a kiss, he dipped his head down to sink his teeth into her throat through her voice box. He wasn't hungry, but he'd told her the truth. The blood of mothers was his favorite. He tossed her body on the floor in front of the stairs. Sampson could use her flesh to regain strength lost in changing those men.

Daniel pulled a handkerchief from his pocket. He wiped his mouth, then made his way calmly and casually up the left staircase.

There was no way Howard wanted to obey Bianco and sit down. Thank God the commotion downstairs gave him an excuse not to. Bersi unlatched the cat cage. Was the old monster crazy? What good would a cat do in a fight? Sure, Bersi thought the cat was important, but why didn't he open the door instead to let the others in? It would be unwise to do that himself. Bianco probably had a gun pointed at his back, and Bersi was the bulletproof one. Time to improvise plan B.

"Boss, we gotta get you out of here." Howard faced Bianco squarely, doing his best imitation of Niccolo. "Someone's attacking the guards downstairs." A crashing sound and the rising wails of men in pain rose from below to support his argument.

"Get me out of this." Bianco took his hand out of his jacket. "But this conversation's not over. You still have to answer for lying to me." Howard nodded and moved past Bianco to unlatch the window.

"No, we go this way." Bianco got up from his seat, oddly shaky for a hardened criminal who'd ordered hundreds of deaths through the years. There was a full-sized portrait of Bradford Durfee on one of the walls. Bianco reached for it, turning his back to Bersi and the cat.

Howard tried to catch Bersi's attention but got distracted. The cat was shapeshifting. So, it was another Changed monster, and one Bersi knew. Bersi smiled at the cat as its legs grew longer and less hairy. Bersi pulled the wooden dentures out of his mouth. His teeth were already growing back. Tiny razor sharp points poked up through the gums. He'd had no idea they could grow back that fast. It wasn't anywhere near as fast as shapeshifting, though. The cat turned into a man, short and wiry with dark hair and eyes. He was built like Jimmy, but short like Oguina. The new monster held his index finger to his lips and looked Howard in the eye. He looked less like a monster than pretty much all of them except Leo.

Howard turned back toward Bianco. The Durfee painting was on hinges and Bianco pulled it aside. The painting had been covering a door with a sturdy lock. Bianco struggled with a key, hands shaking. Howard thought the Mafia Boss was going to pieces until Bianco glared at him.

"I think Daniel has gotten some ideas." Bianco pressed the key into Howard's hand. "We shouldn't stick around to see what they are."

Howard unlocked and opened the door. They stepped through into the next room, which was cold and bare and dusty. There was an enlarged dumbwaiter in the opposite wall. Howard figured it would open in the kitchen pantry near the kennel door. He looked back over his shoulder to see Bersi had opened the door to the upstairs hallway. A raccoon ran into the room. He still had trouble understanding that was Pearl. An owl and a large orange tabby cat followed her. Great, a menagerie. Howard rolled his eyes. He could be Doctor Dolittle after all this was over.

Bianco struggled but managed to open the dumbwaiter. His hands trembled, and his left leg didn't move like it was supposed to. It jerked forward and then backward. Bianco couldn't put it into the small space. He turned and sat on the base, then tried to pull his legs in. The right one went, but the left kept up its repetitive motion. Bianco's expression was blank, his facial muscles immobile. His eyes burned with anger and something else. Shame? Why hadn't Howard noticed this before?

"Bum leg cramped up." Bianco pounded the rebel leg with his left fist. "Help me out here, Howard." Howard took a few steps forward, then saw Bianco's eyes flicker down and to the right. His eyes grew wide, and he blinked, though the rest of his face stayed still. Bianco tremored and twitched, all four limbs of his body hitching and heaving. He glared at a spot over Howard's shoulder. "You."

"Parkinson's, huh?" Leo strode past Howard. "Lousy way to go. In fact, it's worse than anything I can do to you." Leo stepped next to Bianco.

"You mean you didn't know?" Bianco's voice cracked on the last word. "None of them knew."

"Only just sniffed it out now." Leo tapped his nose.

"I'm not sorry." Bianco put his hand in his jacket again, fighting the tics as he tried to grab something in his pocket.

"I didn't expect an apology. But I guess I can afford to

be the bigger man for now." Leo smiled. "Here, let me help you." Leo stood over Bianco, stuffed his leg into the dumbwaiter, then pulled the lever to send it down.

"Wh-wh-what?" Bianco's outraged shout came muffled through the wall. A peal of feminine laughter rose behind him. Howard turned to see Oguina back in her human shape, smirking and chuckling as she took a defensive stance in the doorway.

"Excellent work, cub." Oguina smiled at Leo. Her smile scared Howard in a way Leo's and Bersi's didn't. That laugh of hers was pretty unsettling too, almost as creepy as Daniel's. Why was that? At least she laughed at something that could have been in a Marx Brothers skit instead of a horror show.

"Thanks." Leo winked. "Hey, Pearl? Will you go after old Giacomo and keep an eye on him? We don't want him getting away."

"I can handle that." Pearl raced over to the dumbwaiter, gray and black raccoon hair still vanishing from all the blonde. She jumped down the shaft after Bianco.

Pearl was right. They weren't human, but they were different from the monsters Howard had hunted all these years. They laughed and joked, looked out for each other like family. Even without the whole truth, Father Francis's advice had been spot on. Something crashed in the hall. Howard could think about this stuff later.

"Incoming." Oguina jerked her chin toward the wall between the room and the hall.

"Howard, go with your sister." Leo cracked his knuckles. "We'll handle this."

"No." Howard didn't budge. 'Daniel took my sister from me. He's the reason I do what I do. I'm staying."

"I get it." Leo stood between Howard and the wall. "Just, if things get hinky, leave. You still have a family."

Howard didn't have time to disagree with Leo. Part of the wall between rooms collapsed as the monster who'd been the fluffy cat was thrown through it. He sprung up instantly and back into a fighting stance. Bloody Bess stalked in after him, leering with her teeth bared.

"Pay the price for your cruelty and dishonor, Feral. In the name of God and Rome's Rangers, you face Sir Hrafin." The cat man's voice rang and carried like a general calling a charge on a battlefield. So this was the guy who'd Changed Bersi? Had to be more dangerous than he looked, then.

"There's no place to run now, little man." Bess held up her pinkie finger in a lewd and derogatory gesture.

Hrafin didn't speak, just held his stance and waited. Bess leaped at Hrafin, red hair streaming behind her like a comet. Big mistake. Howard's eyes didn't move fast enough to track their movements, but he could tell Hrafin was the better fighter. In moments, the small, wiry monster was standing still, holding Bess's severed head by the hair.

Leo might be right about him being outclassed. Still, he owed it to Pearl to stick around. If things started to go south too quickly, he had a plan to get Howard out of there.

Bersi knew he had a disadvantage with his teeth still growing back in. At least they'd come halfway back. One of Bianco's bodyguards lurched into the room, and Bersi knew right away he'd been Changed. He smelled of disintegrating teeth and dying flesh. The Changed gangster stared past Bersi, at the doorway. He'd be after food. Howard. Bersi got in his way.

The gangster stopped his shambling and charged, trying to knock him over. Bersi waited, arms outstretched. He caught the man and grappled, effectively immobilizing him. The new Changed bowed his head to push harder against his might. Bersi saw the opportunity and seized it. He cracked the man's still weak skill with his forehead.

The top of the gangster's head dented. He fell to his knees. Bersi put one hand on either side of his head and twisted, ripping that head from the body. The loamy smell of dead blood met his nose for a moment. Then, the flesh on the bodyguard's bones dried up, turning to dust. In seconds, there was only a skeleton. Oguina looked over her shoulder from the doorway behind him.

"So. That is how we die." She stared, stone-faced. "I never knew."

"You'll see more of this before the night is over." Bersi stared into her eyes. "I can hear at least six more of them." He held her gaze as long as he could. He averted his eyes first. Was something wrong with her, different?

They both heard footsteps in the hall as more stomped down. Two newly Changed guards stepped through the door, apparently adjusting better than the last one. They stalked instead of shambled, snarling as they came. Oguina flung herself at the nearest, knocking him down. He couldn't get leverage. Her teeth sank into his throat. She tore, turning her head with each bite to spit any dead blood out. The gangsters were Changed, but they still fought like humans. The other one waited, watching Oguina intently. He'd be a quick learner, given a chance. Bersi couldn't let him have it unless he wasn't Feral.

"Leave or die." Bersi closed the distance between them, glaring and baring his teeth.

They locked gazes. It was like looking a rabid wolf in the eye. The gangster only growled instead of answering. This wasn't a man anymore. In two movements, Bersi tore the Feral creature's head from his shoulders.

In the heat of close combat, Bersi hadn't noticed the man behind his victim until it was too late. He was huge, almost as tall as Bersi and bald with dark skin and eyes. He bolted for the doorway Oguina had left empty, knocking Bersi to the ground as he went.

"Howard, watch out!" Bersi got up, ready to defend the door from the hall. He could hear more coming, and Daniel was still unaccounted for. Another Changed gangster came through the door.

This one had a Tommy gun. Bersi went right for his arms, pulling, so the firearm pointed at the ceiling. Its ratcheting sound muddled his hearing. When he ripped the gunman's arms off, his finger stayed clamped on the trigger. He pointed the arm at the ceiling, waiting for the weapon to run out of ammo before he could do anything else.

Hrafin heard the lightest set of footsteps stop in the hall. He looked over at the large mortal standing in front of the dumb waiter. Men were larger in this day and age. He gave the man a close-lipped grin, then faced the dusty wall. The mortals who'd built this house had cleverly hidden extra exits. Still, that sort of cleverness hadn't taken Changed or any other creature with enhanced senses into account.

Hrafin waited for the creature on the other side of the wall to come to him. Daniel must have sensed his presence by now. Either calculation or cowardice stayed him, probably the former. Daniel must have had a brilliant tactical mind for it to carry over like this.

Something hit Hrafin from behind, and he found himself pinned against the wall by a pair of well-muscled arms.

"You're small for a Knight." Dark eyes studied Hrafin as he struggled. No use, his feet were off the floor. He remembered this Changed from his time tracking Daniel. Sampson. He'd been Haunted then, but now he was either Feral or just on the verge.

Hrafin should have pushed off the memory of that

duel, but that was the price of unlimited memory. Each decade, he had less control of where his mind went.

He smelled the bulky human close to him and the force pressing against him was gone. Hrafin stepped away from the wall. Sampson picked himself up from the rubble from the hole Bess made in the wall a few minutes earlier. He looked down at her bones, blinking. Were those tears at the corners of Sampson's eyes? He pulled the skull from the remains. Along with it came strands of red hair. Sampson's eyes widened, and the tightness around his mouth eased. He looked relieved. Hrafin hadn't seen a Feral act this way in centuries. Perhaps the dark, bald, man wasn't quite gone yet.

"I know you not stranger, but I am in your debt." Hrafin stood between the human and Sampson, taking up a defensive stance.

"Howard. Pearl's brother. You're welcome." Howard's eyebrows flew up in alarm. "Heads up!" Sampson had thrown Bess's skull at him. Thanks to Howard, Hrafin dodged it in time. It hit hard enough to lodge in the plaster.

"Howard?" All the tension came back to Sampson's body. "Pearl wanted you to stay away from her!" He growled, baring his teeth.

"You have some outdated information, pal." Howard's heartbeat increased only slightly, and he laughed. Hrafin felt an instant respect for the fellow. Bravery and honor had clearly been part of his and Pearl's upbringing.

"You're laughing at me." Sampson's voice lowered to a hissing whisper. "You think all this is funny?" He bared his teeth, pointed at them. "You think this happening to us is some kind of joke?"

"Pearl and I had a talk last night." Howard drew a kukri knife from his belt, but held it like a warning, pointed down. "She said you were a good man, not whatever Daniel tried to make you. Fight it."

Sampson's eyes got a look that Hrafin knew meant his mind had gone far away. He leaped at Howard, knocking him down. Howard used momentum against him, rolling, so they ended up on their sides. Sampson raked his forearm with his teeth, trying to press the wound against Howard's mouth. As they struggled, Hrafin heard a scream from outside. Howard hadn't heard it, but Sampson did, and it called him back from whatever past he'd been reliving. He locked his arms, pausing his struggle with Howard.

"Bianco! He must have done something to Pearl!" The young Changed stepped through the doorway. Hrafin had almost forgotten about Oguina's cub. "Help Howard. I'll go take care of whatever's wrong out there. Bianco's mine!"

In a flurry of movement, the cub was gone. He'd moved so fast even Hrafin hadn't been able to track exactly how he'd left.

Leo dropped down on top of the dumbwaiter. Pearl's weight had pushed it all the way down when she followed Bianco. He wriggled through the space between the top of the dumbwaiter and the portal that led to the basement. His feet tapped lightly on the slate floor. The secret door was already open. Pearl must have used it. He raced down the passage and bolted up the rungs sticking out of the wall at the end. He kicked the stone over the hole after climbing out.

Pearl was pinned to the ground by a granite bench. Somehow, it had been knocked over and broke in two. It looked like she'd been thrown into it. Her right hip and left arm were each trapped under a piece of the bench. Bianco crouched next to her, stabbing her legs with teeth from the metal box Howard brought earlier. Each time he made a wound, Bianco licked the cut before it closed, getting a dose of dead blood into his mouth. He smelled much healthier now, though the disease stink hovered around him like a circle of buzzards. Pearl stretched out her right arm, trying to grab a fallen branch just out of reach.

Why wasn't Bianco Changing? He seemed stronger, but how did he knock Pearl down in the first place? Leo hadn't been seen, so he looked around more slowly. There were three syringes with the plungers pushed home by an opening in the hedge maze. They smelled like dead blood. So, Bianco had filled syringes on him. He'd only needed a chance to use them.

Dead blood could Change and heal injuries. It looked like it worked as a treatment for diseases, too. But what else had it done to Bianco? On his first night, Oguina'd said power always comes with a price. The blood gave Bianco power to mask a debilitating disease but, according to Howard he'd gone off the deep end recently. He had no time to continue pondering this puzzle. Right now, Pearl's blood was beefing up Bianco.

Hadn't Bersi used it to help take down a Feral? Leo couldn't afford to let Bianco get juiced up like that.

Bianco gashed Pearl's leg one more time. She clenched her right fist, beating the ground in a fury. She wrinkled her nose and forehead like a seasick passenger on the Titanic. He hooted to get her attention. When their eyes met, Leo smirked, putting a finger to his lips in a shushing gesture. Pearl closed her eyes so she wouldn't give him away, hissing as Bianco gashed her leg again. Leo advanced quietly until Bianco was within pouncing distance.

"Hey, Jacky-momo! You have your guys kill grandmas, but take on teenage girls on your own?"

Bianco sprang up, snarling. His heart ticked like a top-of-the-line Westclox. His eyes reflected the moonlight with a greenish glow. His jacket hung open, flapping in a slight breeze. He held his hands slightly out at his sides, like an outlaw in the Wild West preparing for a quick draw. Bianco had an empty shoulder holster, but no guns strapped to his hips. Instead, two belts ran across his chest and over his hips. Metal staples in the straps held the teeth of dead Changed. There were so many, Leo couldn't get anything like a rough count.

"Holy crow." Leo gulped. "He's a tooth-slinger." He ducked the first two teeth that Bianco hurled at his eyes, trying to think fast about what to do next. "You've got to be kidding me."

Howard couldn't wait; he had to start his holdout plan now that things had gone sideways in here. He glanced at Hrafin. He'd grappled Sampson to pull him away. Howard reached in his coat pocket, grabbing his Nassau push-button lighter and the can of Thorens fluid he had to fill it. He mouthed a Hail Mary under his breath and thumbed open the Thorens bottle, letting flammable naphtha soak into his coat lining. Sampson made a face, apparently smelling something even though Thorens was supposed to be a deodorized lighter fluid.

"Ugh. What's that smell?" Sampson lost a little ground to Hrafin in his distraction.

"Damn the human and his stench, kill him!" The muffled voice from the other side of the wall was Daniel.

Howard laughed, evoking a howl of rage from the pint-sized monster in the hall. Sampson fought against Hrafin's grip, trying to shrug the Knight off while holding Howard by the coat. Howard stopped throwing his weight into his footing. Instead, he shrugged until his arms came halfway out of his sleeves. He gripped the lighter in his right hand, thumb away from the push button for now. Hrafin grappled Sampson around his waist and pulled back. Howard shifted all his weight toward the floor, tucking his chin.

The back seam of the coat came apart with a ragged purr. Howard's head slipped past the coat collar as he fell to the floor. He lifted his right arm, triggered the mechanism to strike the flint, igniting the lighter. The jacket caught fire, the side doused with Thorens blazing up quickly. Sampson's hand was tangled in the jacket, and now he was in serious trouble. Fire was the deadliest element for these monsters. Howard hadn't used it much while working for Bianco because it made tooth recovery difficult. The tactic saved his life more than a few times when he'd worked with Jack.

Hrafin reacted quickly, letting go of Sampson and kicking him into the dumb waiter. He got tangled in the cord hanging from the pulley and flames licked up the rope. The fire spread more quickly than Howard expected. He should have remembered this was an old house with horsehair plaster and not asbestos like modern construction.

"Fire in the hole!" Howard picked himself off the floor, hoping his warning came in time for Bersi and Oguina to get out.

"Your timing is impeccable." Hrafin lifted Howard off the floor, grasping him under the arms the way an adult would lift a toddler. "Daniel was about to break through there." The Knight turned to face the wall shared with the upstairs hall. "He won't bother now that there's a fire in here. Speaking of which, you should be on your way." Hrafin gestured to the doorway again, letting Howard go first. He gave Hrafin a smirk and walked through the door into chaos.

Bersi heard muffled orders barked on the other side of the wall. Howard came through the door behind him, smelling like fire. Two of Bianco's newly Changed thugs came in from the hall. He didn't have the time to ask Howard what happened. A crash and rumble came from the room behind him, but his attention snagged on the desolation in front of him.

Oguina stood closest to the doorway, brushing dust and flakes of shriveling skin from her shirt. She smiled at the thugs, stepping forward almost like a hostess greeting guests. Oguina seized one by the tie and forehead, sinking her teeth into his neck and ripping. She stuck out a foot to trip the other one. The man's body thumped to the floor. She spat the remains of his neck in his face before throwing his severed head against the wall. Then she howled, leaping at the back of the one she'd tripped. The next two thugs coming through the door paused there. Bianco's enforcers used guns and knives, not teeth. These two were outclassed and knew it.

Bersi himself was shocked. Oguina pushed the rising Changed back to the floor and ripped off the back of his skull off with her teeth. She spat dead blood, bone fragments, and hairy gore out of her mouth as her hand went into the hole she'd made and twisted. His flesh withered away. She stood, crushing the rest of the skull to pieces with her heel. Oguina fought like the Ferals in Hrafin's old tales.

The men in the doorway moved at the same time, rushing Oguina in a tandem leap designed to knock her down. It worked, if only because she was small. But Oguina'd fought her way out from under a bear. The two Changed enforcers didn't stand a chance. Howard stood without moving. Canny. He wouldn't want to attract Oguina's attention while she was like this.

The man who stepped in the doorway this time filled it. He held his gun drawn and ready, its hammer cocked back. It was Niccolo, the one who'd shown them in. He pointed his firearm at Bersi, then moved it left and pulled the trigger. Howard tucked and rolled behind Bersi just in time.

"What'd that little bastard offer you, Fallon?" Niccolo cocked the gun again, trying to get a line of sight on Howard. "Where's the Boss? You let some monster Change him too like what happened to me?"

"I'm not working with Daniel, you big lunk." Howard stepped out where Niccolo could see him. Bersi got ready to get in his way. "I warned your Boss about that little bastard. You think Daniel needed me to do a turn before stabbing Bianco in the back?"

"You shoulda warned us too, Jimmy and me." Niccolo let out a hysterical laugh, higher pitched than Bersi would have imagined. "But you warn this monster broad and her monster friend instead?"

"I did warn Jimmy." Howard kept his hands out at his sides, away from his shoulder holster. "He said he tried to talk to you, but you didn't listen."

"Your warning was shit, Fallon." Niccolo spat at Howard's feet. "I wouldn't betray the Boss for a mick and a half-blood. So now I'm a monster. Fine. But I'm the Boss's monster. If you want him, you'll have to get through me first. Yeah, and I know you're a hunter. Big deal. Try and stop me." Niccolo dropped the gun, backpedaling into the hall. Bersi could hear him crash through the half-open window.

Bersi glanced back to where Oguina'd fallen. She stood like a triumphant Berserker over a pile of torn and jumbled limbs, her face and arms were streaked with red and her hair matted with gore. Her eyes glittered with unfamiliar ferocity. She turned her head toward the doorway, sniffing the air. What could she possibly smell underneath the blood and smoke? Then, he caught the cloying scent, too. Familiar, but from where?

Howard gasped, and Bersi turned. The man leaned against the wall near the window, struggling to get air. The fire. His lips were blue because he still needed air. Bersi dragged Howard closer to the window, then broke it open to let the mortal breathe. Howard slumped with his face against the wall, eyes closed. He'd be fine for a few more minutes, but they should all leave soon.

"Woah." A bronze-skinned man in a suit stood in the doorway, hands out flat in front of him at waist height. This must be the rumrunner, Jimmy. His suit was streaked with blood, ashes and plaster dust. "You got them all, except the one in there." He jerked his chin at the room with Bianco's escape route. "Take it easy now, doll. I'm just here to get Fallon out. We got an understanding, right?"

Oguina stared at the man, the snarl fading from her lips. That glittering ferocity in her eyes damped down the longer she looked at Jimmy. Bersi let out a breath he'd been holding since Niccolo left. If this was the memory-fugue, she hadn't turned Feral.

"Ahanu..." Oguina's voice spoke the word like a prayer. Bersi thought it meant laughter in her old tongue.

"Everything's five-by-five, Doll. You showed that Daniel punk cleaned up his mess and all."

Oguina took one shaky step toward Jimmy. She unwound her hands from fists, stretching the fingers out. But her jaw was still clenched. Bersi didn't know what she was remembering. It could be a happy time, but more likely was a vision of death. Bersi couldn't let Oguina kill this man. He shouldn't let her kill anyone else at all. Something was wrong with her and this memory was like a gift from the gods, stopping her at some sort of terrible brink.

"Go. Now." Bersi leaned forward, still trying to prop up Howard. His other hand hovered above Oguina's shoulder. He didn't want to touch her unless he had to, in case it took her out of the memory. "She's still stuck in the past for now. Something's wrong with her, and if she kills you, it will get worse."

Jimmy's mouth dropped open, and he blinked. He glanced at Howard, then nodded. He winced, looking over his shoulder. More smoke billowed in the hall behind him. Jimmy stepped around Oguina and past Bersi to the window. He knocked the last bits of glass out of the frame and put one leg over the sill. He stopped to look back at Bersi.

"Whatever's wrong with her, we're going to fix it, understand?" Jimmy's voice was heavy with determination and anger.

Now it was Bersi's turn to blink and gape. Why would a mortal man be so invested in the fate of a Changed creature centuries older than him? Bersi nodded because he needed the window clear. Jimmy jumped out the window. He heard a crunching noise, a snap, and a muffled "son of a bitch" come up from the ground outside. Bersi didn't have to look down to know that Jimmy had broken an ankle. Still, the man was incredibly lucky.

"Did that actually happen?" Howard winced. Bersi nodded again, watching Oguina's ferocity return as she came back from the memory fugue. He felt Howard's head slump against his arm. He lifted it, boosting Howard's head back up to give him air.

Hrafin waited for Howard to leave. He stood near the wall between him and the hallway, listening. The fire crackled in the dumbwaiter. Something thudded in the shaft. A floorboard creaked out in the hall, followed by a voice ordering "you two" to "get in there now." Hrafin struck the wall, his left arm breaking through. He closed his fist on something cold and rounded. He braced his feet, then pulled as hard as he could.

Daniel came crashing through the wall. He'd pushed with his feet after Hrafin grabbed him, trying to throw him off balance. Hrafin compensated by bringing his arm over his head, pivoting before releasing his grasp. Daniel tumbled toward the smoky fire in the dumbwaiter, landed on his feet, then took a few steps away from the fire. Hrafin countered him, stepping between the Feral and the door into the next room, where he heard Howard arguing with someone.

"Hullo, again, old man." Daniel brushed plaster off his shoulder. A casual gesture, though his feet were planted in a defensive stance. Hrafin finally realized what was so familiar about Daniel.

"Cousin." If Hrafin were right about Daniel's origins, he'd press that knowledge to its full advantage.

Daniel's only reply was a mocking laugh. He feinted toward the hole Sampson had made in the office wall. Hrafin wasn't fooled. The floorboards told him where Daniel's weight really was. He shifted slightly, countering with a feint of his own.

Hrafin blocked Daniel from Bianco's office, countering with a shove toward the burning shaft of the dumbwaiter. Daniel grappled Hrafin's arm, trying to unbalance and toss him. Hrafin pushed through, robbing him of the desired point of leverage. They both ended up closer to the fire.

Daniel tried to let go of his arm, but Hrafin had clasped his in return. For a moment, they stared at each other, locked in a pose an outsider might mistake as a friendly greeting. They pushed against each other, neither gaining any sort of advantage. Hrafin could see, hear, and smell the fire growing behind Daniel. It called out to something from his past. Alexandria burning. He clenched his jaw, not even daring to blink. Closing his eyes even once might let in the memory that threatened to overtake him. If he gave in, Daniel would end him.

"Go on, old man." Daniel grinned amiably. "Go on back to wherever it is you're thinking of."

"Some night decades from now, I'll be going back to this event. I'll smile remembering your demise, cousin." Hrafin didn't smile now. He clasped Daniel's other arm, squaring their grapple.

"Stop calling me that!" Daniel snarled. "I'm as far removed from you as men are from worms." The familial jab was as effective as it had been last month. Pressing this line of verbal attack was likely to get Hrafin confirmation of Daniel's origins. He had to know.

"You ought not to be. We're here to remember, not murder." Hrafin pushed Daniel, trying to make him step backward, but the Feral matched Hrafin's effort. "Lacertus would be ashamed, seeing you now. Have you no memory of him?"

"That's all he is, a memory. Has been for the last hundred years or so." Daniel's grip tightened on Hrafin's arms, but his foot slipped. "He was stupid, soft-hearted. He pitied me, didn't realize what a dangerous fellow he was Changing." So, Hrafin's old comrade had Changed this boy. But where was he now?

"He's worth a hundred of you, a fact that will never be forgotten as long as I exist." Hrafin watched Daniel's face, and he saw a twitch under one of his eyes. The younger Changed blinked. Hrafin knew he was almost at a breaking point. "I can't wait to tell him about how I killed you myself."

"Then die, and meet him." Daniel pushed with renewed strength that could only come from the flesh of living human victims. With such hunger for power, no wonder he'd turned Feral. Hrafin's feet slid along the bare wood floor toward the open door, but this was exactly what he wanted.

Hrafin pushed back, using only his natural strength, and the backward slide stopped. He used his slightly greater height as leverage along with his strength and managed to force Daniel back along about a quarter of the ground that he had gained.

"Think back. Are you sure Lacertus is dead? I didn't feel him die. Did you, little Cousin?" Hrafin couldn't have felt Lacertus's death himself across the Atlantic. Daniel laughed, but outrage lurked at the core of that sound.

"Little is hardly an insult from you, fallen knight." All expression vanished from Daniel's face. "I know all about your Cloistered Lady and how you betrayed your Liege for her. Like little Matty Groves in all the old ballads. Perhaps that was actually you."

"Someone's got his stories all topsy-turvy," Hrafin spoke too quickly because Daniel had hit close to the quick of the matter. Hrafin wasn't sure if he was the source of that story, but its similarity to his history had always disturbed him. This exercise in verbal sparring was working both ways. He had to stop it before Daniel got the upper hand. Such a shame a clever fellow like Daniel went Feral. He would have made a fantastic Ranger.

"Wouldn't your Lady be so proud?" Daniel smiled, teeth glinting red in the firelight. "Will you sacrifice yourself to kill me? How painfully dull of you."

"Pride has nothing to do with the honorable course." said Hrafin, "But you're a dishonorable creature. You wouldn't know." He pushed again, gaining more ground. Something thumped just inside the dumbwaiter shaft.

"I expected you to fail. The strongest Changed I know started off as scoundrels, not Knights." Daniel managed to stop his backward slide again. That thud sounded again, and Hrafin saw a large ebony hand grip the lip of the shaft behind Daniel. Worry fell away from Hrafin's heart. Hope flooded through him, bathing his muscles and bones with more strength than even human blood could supply.

"Most Changed you know are your own mistakes, Cousin. Take care they don't make you their mark." Hrafin released Daniel's arms, giving one more push with flat palms to break Daniel's hold on him.

Daniel lost his balance and inhaled a completely unnecessary breath. Enraged, the Feral tried to take a step forward. Hrafin watched dismay and fear cross Daniel's face as he looked down. Sampson's hand clamped around his ankle like a manacle. He'd dragged himself through the flames in the dumbwaiter and was holding on to him in a desperate attempt to bring him down. The Feral gleam had left Sampson's eyes; only grim determination was left. The flames had spread through most of the room, blocking both holes in the walls.

"He won't make it out. Go tell Pearl she was right. I'll see her again some night, God willing."

Hrafin nodded, giving Sampson a slight bow as he made his escape through the doorway into Bianco's office. He didn't think any Changed could make it out of a fire that hot, but he wouldn't argue with Sampson. Stranger things had happened. The sound of a support beam crashing down came from behind him as he saw Oguina standing over a large pile of dusty Changed bones. Bersi held an unconscious Howard next to the window.

"The smoke's gotten to him." said Bersi holding the mortal's head up.

Oguina hissed and stared at the room Hrafin had just

vacated. "Daniel's still in there." She took a step toward the door. Hrafin studied Oguina gravely. She was in a bad way.

"He's paying the consequence for unwise decisions. We must leave, or we'll die with him." Hrafin had seen Changed on the edge of going feral before and Oguina stood squarely at the point of no return. "Come away." Hrafin gestured toward the now open window.

"Bersadottir, think of your Cub out there fighting Bianco and who knows what else. Let's go and help him."

Oguina nodded her head a single time. "I'll follow you."

"A man doesn't leave a burning building before a woman, Bersadottir," Bersi smirked. Oguina rolled her eyes and leaped out the window. Her expression looked genuine, but Hrafin would keep a close eye on her. "Hrafin, carry Howard." Bersi kept his head turned away from the human. "I'm too hungry to bear him any longer."

Hrafin took Howard, then went out the window himself. He landed near Oguina, who was hissing at one of the dogs that had come too close. A broken rosebush and tracks indicated a man with a wounded leg had gone toward an entrance to the hedge maze. Looking back to the building, Hrafin saw Bersi turn in mid-air and land on the dog, making short work of it. Judging from what he'd seen in the office, an entire pack of the animals might not be enough.

Something human moved at the far end of the hedge maze but, before Hrafin could investigate it, a high pitched scream came again from the back line of the property. All three Changed ran for the hedges. They leaped them like hurdles, with Howard Fallon a sleeping passenger on Hrafin's shoulders.

Pearl struggled under the stones as Bianco threw teeth at Leo. What good would she be even if she got free? She wasn't a fighter, at least not the way Leo and Bianco were. Maybe Leo could handle this on his own.

Leo hissed. A tooth hit his left shoulder, sticking out like a porcupine spine sticks in a dog's muzzle. Giacomo Bianco was like a porcupine. He was prickly, and all the Changed had underestimated him, herself included. Bianco smelled sick. None of Daniel's people knew dead blood healed people. Bianco had figured it out somehow. He hadn't wanted the blood to exterminate Changed; he wanted to cure his disease. Whatever he had, the blood only had a temporary effect.

Leo pulled the tooth out, growling. Good. It'd get stuck if he healed around it. Pearl knew all about that from the "endurance exercises" Daniel made them do. He'd stuck nails, razors, and wire through their skin then challenged them to rip it out. He'd also done another exercise he'd called "lizard tails." She could actually use that now.

Pearl tried to catch Leo's eye, let him know she'd try and help. Bianco threw another tooth, this time at Leo's throat. Leo dodged, so it hit under his left collarbone instead. This was a bad situation. Bianco wasn't as strong as the Changed, but the teeth were so sharp he only had to be a good shot. And he was. The man was full of ideas. Blood for medicine and teeth for weapons. He'd even used Howard to get them at no risk to himself.

Leo pulled this tooth out, too. Bianco threw again, barely giving him time to do it. The back of Leo's bony right shoulder was open. The tooth stuck in a spot he couldn't reach. Leo was going to be in trouble if she couldn't get up. Pearl shrugged her left shoulder, pressing upward and grinding it against the rock. She clenched her jaw, turning the scream in her throat into a whimper she hoped Bianco couldn't hear.

Pearl thought about separation. She imagined all types of parting, from the Biblical Red Sea to children leaving for school each morning, a woman estranged from her family. Fabric tore. Flesh and muscle flaked off her shoulder, bits curling and crumbling like pine needles in a fire. Her shoulder burned where it rubbed the rock, but her hand and the rest of the arm felt farther away. Soon. She'd have to focus, be ready after the arm came off. At least she had practice.

At last. Pearl sat up. She reached over her body. Grabbing her severed arm was like picking up a tree branch. She tried not to look too long at the round bone that went in the socket of her shoulder. She held it up against the wounded stump. Then Pearl slammed against the rock, feeling something snap into place. She itched like crazy with a tingle that went from her neck all the way down to her pinkie finger. She wasn't sure it was on exactly right but didn't have time to worry. Pearl pushed the other piece of stone off her left hip.

The rock made a noise as it tumbled away. Bianco glanced down at her. He flicked his right wrist, then his left. A tooth hurtled toward her head but she ducked, and it whistled past her ear. Another flew at her chest. Pearl rolled to the side, the tooth twanging against a stepping-stone. Bianco was fast; she'd have to watch herself.

Leo was in trouble. He couldn't reach the tooth in his shoulder and Bianco had hit him two more times. Fortunately, Leo was being himself and using his head. He crouched in a sidestepping run toward the fountain. She'd have to get there, too. They could use it as cover.

Pearl hollered and pushed the rock at Bianco, hoping to distract him. He dodged it without looking and threw another tooth at Leo. That dodge took Bianco closer to the hedges. She heard his heart beat faster. Her mouth dropped open, but Pearl only breathed through her nose. She went several paces toward Bianco instead of Leo and cover.

Pearl had been shapeshifting and running all night before Bianco trapped her and took a bunch of her blood. Then she'd done the stunt with her arm. She couldn't focus on anything but hot blood. Her fingers curled as she lifted her arms and took another step toward Bianco. He aimed one hand at Leo and the other at Pearl. She had to dodge, but her body wasn't listening. She'd walk right into Bianco's attack if she couldn't stop. She blinked, hearing a small, fast heartbeat on the other side of the hedge beside her. Pearl deliberately sniffed. Dog.

Her footsteps paused, then she punched through the hedge.

A canine yelp made Bianco jump, spoiling his aim. The tooth meant for Pearl's forehead went wide. Pearl pulled the Doberman through the hedge, looking Bianco in the eye as she tore out its throat. She expected fear, but Bianco's face wrinkled in disgust, and he spat at her. He forked his fingers in the sign of the evil eye. A crime boss was judging her for killing a half-starved guard dog? What a hypocrite. She silently thanked the dog for strengthening her as she devoured it. Weak, Daniel would say. Pearl kept her face free of pity for the dog, then dropped its remains at her feet. She smiled at Bianco as widely as she could. She smiled so big her cheeks hurt. He flinched, looking away from her and back to where he'd last seen Leo.

Leo's giggle echoed from behind the fountain. She sprinted around the other side to join him. He looked punchy, like a man who'd had a few too many drinks. The root of a tooth jutted out from his temple; the tip lodged in his brain. Bianco skulked around the side of the fountain, taking aim with another tooth. It was too late to help Leo remove the teeth. It was Pearl Fallon versus Giacomo Bianco. Which one of them would come off like Jack Dempsey? She barked out an ironic little laugh. A face-off between the weakest Changed and a terminally-ill man hopped up on dead blood like cocaine. Had that ever happened in the history of the world? She could ask Hrafin later if they lived through this.

If she closed with him, he wouldn't be able to throw.

Pearl rushed Bianco, taking a jump when she reached full speed. They clashed in a jumble of limbs, and they hit the ground, tearing up frosty clumps of well-maintained turf. She slapped at Bianco's hands, managing to grab his wrist. She squeezed, forcing him to drop a tooth.

She felt a sharp pain in her side. He'd stabbed her with the tooth in his other hand, of course. This was hundreds of times worse than the scrapes he'd made on her legs earlier. She screamed in pain. He chuckled, twisting the tooth. If she'd been human, she would have passed out.

Out of the corner of her eye, she saw Leo crawl around the fountain. He stopped to rest, leaning against the fountain. His lips pulled back from his teeth in a grimace, and his eyes narrowed in pain. Bianco shifted his weight under her. She managed to block his hands from reaching the belts full of teeth, but he'd get enough leverage to fight her off soon.

If someone from the house didn't show up, she'd be stuck on a cot in another attic somewhere, and Leo would be lying right next to her. She didn't want to let that happen, but she wasn't sure Leo could help. The chance she could defeat Bianco on her own was slim to none. And then things got worse.

"Boss." Pearl didn't recognize the voice behind her, but the speaker wasn't alive. "That little bastard Changed me, and.... Oh. Let me help you with that." Pearl looked over her shoulder. A man, the size of her brother, stood looking down at them. She watched him pull back his foot, then felt it hit her on the side.

Pearl didn't have time to brace or even roll with the kick. She lost her grip on Bianco, flying through the air toward Leo. She crashed into him, and felt two more teeth hit her in the leg; one in the hip.

Three guard dogs wandered the maze. Oguina stopped and took them all. She didn't bother snapping their necks before feeding. What was the point?

Bersi was too busy with Howard to notice. Hrafin glanced at her as she fed, but he didn't say anything. Why would he care about how a few dogs died?

She smelled a living man in the maze, too. He was injured, limping. He smelled familiar somehow. She almost went for him, too. Wasn't there a reason she shouldn't? It didn't matter, they were there.

Pearl crouched over Leo behind a tangle of rose bushes next to the stone fountain. A large man, newly Changed, helped Bianco to his feet. He lived, but his blood smelled all wrong. She heard it move in him differently than other humans, even other creatures. Bianco wasn't exactly human anymore.

Hrafin clung to the shadows, heading around the fountain in a direction behind Bianco's bodyguard. She followed. Bersi jumped down from the hedge, drawing the crime boss's attention. Bianco drew thin, sharp weapons from inside his jacket and flung them at Bersi. He dodged them, laughing.

"Niccolo, take him out." Bianco's voice cracked with

rage.

"You don't touch the Boss." Niccolo rushed Bersi, arms stretched out with hands curved for grappling.

Bersi responded wordlessly, snarling as he stood his ground. He threw his shoulder, leaning forward and heaving. Niccolo went over Bersi's head like a bale of hay, carried by his own momentum. He hit the hedge, tangling in evergreen branches and bare ivy vines.

"He hit us with teeth. Get the one in his head." Pearl pointed shakily at Leo as she murmured. Her dress was dirty and torn, missing the left sleeve. Leo looked worse, roots of Changed teeth bristling from his shoulders and legs like he'd wrestled a porcupine. Oguina shook her head. She should have followed Bianco instead of sending these children.

Oguina reached out, yanking the tooth out of Leo's head. He screamed, thrashing in pain. Oguina didn't even blink. She grasped another one lodged in his shoulder. Pearl stopped her, dragging herself to Leo's other side and holding her hand over his mouth. Oguina pulled, studying the pain flickering like fireflies in Leo's eyes. What could pain like that teach her? She reached for a third tooth lodged in his collarbone.

"Try and relax," Pearl whispered, "take a breath before she pulls if you want." Pearl breathed in, then pulled a tooth from her own side. She hissed instead of screaming. "Like that."

"Good idea." Hrafin put a hand on Pearl's shoulder. He looked past her and Leo, meeting Oguina's gaze. "Gently, friend."

She blinked, puzzled. What was the point of

gentleness in a world with creatures like her that could tear people in two? She blinked again, shook her head.

"I'll handle this, then." Hrafin reached around Leo, pulled the tooth from his collarbone and one from his hip at the same time.

Oguina heard a thud behind her, then Bianco's laugh. She turned. Bersi had tackled Bianco, teeth clamped on his shoulder. Bersi's arms stiffened and shook, unable to support his weight. Bianco pushed him aside, letting Bersi's teeth shear skin and muscle right off his shoulder. Bianco jabbed Bersi's neck with a syringe, drew back the plunger. He pulled it out and stuck it in the wound, bathing it with dead blood. The meat of his shoulder wove together as it healed, shiny pink skin blanketing it seconds later.

Bersi's eyes glittered with anger. He tried to move, but his legs and arms only quivered, tiny tremors rippling the muscles under his skin. He couldn't even open his mouth but growled around a chunk of Bianco's shoulder. The rumbling sound sputtered to a stop, like a stalling automobile. His eyelid twitched. He couldn't even blink. Oguina gasped, her hands forming fists like knots.

"This is Leo's fight. Stop her." Hrafin's command was followed by Pearl's arms clamping around her legs. Oguina didn't bother breaking free.

Leo hurtled past her like a locomotive, howling rage at the sky. He pounced on Bianco like a cougar.

"Don't drink." Hrafin's warning echoed off the fountain and the stone wall at the back of the clearing.

That off smell wafted off Bianco in the air churned by

Leo's pounce. The dead blood must have combined with his illness into some kind of paralyzing bane.

Leo and Bianco wrestled on the ground, kicking up clumps of yellowed grass and dusty earth. Leo had speed and grace and raw power. Bianco didn't need any of that. He had guile. He flailed with his left arm, feigning desperation as he struggled. His face was like a frozen pond, giving no hint that his right hand inched the syringe toward Leo's neck.

"Left, Cub!" Oguina's warning startled Leo, but he slammed Bianco's forearm with his shoulder just in time.

Leo grasped Bianco's fist, holding it closed. The tooth-tipped syringe tickled the soft spot between Bianco's jaw and ear. Leo locked his joints, pinning Bianco in place at least for now. Why did he hesitate? Couldn't he kill? Wasn't that what Changed were made for?

Hrafin flew through the air, landing in front of Niccolo. He met the bodyguard's lunge, stopping Niccolo from interfering. Hrafin shouldn't have been able to hold the big man back, but he did. Time, skill, or something else gave Hrafin an advantage. Who knew? Who cared? Perhaps Leo might once he killed Bianco.

"You're no killer, kid." Bianco shouldn't have been talking. Oguina saw he and Leo still locked together on the ground.

"Fuck you." Leo's voice cracked.

"You're going to let me go." Bianco smiled, glanced up at the column of smoke from his burning house. "It's all up in smoke, now. Without you monsters, I'll just be an old guy in a hospital somewhere. All you have to do is hide from me for a few months. This damn disease will do the rest."

"Bullshit." Leo sighed. He should have roared, screamed, just killed Bianco already. "You'll run to Providence or something. Find old friends. Start this racket up again. I'm smarter than you. You're not just curing yourself. This was an experiment. You want to use Changed to make drugs. We can't let you go."

"Neither can I." Jimmy stood by the hedge with one leg bent, like a crane, smirking at Leo. "This is my kind of gig, kid. Let me play."

"Jimmy, what the Hell?" Niccolo's voice rasped as he strained against Hrafin's grapple.

"Giacomo's nuts." Jimmy drew his pistol and cocked it. "I shoulda done something months ago. He ain't been fit to lead since he took up with Daniel." He aimed at Bianco's head.

"You can't shoot him, Jimmy."

"Sure, I can. The Riley kid's right. He'll take his idea somewhere else."

"I still say you can't shoot him." Niccolo dropped his shoulder, trying a different angle against Hrafin. Bianco smiled. Leo looked like he'd be sick.

"Why?"

"His cousin Esmeralda will go to Providence. They'll either put a hit out on you or blame Boston and start a war. Yeah, he has to die, but you can't shoot him."

"Good luck with that." Bianco laughed. "This kid can't do it. You're occupied. Fallon's out like a light. Who's going to stop me, this broad?"

Rage burned in Oguina's chest. Before she could think, her feet carried her to Leo's side in three fluid steps. She smiled down like a new mother over a newborn.

Bianco's face paled enough to match the moon. Oguina's hand flew from her side, striking Leo in the shoulder. Her blow shocked him, and he broke his grasp, flying through the air to crash into the fountain.

"Oguina, no!" She didn't care about Hrafin's warning or much of anything.

"Get up."

Bianco stood, drawing teeth from belts strapped under his jacket. He smiled, lifting both arms to throw. "Bring it, broad."

"No, Oguina! Don't!" Pearl tried to get up, but teeth still bristled from her side.

"I became what I am to kill white men from boats. What's one more?" Oguina plucked the teeth out of Bianco's hands like a vigilant mother might take an arrowhead from a toddler.

"She's right, Doll. Don't you do it. You'll be like Daniel." Jimmy turned to Hrafin. "Do something!"

Hrafin was too slow. Oguina plunged the teeth into Bianco's neck, piercing his voice box. She pulled back and stabbed again, marking his throat like a wolf might, or maybe a guard dog. His tainted blood spurted, staining the broken bench, the grass, Oguina's hands and face.

She threw back her head, trying to laugh. All she could do was howl. Her nostrils flared. Oguina hungered, but the flesh and blood in front of her was all poison. Something living and injured moved behind her. She whirled, then crouched to pounce. Her gaze snagged on something bushy and orange-red, a face framed by red hair and a beard. Blue eyes glittered with anger, rolling heavenward and then right at her. Bersi. Why did he look at her like that? Hunger squeezed tight in her belly. She lunged at the human with the broken ankle. His gun couldn't hurt her.

Nothing could hurt Oguina anymore.

Leo ripped through Bianco's pockets, praying while he searched. He found it, a syringe full of dead blood.

"I can't let her kill you, but you're still gonna pay, Hooch."

Leo ran to Oguina, stabbing her in the side with the syringe and pushing the plunger home as he passed. She dropped at Jimmy's feet. He doubled back to stand over his mentor, glaring at Jimmy.

"Kid. We've played this tune already tonight. You're no killer." Jimmy holstered his gun and held his hands out, palms up.

"You can pay without dying, Hooch. What's the going rate for a family of five these days?" Leo bared his teeth in a grimace. "Maybe a leg. Maybe both."

"Three, kid." Jimmy glanced down at Oguina. "Two of you Rileys are still standing."

"What?"

"Three." Niccolo stepped up next to Jimmy. "That's how many died. And he didn't do it. I did."

"You explain this to me right now, or Hooch spends the rest of his life in a chair."

"When the Boss ordered the hit on your family, we

were confused. There're no Rileys in business around here, or even in Providence or Boston." Niccolo shook his head.

"Bianco ordered me to do it." Jimmy twitched his cheek as sweat trickled a line in the soot on his temple. "I went in expecting a bunch of guys, but I saw women in there, washing dishes. So, I called Niccolo."

"So the Boss tells me your family had some kind of dirt on him, that they'd take it to the cops, that we had to kill everyone in the house." Niccolo hung his head. "I went and did Jimmy's job for him. But after, I heard a baby cry."

"Colin." Leo's voice came out in a whisper.

"It was all wrong." Jimmy's outstretched hands trembled like November's last leaves. "It's when I was sure Bianco lost his marbles. I called Father Francis."

"Colin's alive, with the Father? Why should I take your word?" Leo was so overcome, he barely noticed the footsteps behind him.

"You don't have to." Pearl put her free hand on Leo's shoulder. "You're Changed. We all have the power to go back in time with the fugue."

"But I wasn't Changed that night, not yet."

"That doesn't matter." Hrafin stepped out from behind Niccolo. "We get to keep all the memories from before. We remember everything. Our scholars believe that's what Changed are for. To remember."

Leo gazed down at Oguina. She'd been a creature of vengeance. He didn't know whether she'd ever come back from that. It'd be easy to act as she might, take Jimmy's legs off and be done with it. He glanced at Pearl.

She looked weary but clutched her brother like a lifeline. She'd endured Daniel and Bianco with a different kind of strength.

Leo pulled the paper with its red stamp from his pocket. He stared at his name on the top line, and his mind skipped back a month.

His new Changed senses enhanced the memory. He could see better, and the burning smell was stronger this time. He couldn't alter his actions or course toward the street he'd grown up on, but he noticed something new.

A white-haired old man passed him on the other side of the street. He wore all black and Leo saw a flash of white at his throat, a Priest's collar. His tread was cumbersome and uneven, weighted by the big black bag he carried. The man passed out of view, and Leo couldn't turn his head to see more. Instead, he listened.

Something rustled inside the bag. Leo had to strain his ears, even with Changed hearing. A muffled gurgle, a clear shush, then a muffled coo. He had to know more, so he scented the air. Old oiled leather over a dirty nappy, a faint hint of lye and boiled cabbage.

Leo believed.

"Fine, Jimmy." Leo blinked the past out of his eyes. "Bianco's dead, and he gave the order. You didn't kill them. But he did." Leo jerked his chin at Niccolo. "He should pay."

"Yeah, I should." Niccolo stepped forward. "Go ahead. Take a shot, or whatever kills monsters." Niccolo dropped to his knees and folded his hands, murmuring. "The Lord is my shepherd, I shall not want."

"Jeeze, get up Niccolo." Leo shifted his weight from

one foot to the other. "Everyone here knows I don't kill people."

"But I ain't people no more."

"Yes, you are." The three words were too much too soon for Howard. He coughed before looking at Hrafin and speaking again. "Your people have scholars. You got prisons, too?"

"After a fashion. We put the penitent to work at the Cloister near Milago."

"In Italy? I come all the way here just to go back there." Niccolo snorted. "If that's the thing to do, I'll go."

"I know what kind of arrangements to make, but not how to make them in this time." Hrafin faced Leo. "Will you help?"

"If he won't, I will." Leo glared at Jimmy. The rumrunner just blinked. "What? You're too good for my help? I know almost everything about shipping cargo and hiding what's in it. People owe me favors, too."

"You'd do that for me? After all this?" Niccolo's mouth dropped open. When Jimmy's eyes widened, he shut it.

"Not just for you. Bianco left a big mess, needs to be cleaned up." Jimmy limped to Bianco's body. He sat on the ground, removed the tooth belts and searched his pockets. "I got to get rid of the teeth, the syringes, the blood. I can't leave any of this for the fuzz to find, can't let Providence or Boston find out about you people. Things would get bad all over, uglier than here. And I got the idea you're not the only one who has to go over there." Jimmy glanced over at Bersi and Oguina.

"You're right about the mess." Howard stood up

more, leaning less on Pearl. "I'll help with that. I know some of Bianco's holdouts, places he stashed this kind of equipment."

"And I know how to find the rest of Daniel's people." Pearl captured strands of escaped hair, tucking them behind her ear. "Most of them will want to go with you, Niccolo. But the rest...." Pearl glanced at Howard, shaking her head. "We can't leave them hanging around the city."

"Agreed." Leo crossed his arms over his chest. "It'll get done better and faster if we do it together. I'll even work with you if I have to, Hooch."

"Back at you, kid."

Pearl let Leo and Jimmy glare at each other for a moment, but that was all the time she could give them.

"It's getting close to dawn." Pearl put a hand on Leo's shoulder. "The police must be on their way by now. We need to get away from here."

"Agreed, Lady Pearl." Hrafin looked at Oguina and Bersi. "We'll have to carry them. They've been staying somewhere?"

"Yes." Pearl nodded.

"We're not bringing these wise guys with us." Leo's tone was flat and final.

"Us wise guys don't want to go with you anyway." Jimmy picked up a fallen branch, testing its strength by leaning on it. "I got a place you can hide out, Niccolo."

"Good." Leo moved to Oguina's side.

"What about your brother?' Hrafin glanced at Howard. "Forgive me, but we haven't been introduced."

"Howard. And I'll get out on my own. I'll make it before the police show up."

"As you will." Hrafin crossed the grass and leaned over Bersi. "Thank you for your assistance, Howard. I might have died in that cage if you hadn't given Bersi a chance to get me out of it."

"Um, you're welcome I guess." Howard folded his hands and tapped his thumbs together, a fidget Pearl hadn't seen in decades. "I didn't know you were anything but a regular cat. Look, I have to talk to my sister. It won't take long."

Hrafin nodded, grinning without letting any of his teeth show. He put a hand on Bersi's forehead, moved it to his jaw, then his shoulders. Hrafin shook his head and murmured, "the Cloister it is." He lifted Bersi in his arms, moving him closer to Oguina and Leo.

"Pearl." Howard stepped in front of her, blocking the view of her friends. "Daniel's gone. You're free now, to do what you want. And these people of Leo's seem like they won't be trouble. But..." He took a deep breath, squaring his shoulders. He opened his mouth but closed it again without speaking. His eyes closed too.

"Howard, whatever it is you have to say, I can take it."

"You're my sister. We're family, and nothing's ever going to change that." His hands did that folding and tapping fidget again. "But things are different now. Dad passed on a few years back; Mom's alive but not really with us. She's not doing so good. You probably want to see her, and I want that, too. But she's in pain most of the time. She's not even sure who I am half the time." Howard blinked, his eyes looking off into the distance behind her and rimmed with tears. "But it's important that she stays human, especially after all this." He glanced down at Bianco's bloodied body. "We shouldn't give her dead blood. And Mom shouldn't be Changed, no matter how much of a mercy it might seem."

"I understand. I don't want to Change her."

"I want your promise that you won't." Howard swallowed. "You said you didn't want to be Changed either, but that's what happened."

"I won't Change Mom; you have my word." Pearl watched Howard let out a breath, his shoulders lowering as his jaw unclenched. She grinned gently. Both of them could use a little gentleness in their lives. He smiled back and it was her turn to let out a breath of relief. She didn't have to hide from Howard anymore. "You should go. Get to your car before the police block the road. I'll meet you tomorrow night, in the park across from Saint Anne's."

"Take care of them." He jerked his chin at Bersi and Hrafin, then jogged across the side of the lawn with the old oak tree.

Pearl glanced back at the brightly burning house, seeing two silhouettes against the flames; one large and one small. Jimmy and Niccolo, getting out. She watched them head around the side of the garage. She found herself saying a quick prayer for the big mobster, wondering again whether God could hear her or would care if He did.

She turned back to see Hrafin lift Bersi. He did it with ease, grace, and tenderness. He stood waiting, but Leo hesitated over Oguina. Pearl went to his side, put a hand on his shoulder.

"Let me help."

"No one can help." Leo's eyelids fluttered as he whispered. "It's too late for Oguina."

"Maybe not. We should do whatever we can for her."

"I shouldn't. This is all my fault."

"Why? Because you asked for help and she gave it? That was her choice."

"No. Because I couldn't do it. I wanted this battle, and then when I got here, I couldn't do it."

"I know. I saw. I've also been where you are. Someone ruined my life years ago, and I went with Daniel to get away from him. Howard doesn't even know."

"But vengeance was my idea from the beginning. It's why I asked Oguina to Change me. And because of me, all those guys in there are dead." He flopped one hand in the vague direction of the house. "A bunch of other folks have to deal with the fact that their sons or dads or brothers are dead because of me."

"Leo, you didn't kill them. That's Daniel's fault." Pearl sighed as Leo hung his head and shrugged her hand off his shoulder. "You want to know what is your fault? It's your fault those guys aren't out rampaging through Fall River tonight. It's your fault Daniel burned up in that building. It's your fault Howard and Jimmy weren't Changed. It's your fault Hrafin and I aren't back there going up in flames right now. We came here to do the right thing." Pearl glanced down at Bersi. "All of us made mistakes tonight. We're stronger and faster, but we're still like humans. Not perfect. All we can do is our best, and that's exactly what we all did. So stop throwing sandbags on your soul. I've seen evil Changed. You're not one of those."

"But because of me, Oguina is." Leo looked like a cat stuck out in the rain.

"Perhaps not." Hrafin crossed the distance between them and the stone wall. "She might recover. I've seen such a thing before." Hrafin's dark eyes met hers.

"Sampson?"

"Yes. Leo, you and Pearl are Oguina's best hope, just as the Cloister is Bersi's. But we must get away before we're seen."

"You'll have to tell me about Sampson." Leo lifted Oguina so he could carry her over his shoulder.

"All you want."

They didn't bother with the gate, just leaped the wall and raced the dawn home.

This story is far from over. What kind of impact will a power vacuum in Fall River have on other organized crime operations? Find out in the next book, Wiser Guys, available now.

Thank you for reading! You can find the rest of my books, including two other series on my Amazon Author Central Page.

I've also got pieces published in some charity anthologies. The Longest Night Watch is a charity publication benefiting The Alzheimer's Association in honor of Sir Terry Pratchett. You can find Volume Two here. Stardust, Always benefits St. Jude's Research in honor of David Bowie and Alan Rickman.

Please check out my website! You'll find more information about my other works there, discover more authors on my blog page, and can sign up for my newsletter to stay on top of new releases, contests, and freebies. http://www.drperryauthor.com/